WOMAN ON WARD 13

IRIS LOWE MYSTERIES BOOK 1

DELPHINE WOODS

PEPPER POT PUBLISHING

Copyright © 2020 by Delphine Woods

All rights reserved.

No part of this book may be reproduced in any form or by any electronic or mechanical means, including information storage and retrieval systems, without written permission from the author, except for the use of brief quotations in a book review.

❦ Created with Vellum

PROLOGUE
1870

The hammer slips out of my hands.

I stagger back, stumble over the side, land in the water. My skirts drag against my legs as I climb out, and then I run.

The water drips from my gown, the wet material weighing me down, catching on the grasses. Nettles sting my palms. The ground is uneven, hard in places, soft in others; my feet crash into ridges or slide in the sludge.

The bridge is in sight. I scramble up to it, tearing my flesh on the gravel and the brambles so that my blood is mixed with his.

My shoes pound on the road. The autumn wind slices my face. My breath rips my lungs.

Past the groundkeeper's cottage. A twitch from the window? I do not care who sees me, who hears me. Is it me who screams, or is it the sound of his soul sweeping away?

I sprint for the house, crash through the oak door. My

heels echo on the flagstones of the great hall, and the eyes of the dead watch me as I dash for the stairs.

The flash of my son's milk-pale face, eyes bulging. The whisper of his governess's voice, telling him to come away. The thud of their door, the clink of a lock. Safe, away from me.

Round and round the staircase. I fear I am lost in hell already, cursed to spend eternity spiralling, searching, sobbing.

Then the light from the gallery windows. He will be in the library, so I run again and slam into the room.

He starts, drops the book in his lap, his mouth agape. 'What has happened?'

I hold out my shaking hands. The blood is growing sticky, staining my own white flesh.

'I have killed him.'

1

1956

'Wasting your money on flowers,' Iris's mother said. She was in her worn-out dressing gown, the cotton so thin that Iris could see the floral patterns of her nightdress underneath it.

'I haven't wasted my money. I picked them from the woods yesterday.' Iris scooped up the handful of bluebells and ferns that had been lying on the kitchen table next to her mother's cup of tea.

'Never get your mother any flowers.'

'I'll pick you some on my way home tonight.'

'You shall not. Don't you get going in them woods at nighttime. Lord knows who might be lurking.'

'Fine.' Iris finished her tea. 'I won't get you any flowers.'

'Bet *they* won't even know what they are.'

Iris checked her watch. She needed to go. She threw her cloak over her shoulders. 'Actually, they know lots of flowers. They're the only things that make them smile.'

Her mother muttered something, but Iris couldn't catch it. 'I'll see you tonight.'

'I hope they like them,' her mum called as Iris walked out through the back door.

The sun hadn't managed to break over the walls of their backyard yet. The cramped space, complete with a few old plant pots and the mangle and wash bucket, was gloomy and dank. She always felt she could breathe better once she had hurried down the alley at the back of their row of houses and out into the lanes.

It was a relatively short walk to Smedley from their house, something that was a relief to her and a cause for concern for her mother; too close to the loonies. Her mother often recounted the time when one of them had escaped and she had found him in their yard, naked from the waist down. She'd kept the yard door bolted ever since.

Smedley soon loomed ahead. Iris passed through its open iron gates and strolled beside the avenue of trimmed lime trees as the hospital's golden stonework blocked out the morning sunshine and left her in the shadows. She climbed the steps and dashed through the door as one of the junior doctors held it open for her, smiling her thanks, but he had already moved on before glancing back at her.

In the main corridor, people were creeping around like ants. She turned right and trekked to Ward 13.

She nodded and smiled at the nurses she always saw at this time in the morning, the ones with the dark patches under their eyes and creased uniforms after a night shift. She said hello to patients who sat in the chairs outside their wards, still in their night clothes, hair unbrushed. Some of them said hello back; most didn't.

The sounds of the hospital were beginning to strengthen the further down the corridor she went. A long wail rang from a ward to her right, and through the window in the door, she could see one middle-aged lady swatting at a nurse who was trying to remove her bedsheets.

The corridor veered left, and her ward door came into view at the very end of the tiled walkway. Then the smell hit her. She brought the flowers to her nose and inhaled their freshness, knowing that soon there would be only the scent of stale urine, faeces, and old age. She winced as she opened the door.

She blinked, her eyes finally adjusting to the dimness. The curtains were still closed, and the patients were still in their beds. But they knew morning was coming; the stiff sheets snapped like cardboard as they started fidgeting.

Iris tiptoed to the staff room, where the night nurses were gathering their cloaks and her fellow colleagues were hanging up their bags. She whispered good morning to them all.

'Maeve's been up all night. I gave her glutethimide,' Nurse Rattan said as she yawned, 'so you'll have no trouble today.'

'Very well.' Miss Carmichael, the charge nurse, straightened her white cap, which had been knocked askew as she removed her coat. 'See you tonight.'

Miss Rattan and the other couple of nurses clomped out through the ward.

'They're nice,' Shirley – Nurse Temperton, when on duty – whispered to Iris and nodded at the flowers on the desk.

'Thought they'd brighten the place up a bit.'

'There always used to be so many flowers, didn't there?' Shirley said to Nurse Shaw.

'Well, when you go and pick us some, Temperton, there'll be some more, won't there?'

In the ward, Iris fixed the flowers in a vase and set them on the table beside Kath's bed. The old woman smiled at them then started coughing. Iris gave her a tissue and, once Kath was quiet again, opened the curtains.

The women squinted at the brightness, their toothless mouths grimacing for something to drink. With the light, Iris could see the beds that had been soiled, the women who would need to be wiped clean, the parts of the wooden floor that would have to be mopped.

Starting at the far end of the room, Shirley helped with the commode, and together, she and Iris lifted the old ladies out of their beds, one at a time, and sat them on the stool. The only person they did not wake was Maeve.

'Still free Friday?' Iris said as she placed Celia back into bed and stroked the old woman's hair when she grumbled to get up again.

'Iris! I'm so sorry.'

'Oh, it's no matter.' Iris pulled the sheet up under Celia's chin. 'We can go another time.'

They moved to the next bed, and Iris tried not to be so disappointed, but she couldn't help the sting of annoyance in her stomach. She had been looking forward to going to the pictures, to having a night away from the ward, to seeing the real world. It had been so long since she'd last had a free evening.

'Well?' Shirley smirked as she hoisted Flo upright.

'Aren't you going to ask me why?' They sat Flo on the stool. Shirley leant across the woman's white head and whispered, 'Dr Brown is taking me out.'

Flo slipped to the side, and Iris jumped to steady the woman. 'You're all right, Flo. Are you finished?'

The old woman nodded, and they lifted her to her feet so Iris could wipe her.

'In you get.' Iris laid Flo in bed whilst Shirley sauntered off with the full pan. 'There, now, that's a good girl.' Flo's hands, marked with brown age spots that looked like clumps of mud, clutched Iris.

'Next one,' Shirley said as she returned, and Iris prised herself out of Flo's grip.

'That explains the lipstick,' Iris said. 'And new rouge?'

'What do you mean? Mr Brown likes me for my inner beauty.' Shirley grinned wickedly, showing off her enviable white teeth. She was the opposite of Iris. She could have been made for the screen, and on more than one occasion, people had mentioned her likeness to Marilyn Monroe.

'I don't know how you find the time.'

'You make time, Iris. How else do you think you'll get a husband?'

'Well, I hope you enjoy the film.'

'You could come too, if you bring someone along.'

'I'm fine, thank you.'

'Come on, Iris. There must be someone?'

Iris shook her head. Everyone was so interested in finding her a man. The only thing her mother liked about her working at Smedley was the opportunity for her to meet a nice, young doctor. But the doctors never looked at Iris. She was too plain, too serious. She only spoke to them about patients and treatments, and she was grateful none of them had patted her bottom like they did to other nurses.

She pulled back Nora's sheets to find them smeared in faeces. They rolled the woman onto her side and wiped the worst of it off, then sat her on the stool and stripped the bed.

'You wouldn't have to do this if you married a doctor.'

Iris bundled the soiled linen in her arms and strode for the wash basket. 'Exactly!'

Inside the day room, the wireless buzzed with war-time tunes. Some of the women hummed along whilst Iris collected their lunch plates. She still had not got used to this time of day, after lunch, when the main duties had been done and a lull came over the women. Hours of nothing, of staring at walls, of watching their tea turn cold.

She loaded the plates and blunt knives and forks onto the trolley, then made her way round with a cloth to wipe the food off the ladies' chins. There was a bit of wailing and moaning, but most let her clean them as if they were babes.

In this ward, there was very little trouble. The women, all sixty and above, were chronic patients. Most would die here. Nurse Carmichael had warned her about that when she first arrived, and had stared at her to see if she would flinch, but Iris just nodded. She was not scared of death; in this ward, she imagined it would be a welcome relief.

She set about making some tea.

'Can I help?' Kath said, as she always did. She took a cup and saucer in each trembling hand and began placing them on the dining tables in front of her fellow patients. The action led to another coughing fit; she dragged in an unsteady breath, then returned for the milk jug.

'You're very kind, Kath,' Iris said.

Kath nodded and lifted her eyes from the floor for a second. They were the palest blue, like forget-me-nots. What a beauty Kath must have been in her youth. Her hair was thick and fell straight to her shoulders, although completely white. Her features could have been described as dainty, if years in the hospital had not made her skin grey and drawn.

Iris followed after Kath, filling up cups with weak tea as relatives came to visit. Most of the visitors were the daughters of the patients, and they'd bring sweets or birthday cards, or they'd brush their mother's hair just for something to do. The day room grew louder then, for the visitors were never used to talking in hushed tones. Their arrival always caused a stir. A few of the patients started to cry, and Iris saw to Dot who had begun to bang against her dining chair.

'That's enough of that, Dot. You'll hurt yourself.'

Dot's face was screwed so tightly into itself that her lips had whitened. Iris took hold of her shoulders, feeling the bones underneath her cotton top, and tried to make her be still. For such a skinny woman, Dot had a lot of strength.

'Dot, you need to calm down.' Iris was losing the battle. 'Nurse Temperton?'

Shirley emerged from the back room and came trotting over.

'This won't do, Dot. Come on, stop this.' Shirley took Dot's other shoulder and yanked her into place, but Dot continued to struggle. 'You're being silly now. Just calm yourself. What will your daughter think?'

'Sally?' Dot stopped fighting them.

'Yes, Sally's coming this afternoon. Don't you remember? She told you that on Monday.'

'Sally?' Dot said, and her face un-creased itself.

'That's right. And she won't want to see you if you're being silly, will she?'

Dot pinched her lips together and held a finger over them, like a child.

Shirley smiled at Iris. 'You know your problem? Too nice.' Then she wiggled away.

Iris refilled the teapot, leaving Dot in her chair. Just as she was about to start the tea round again, the door opened. She was expecting to see Sally, a forty-something carpet factory worker who was almost as tall as the door frame and just as wide, but instead she found a man, so stooped he was almost doubled over. He held his cap in his hands, and a few grey hairs stretched over his otherwise bald head. His dark green suit was worn at the knees, and he lingered in the doorway, his eyes straining to see before him.

'Hello, sir. Can I help you?' Iris said.

He tilted his head to the side so that he could see her better. 'I'm looking for Katy.'

'Katy? We don't have a Katy here, sir.'

The man frowned at his cap. 'I was told she would be here. Katherine Owen?'

It took a while for Iris to understand that the man was talking about Kath. The whole time Iris had worked there, Kath had never had a single visitor. Iris had even asked Nurse Shaw, who had been on the ward for six years, about it, and even she had never known Kath to have any friends or family.

'Can I ask who you are to Kath, sir?'

'I... I'm an old friend. Albert Jones.'

'I'll just see...' Iris found Kath sat beside the window at the far end of the day room, looking out at the oak tree, her favourite view.

'Bertie,' the man called, 'she'll know me as Bertie.'

'Kath?' Iris took the seat next to the woman and touched her hand. 'There's someone here to see you.'

Kath didn't move.

'Bertie is here to see you.'

Kath blinked. 'Bertie Blackbird.'

Iris followed her gaze and saw a blackbird hopping between the thick roots of the oak tree. 'Do you know Bertie, Kath?'

'Bertie.' Kath closed her eyes, and when she opened them again, they were misty. 'Bertie Blackbird.'

'Do you want to see him?'

Kath jerked her head towards Iris. 'Bertie's here?'

'That's right. He's here to see you.'

Iris couldn't bear to look into Kath's wide, watery eyes a moment longer. She sprang to her feet and beckoned Albert to come over. He walked as if his legs were made of iron rods, and it seemed to take an age for him to cross the floor. He waited beside Iris, looking at Kath from over her shoulder.

'Is this her?'

Iris nodded and gestured for him to take a seat. He swallowed, then sat, and finally, she could see his face more clearly. He did not manage to hide his shock.

'How are you, Katy?'

Kath took him all in, a frown thick on her forehead.

'Do you remember me, Katy?'

'Bertie Blackbird?'

A smile broke over his face. 'That's right. How are you?'

'Where is he?' Kath said, her frown gone.

Bertie wrung his cap between his hands. 'Who do you mean?'

'You know.' Kath leant forward in her chair. The eyes that had threatened tears were now sharp.

'He's fine,' Bertie said, after he had cleared his throat.

'Where is he?'

'I didn't come to talk about him, Katy. That's not why I'm here—'

'Where is he, Bertie?'

'I'm here because... well, because Mabel died.'

Kath slumped back against her chair.

'She died in January. Heart attack.'

Iris waited nearby. She should let them have some privacy, but she could not peel herself away. She was only doing her duty, she told herself; it would be no good for Kath to be upset by a stranger.

'It was quick.'

'I don't care.' Kath turned her face to the window.

'No.' Bertie sniffed and pressed his cap into his lap. 'No, I know you don't, but I... I wanted to ask if you would like to... if you would like to get out of here and come and live with me?'

Iris dropped the teapot. The question brought Kath up short as well.

'Live with you?'

'That's right.'

Iris dabbed the pool of stewed tea on the table top.

'Leave?' Kath craned her neck and caught Iris's gaze. She was petrified. 'I can't leave here.'

'It's not far. I'm only in Sandhill now. I... I thought you'd want to. I thought you'd want to get out of here.' Bertie reached for her hand. Kath tried to pull away but gave up. 'I'm sorry, Katy. I'm so sorry.'

'Where is he?'

Bertie dropped her hand and wiped his eyes with his fingers. 'I'm sorry.' He staggered to his feet, and for a moment, Iris thought she might have to save him from falling over, but he steadied himself by taking hold of the back of his chair. He stumbled out of the room without another word to anyone.

Kath continued to watch the blackbird by the oak tree, but Iris could see the hem of her cotton dress quivering. Iris was about to go to her, when Nurse Carmichael called her over.

'Who was that?'

'Albert Jones.'

'And what relation did he say he was to Kath?'

'An old friend.'

'I've never seen him before. Has he upset her?'

'I... I don't think so, ma'am.'

'Right.' Miss Carmichael's lips pursed.

'He asked her to live with him.'

Nurse Carmichael laughed. 'That's absurd. And it's not his decision to make.'

'Have you seen him before?'

'Kath has never had a visitor.' Carmichael shook her head, bemused.

'She knew him. She definitely knew him. How long has she been here?'

'Fifteen years in Ward 13.'

Iris tried to conceal her gasp, but it was too late.

Miss Carmichael smiled wearily at her. 'Katherine Owen has been at Smedley hospital since 1901.'

2

1956

Sunday's church service had been unbearable. The normally cool stone walls and wooden pews had not held back the heat, and as Iris sat next to her mother, her eyelids had wilted like scorched daisies. The vicar had droned on from the pulpit, the sweat on his face glimmering in the rainbow light from the stained windows. When they had finally been released, Iris had raced into the shade of a yew tree and waited for her parents.

Her mother had tutted at her. Why did she have to be so ungainly? Why couldn't she stand straighter? It was no wonder she hadn't caught anyone's eye yet. Her dad had smiled, given Iris his arm, and strolled them away as her mum chatted to the neighbours she would gossip about later.

Now, Iris's dinner – a mountain of boiled spuds and roast lamb and thick, lumpy gravy – was only just beginning to go down. The three of them sprawled in the living room, the windows thrown as far open as they would go, listening to the wireless. Her mum's knitting needles clicked slowly, and her dad's mouth hung open, sucking in air, his cheeks wobbling as he napped.

What would Shirley be doing now? Iris wondered. Something infinitely more exciting, she expected.

Shirley's date with Dr Brown had gone well; they'd kissed on the back seats at the picture-house, and he'd walked her home. Shirley had said he hadn't even batted an eyelid when he found out she lived on the Brookside estate. Ever such a gentleman.

Iris closed her eyes. What would it be like to be in love? She'd never been in love, never even fancied any of the boys at school. There was one, Richard, who had made her giggle – over what, she can't remember now – but she recalled how he'd touched her arm one time on the walk home from school and it had felt like a bee had stung her there. It had made her tummy turn. But then Richard had moved away to Chester, and she'd never thought about him again, until now.

What if Richard came back? Would she recognise him? They had only been eleven years old, still too round in the cheeks. What would he look like now they were twenty-one? She imagined him tall, with dark hair in the fashionable style, clean shaven, wearing denim jeans and a leather jacket. He would smell of cigarettes and would drive a motorcycle with a side-car, and he'd take her out on a Saturday night and kiss her on the back seats at the picture-house...

She opened her eyes. She didn't want Richard, neither real Richard nor imagined Richard.

'I might go out for a ride,' she whispered to her mum, trying not to wake her father.

'In this heat?' her mother cried, and Dad jerked

upright, wiping his hand over his face, and staring about himself as if the place had been bombed out.

'What? What's going on?'

'Iris wants to go on the bike.'

'Oh.' Dad settled into his chair again.

'It's too hot. You'll overheat. If you want to do something, you can make a start on that washing.'

'But it's Sunday,' Iris moaned. It was rare she got a day off as it was, and how many times had Mum propped her feet on that little footstool and declared Sunday a day of rest?

'Let her go, Pearl.' Dad unfastened the top button of his shirt and pulled his collar away from his neck.

The knitting needles clattered together, faster and faster. 'Fine. Go. What do I know? You go out and boil to death, see if I care. Then you can go and fetch her, Colin, because I shan't be stepping one foot outside in this heat.'

Iris was already brushing the creases out of her skirt. She kissed her dad on his bald head, then caught her mother's cheek as it turned away from her.

'I'll stay in the shade.'

'Alan's round at six for tea, don't you forget. I want you back here before then.'

'Yes, Mum.'

As it happened, there wasn't much shade on the way to Sandhills. Iris had followed the main roads in fear of getting lost on the back lanes, and the only trees which lined the pavements had been near-on saplings. By the time the sign for Sandhills had come into view, Iris had been peddling for an hour and a half, and she did not need to see her cheeks to know they were scarlet.

Sandhills was one of the newly built estates on the outskirts of town. The persistent squeaking of her wheels echoed off the bright-red brick houses as she meandered down the road, and although it wasn't a large estate – perhaps fifty houses at most – she hadn't a clue which one belonged to Albert Jones. It was then, with the air catching in her parched mouth, she cursed herself for being such a fool.

It had been an impulse to find out just who the mysterious Bertie Blackbird was. For the last three days, his and Kath's words on the ward had been repeating in her mind, and Kath had not been herself since. She had been staying in bed as much as possible, though the nurses roused her out of it eventually. She had not helped with the tea; she had simply sat beside the window, staring, her fingers plucking at her lips until they bled. And when Iris had nudged her, it was like waking someone from a nightmare; the horror was plain in the roundness of her eyes, in the whiteness of her skin.

Iris reached the end of the estate. She could hear the giggles and screams of children as they played in their back gardens, but there was no one walking on the pavement whom she could ask. She tried peering into some of the windows, wondering what Albert's home might look like inside, but the sun was too bright and bounced off the glass.

It was ridiculous. She should never have come. Hadn't her training told her to remain detached? To keep a distance from her patients? It did no one any good to start interfering in business that didn't belong to them. She started peddling for home.

Just as she was about to turn out of the estate, the very end house's back gate opened. Albert, with a watering can weighing down his right arm, hobbled in that peculiar way of his towards the pots of roses lining the front of his house.

She stopped. She should leave. Hadn't she just told herself what a bad idea this was?

She should not be pestering an old man on a quiet Sunday afternoon.

But...

'Excuse me, sir?'

Albert turned towards her as she dismounted and pushed her bike up the drive. He tipped his head to the side, the way he had before, so he could see her.

'Can I help you, dear?'

'Yes. Sorry. I hope you can.' Her tongue stuck to the roof of her mouth for a moment, making her swallow air and cough.

'Are you lost? It's too hot to be riding a bike in this weather. Should you like a drink? I've just made lemonade.'

'Oh. Well, yes, if you don't mind me...'

He motioned for her to step inside.

The place was blissfully cool. The tang of citrus fruit hit her nostrils. He led her into the living room, which merged with the dining room in the modern, open-plan way, but the furniture was decidedly old fashioned. China dogs lay on the windowsill, two green chairs sat beside the fireplace, and the walls were lined with cross-stitched pictures and black-and-white photographs.

She studied one photograph of a couple on their wedding day. She recognised the man as Albert; his hair had been thick and pitch-black in his youth, and his spine had been straight. Standing rigid beside him and holding a bouquet of wildflowers was a tall woman in a long-sleeved, high-collared white dress. Her frizzy brown hair was pinned up high on her head, and she had a face that could best be described as masculine.

'Here you are.' Albert handed her a squat glass of lemonade. He had his own on the little table beside his chair. 'Have a seat and rest awhile.'

She did as she was told and sipped the lemonade, the sharpness tingling on her tongue. 'It's delicious, and very kind of you.'

'It's an old recipe, my wife's. Were you lost?'

'Actually,' she put her glass next to his on the table, 'I was looking for you.'

He tried to twist his head further to take her all in. 'I'm sorry, dear, do I know you?'

'You came to Smedley on Wednesday, to see Katherine? I was the nurse who showed you to her.'

'Oh, I'm sorry – my eyes.'

'Don't worry. I didn't expect you to remember me.'

'Is everything all right with Katy? Is that why you're here? Is something wrong?'

'No, no. Well, she's been a bit out of sorts since your visit.'

'I didn't want to upset her.'

'You didn't,' Iris lied. She couldn't make this little old man, who had made his own lemonade and sat on his own all day, feel bad. 'It was just a change that she's not used to. Change can upset them sometimes.'

'Will she come here, do you think?'

Iris could not imagine Kath in this house at all. Bertie's dead wife's presence emanated from the photos, the furniture, the food, and drinks.

'I think that probably won't be possible.'

Albert nodded as if he had expected her response. He drank some lemonade.

'I'm sorry, dear, I don't wish to sound rude, but if there is nothing wrong with Katy and she can't move in with me, why are you here?'

She took a deep breath. 'As I said, Kath's been a little out of sorts since you came. It's very difficult for me to speak to her sometimes, what with the other patients needing seeing to, so I haven't had the chance to ask her...'

'What our conversation was about?'

Iris felt her cheeks flush. 'I only want to understand.'

'But is it any of your business?'

There was no malice in the way he said it, but it made Iris freeze. 'I'm sorry, you're right, I shouldn't have come.'

He reached for her hand as she went to stand.

'I didn't mean to offend. No one has taken any interest in Katy for years – decades. Me being one of them. They put her in there, and no one thought to take her out again. Just left, forgotten.' He shook his head as he stared at the bottom of his glass. 'I never forgot, but I'd done what I'd done, couldn't undo it.'

'What happened to Kath?'

'You not been reading your notes?' He was teasing her; his smile told her so. 'Delusions. Hysteria. Mania,' he said with a shrug.

Iris thought of the sensible, caring old woman, and

could not imagine it. Iris's notes said very little about each patient.

'Was there something that started her delusions? A trigger or something like that?'

A ghost of a smile played on his lips. 'It's a very long time ago. Lots of things happened, bad things, things she would have been better forgetting. I hope she has forgotten them.'

'What?'

'I don't know it all. I was only part of it, you see.' He sighed and sagged back in his chair. 'No one talked about her after it happened, not her family, not the village. Katy was never mentioned again. She was our secret, and if we didn't think about her, we wouldn't have to think about what we'd all done. You can trick yourself into believing anything.' He grinned. Iris shivered. 'But what's the point of pretending now? We're all dead.' He dragged himself to his feet.

Iris was losing time; he would show her out, and her chance would be lost. She followed him into the hallway, desperately trying to think of something to say that might make him tell her what had really happened, but just as she thought he was going to reach for the door, he turned left instead and began climbing the stairs.

'She gave the last of her personal things to me. I've kept them safe. If you want to find out what happened to Katy, you need to read her diary.'

It was half past six when Iris clattered into the back yard. She was dismounting before the bike had come to a halt. She stuffed the diary down her dress and ran inside.

'Where the blooming heck have you been?' Mum shouted. Everyone sat around the kitchen table, fanning themselves with their hands or old copies of *The Mirror*.

'Got herself a fancy man, I reckon,' Alan said. Her brother loomed over the kitchen table, his bare arms thick with muscle and slick with sweat, as he pulled her into a hug. He was such a hulk of a man; how he had ever fitted into this two-up-two-down, Iris would never know. 'Who is it then?'

'Don't be daft, Alan,' Mum said.

Alan winked at Iris, then continued his conversation. 'You should have a look. We love ours.'

'Too modern for us.'

'But space, Mam. There's so much space!'

'Your brother's trying to get us to move into one of them new builds.' Dad rolled his eyes.

'You'd love it, Iris. You could sneak your boyfriend in through the window, and Mam wouldn't have a clue.'

Her mother swatted him with a tea towel.

Adam careered into Iris's legs. She prised away her nephew's hot, sticky body and saw the gaps where his milk teeth had begun to fall out as he beamed at her.

'Come away, Adam. Give your aunty some space. She's as red as a cock,' Janet said.

Iris smiled at her sister-in-law, whose pregnant belly pressed against the table. Chalk and cheese, Mum had described Iris and Janet, but even so, Iris got on rather well with her, despite her loudness and crass language. Her mother had still not adjusted to Janet's ways.

Alan scooped himself a spoonful of red jelly. 'Sit yourself down, then.'

The diary was digging into her ribs, and Iris was sure

that if her parents weren't so besotted with their first grandson, they'd have spotted the bulk under her dress by now. 'I'll just change.'

She ran upstairs. The leather-bound diary was wet with her sweat when she slipped it out under her skirt. She placed it on her bed and stared at it.

To read someone else's diary was a traitorous thing to do.

She thought of her own, secured beneath her mattress, the words flying across the page of dreams to become a charge nurse, a matron, a doctor, even. Her mother had been so close to reading it once. In her tiredness, Iris had forgotten to bury it, and she'd come back from work to find Mum hovering beside her un-made bed, the diary cocooned in the duvet, just inches from her mother's fingers. Iris had said that Dad was eating the ham on the table, and Mum had stormed downstairs, ready to bat him off the family tea. It had given Iris time to lift the mattress and hide the diary.

What would Kath say if she knew Iris was about to read her innermost thoughts? Would Kath even remember she had written a diary?

'You died up there?' Alan shouted from the bottom of the stairs.

Iris lifted the mattress and shoved the diary beside her own, then tore off her dress and dragged on yesterday's which hung on the back of the door.

'Coming,' she called.

3

1956

Iris buttered white bread, ensuring it reached to the edges – other members of staff didn't bother. They slapped the butter and corned beef on sloppily, getting the job done as quickly as possible, so that the patients would have to endlessly chew the dry bread, unable to swallow. They all liked Iris's sandwiches best.

'He hasn't telephoned me.'

Shirley hacked the sandwiches into four butchered pieces.

'Who?'

'John! Who else do you think I mean?'

'Sorry.'

'What's wrong with you today?'

'Nothing.' Iris held in her sigh. It was too hot for arguments, too hot to be as uptight as Shirley. And anyway, she hadn't been listening to Shirley. She'd been watching Kath, who sat by the window, unmoving.

'He said he'd call me.'

'When?'

'When he walked me home.'

'No, I mean, when will he call, did he say?'

Shirley's knife stopped. 'No.'

'There you go then.' Iris placed a slice of bread on the final sandwich and wiped her hands on a tea towel. 'He could still call. Stop worrying.'

'I'm not worrying,' Shirley muttered to herself as Iris walked away from the tea trolley to get the patients to their tables.

She waited at the side of Kath's chair and looked at the view. The blackbird, with its yellow beak opening into song, jumped about amidst the roots of the oak tree.

'Bertie Blackbird,' Iris whispered.

Kath turned, her eyes wide and straining to see past Iris. 'Is he here?'

'No. Sorry, I didn't mean to startle you.'

'I wanted to speak to him.'

'He's well.' Iris hesitated. 'I visited him yesterday, at his home.'

Kath eyed her suspiciously. 'What did he tell you?'

'Nothing, but he has your diary.'

The edges of Kath's lips flicked upwards. 'He kept it.'

'He said I could have it, but I don't think it's right for him to give me your personal things.'

'Why would you want it?'

Because she was nosey, that was the truth, no matter how much she hated to admit it.

'I want to understand what happened to you, Kath. Why you're here. I know I shouldn't, but—'

'I'm not mad.'

The frankness in Kath's face, the set of her lips, the

brightness of her eyes; Iris had known it for months. She swallowed the feeling of nausea.

'How can I help you?'

Kath looked to the blackbird. 'I don't want to live with Bertie. I can't leave.'

'I could try to get you reassessed. Smedley is improving its recovery rates all the time. Lots of patients are now living in the community—'

'I don't want to leave,' Kath said. 'This is my home.'

How could anyone call this ward home? All around them, the other patients were moaning, banging against the chairs in protest as Shirley tried to force them to the table. Every day was the same, life on a cycle until death came.

Kath coughed, dragging up something from her lungs and swallowing it. 'I shan't be here for long. I can feel it.' She patted her chest. 'I want to see him. Before I die, I want to see him.'

'Bertie?'

Kath shook her head.

'Who?'

'Nurse Lowe,' Shirley's nasal voice rammed into their conversation. 'A little help, if it wouldn't be too much trouble for you?'

Kath grinned and let Iris help her to her feet. 'Read the diary.'

Iris ran home. Tea was on the table, a cold plate of stew and dumplings. The last thing she wanted to eat, but she couldn't leave it. Her mum made sure nothing went to waste. *Remember rationing?*

Iris shovelled it in her mouth until her stomach ached. She washed the dishes, splashing water everywhere in her haste, leaving crusted food on the saucepan, which she hoped her mother's failing eyesight wouldn't notice.

Then she was free. She bounded up the stairs, lifted the mattress, and began.

4

1900

Monday, September 24th

I've started a new book for this job. I thought it best. A new book and a new start.

My eyelids are falling already, and it's still light out, but I'll write what I can before I drop off.

This morning seems like ten years ago. How can it be that I was still in the village when the sun rose today? I feel a hundred miles away from home.

Bertie saw me off, like he said he would. I said he didn't need to, for it made the leaving all the harder to have spent the hour together, hand in hand, blissfully alone, but he insisted.

'Here's halfway,' he said.

It was a dense patch of woodland beside the stream. The sun was low and warm, like it has been this whole month. By his pocket watch, it was just after eight o'clock, and I'd no need to be there until ten, so we sat on a tree stump.

It was quiet for a while, nothing but the birds chirping around us, and I suddenly thought how I shouldn't be able to hear his voice for days. I thought how much I was going to miss that lovely voice of his, soft, as if he could be a choir boy.

'Say something,' I said.

'What do you want me to say?'

'Anything.'

He smiled at me from the side, like he does when he thinks I'm being daft. I stroked his cheek.

'I just hope it's not catching,' he said.

'What?'

He tapped the side of his head and pulled a face. I slapped him on the leg, and he laughed and put his arm around me.

'I'll miss you, Katy.'

I rested my forehead against his, and I thought, as I closed my eyes, that I could have stayed like that for all of time.

But he knows why I'm going, and I said again to him that I won't be away long. A year, maybe, just something to do until we've got the money to get wed. He kissed me then. He tasted of bacon and strong tea, no milk, just how he likes it. I thought, stop crying, you daft fool, you'll be making his tea and burning his bacon soon enough, but I couldn't help myself.

'I'll wait for you here every time you have an afternoon free, just write to me.'

'Your da won't let you go.'

'I don't care about Da.' His soft, cool hand rested on the back of my neck. 'I have to see you, Katy.'

I kissed him again, wishing that our time wasn't running out. When I was at the reverend's, I saw him almost every day, what with him delivering the meat. A whole week without him just seemed impossible. It still seems impossible. If I close my eyes now and think really hard, I'm sure I can taste the bacon on my tongue, feel the cold patch on my neck from his hand.

He waved me goodbye. I kept turning, and he was still standing there by the trees, twisting his hat out of shape as he watched me, but then the stream bent, and he disappeared.

I felt ever so alone then. The cows in the fields made me jumpy, not like they did when Bertie was with me. I kept to the side of the stream until the track climbed out of the valley. Even with the cool breeze I got sticky. I thought what a terrible impression I'll make, turning up all red in the face, my dress wet under my pits, so I slowed down a bit and steadied my breathing, but it's a whopping great hill up to here. I thought, whoever built a house on top of such a hill should be hanged, but when I got through the gates, once I was out from between the high hedgerows, I could see why.

Shropshire swept into the distance; great big fields of green and yellow, the cattle and sheep and horses all tiny dots. I couldn't even see the stream I'd followed, just the dark line of trees that clung to its banks.

And the sky! I've never seen the sky so big before. It was like I was in the heavens rather than on the earth, and then a buzzard crossed the blueness and reminded me of home.

I followed the drive up towards the house. The lawns

are all neat and green, not a plant or weed out of place, and I remembered Reverend Cotton's wife always moaning about the state of their modest little patch, how whenever she turned her back another daisy would sprout up.

The drive is hidden behind a border of trees, so it wasn't until I got closer to the house that I saw it, and then it was so big that it startled me. It's huge and clean white, with three pillars in the middle and lots of tall windows. So many windows! And they all glitter with the sunshine. Even the metal bars on them gleam.

The drive stops at the foot of a great many stone steps which lead to the main door. It was so quiet that I could hear my shoes on the stone as loud as if someone was pelting it with rocks, and I'm sure if the sun hadn't been bouncing off the glass, I would have seen faces staring at me from the windows.

Mrs Thorpe – the matron, so I quickly discovered – showed me around when I arrived. She's a sharp woman, as I'd expect from a matron, but much thinner than what I'd had in mind, and she's a nose like a beak. She asked me if I'd found the place without problem and that Dr Basildon wanted to see me when we'd finished the tour.

The house is divided into three, she told me. The main bit is where Dr and Mrs Basildon live and where the patients take their evening meals and where concerts and dances are held.

To the left is the male wing. I'm not to go in there. It's identical to the female wing, which is on the right as you look at the house. There's a great big day room and a library on the ground floor. The bedrooms, closets, bathing rooms, and desk for the night attendant are upstairs. There are no dormitories like in a county asylum, Mrs Thorpe said. The ladies here are all of high breeding and require privacy and quiet. I'm to call them all *Miss* or *Ma'am* and curtsey to them, as if they weren't at all mad.

I had to curtsey for one old woman we met in the day room. Mrs Thorpe introduced her as Mrs Leverton and said we'd soon be getting to know each other, but before I could speak, Mrs Thorpe had me by the arm and was taking me to the main part of the house again. She led me up the carpeted stairs and had me sit on a chair outside one of the many polished wooden doors. She knocked and, before it opened, strode off downstairs. A few minutes later, it opened.

I know it's not right to comment on our employers for the way they look, but Dr Basildon is a very striking man.

He ushered me inside what must be his study and asked me to sit opposite him across his desk. It's a fairly small room for the size of the house, and the walls are all dark with grand books whose titles I couldn't make out. There's one very large window at the end of the room, which Dr Basildon sat in front of in his big chair, so that, until my eyes adjusted, he was just a black outline. And whilst in that outline, it was hard not to notice his ears, which stick out from his head in an unfortunate manner.

He has a nice voice though, and I thought that the patients must find it soothing to be talked to by him. He says everything very slowly and clearly, and his accent is much posher than any I've heard round here before.

He asked me if I'd found the place all right, and I said, again, that it had been no trouble. He asked what experience I had of working with the mentally unsound, and I said I had very little. I thought, then, that he might send me home, that I was not experienced enough, and I thought, if that was the case, why agree to employ me in the first place? Surely Reverend Cotton had told him I had only ever worked as a maid? And as I was thinking all this, he rummaged in a desk drawer and took out a small, red book which said *Handbook for Attendants of the Insane*.

'You shall have to study this very carefully.' He leaned forward to hand it to me. In that moment, he came into the light, and I could see the fine lines around his eyes and at the sides of his mouth. Mostly, I was struck by the blueness of his eyes, as bright and sharp as lightning.

'You will have a week's trial, after which we will discuss your progress and if you are suitable for this kind of work. You will follow Matron's orders completely. You will not give any medicine for the time being. You must be observant, learn quickly, but, most importantly, you must set an example.'

'Yes, sir,' I said, and stopped looking at his face, which is not really handsome but somehow fascinating. I looked instead at the fat book in my hands and wondered whether I should leave. I have never been a fast learner. Da would always sigh and shake his head at the times I'd stumbled over my reading and writing when he'd tried to teach me better than they did at school.

'You worked for Reverend Cotton.'

'Yes, sir.'

'How long did you work for him?'

'Just over three years, sir, as a maid-of-all-work. Before that I was at Eastley Manor, as a scullery maid.'

'Why did you leave Reverend Cotton?' He was leaning

forward again, and I could have sworn he was smirking at me, though his lips were straight.

'They found another girl.'

'You were sacked?'

I stared at the book in my hands.

'Reverend Cotton spoke very favourably of you.' He leant back in his chair and disappeared into the darkness. 'I trust a clergyman.'

I smiled as best as I could, hoping that the meeting was over, but he continued.

'We run a small establishment here. We pride ourselves on the quality of care, the quality of life that our patients can expect. There are no padded cells or ball and chains here, Miss Owen. It is all very civilised. There are six attendants to five patients, plus Matron. You shall have the privilege of attending almost exclusively to Mrs Leverton. You shall only be required to keep an eye on the other patients if or when their own attendants are away, and you shall be in charge of the night duty one night per month. You shall have three afternoons per month to do as you please.'

My head had been nodding all the way through his speech and I wished I'd had a piece of paper on which to write these things down, for I didn't know how I would remember it all.

'Mrs Leverton's previous attendant had been with her since she first came here. She sadly passed away two weeks ago, leaving Mrs Leverton rather bereft. It was all very sudden and could not be expected. Mrs Leverton is now suffering from a bout of melancholia, which requires constant supervision. You should read about this affliction tonight at the latest. It is in the book.'

I nodded again.

He reached for the bell to summon a maid.

'You must introduce yourself to Mrs Leverton once you have changed. It is important that you form a relationship with her, so that she can trust you and try to emulate your habits, but you must not become too close to her. It does them no good to form such attachments to those who can leave so quickly.'

The maid came in then, and she was holding a folded, grey uniform. She dipped a curtsey to the doctor, and I rose from my seat. I curtseyed again and thanked him, then left to change.

Mrs Leverton said very little to me. She's a short woman, no taller than me, but the straightness of her back and the way she holds herself makes me feel very small indeed. She has a little Jack Russell bitch called Annie, which sits by her feet at all times. Her hair has not a single grey strand, despite her age, which I discovered is fifty-five. Her eyes are just as dark as her hair and very hard. She doesn't look mad in the slightest, just old and posh.

As it happens, I only sat in the day room with her for half an hour. After that, I followed Matron round as she showed me the cleaning cupboards and where the medicines are kept. She has a huge ring of keys attached to a string about her waist, and they smash into each other when she walks.

There is a key for everything! For each bedroom, for the bathing room, for the medicine cabinet, for the cleaning cupboard, even for the cupboard which holds the fire guards and pokers. Everything must be locked and secured, for the safety of the patients.

'There is a lake in the grounds,' Mrs Thorpe said, as we stood under the veranda and stared at the view before us as the sun simmered low in the sky. 'It is a distance away and we do not normally walk past it, but if you happen to go for a longer walk, you must keep the patients away from it.'

'Why?' I asked, my ignorance earning me a tut of disapproval.

'A few patients have drowned themselves as a result of a lazy attendant. I can assure you that the attendant was soon dismissed and prosecuted.'

I held my tongue from then on.

Soon after that, it was time for dinner. All the patients take their meals with the Basildons, as a group, Mrs Thorpe told me, which I find most bizarre. They change their dress to formal wear and go down for dinner at six o'clock each evening and enjoy wine and meat and puddings, as long as it doesn't upset their balances, in which case they are served plainer meals without alcohol. Mrs Thorpe explained that the attendants are present in case of any trouble and sit at the sides of the room while the servants serve the patients their food.

I didn't go to dinner, though, as I was excused for the evening. I was sent, with a cold plate of supper, to my bedroom, which is housed in an extension from the female wing. Below me is the laundry and ironing room. I share this room in the eves with two other attendants, Miss Marion Rowley, who is only two years my senior and has already smiled at me, and the night nurse, Miss York, who is sleeping behind a separating curtain right now, as I write this.

I have read almost half of the handbook already, which I must say I am rather pleased about. It is not quite as difficult or as complicated as I thought. I have to be up at six o'clock tomorrow morning, when I shall begin my first day properly. I pray it is a success.

Monday, 1st October

I am sorry for my lack of writing – this last week has been never-ending. I have woken at six each morning and gone to bed at ten. There is very little time in which for me to pen my thoughts, but I have a candle now beside me that is still high, and I do not wish to waste the light. Marion says she doesn't mind the scratching either; she says she could fall asleep standing up.

Where to begin?

This week has become somewhat of a blur.

I shall begin with my patient, Mrs Leverton.

It seems the death of her previous attendant has been hard for her. For the first few days, she would not meet my eye. Nothing was ever right, and she spoke harshly to me. My strides were too small when we walked Annie. I did not fasten her corset tight enough. The water in her bath was too cold, though I had the thermometer in it, like Mrs Thorpe told me I must, and I made sure she was removed as soon as the temperature dipped.

I blushed the first time I had to bathe her. To see your mistress naked is awful. Mrs Leverton didn't seem to care. She took off her nightdress and stood there before me, waiting for me to allow her into the tub. Then she sat upright, unmoving and silent, until I saw the brush and soap and started to wash her.

Her skin is quite loose, the muscles completely undefined, but her hair is wonderful. It reaches to her waist and is as glossy as a chestnut. I washed it with lavender water and finally, as my hands ran from the top of her head to the tip her hair, she began to relax.

Annie goes everywhere with her. Every morning after breakfast, we begin our walk of the grounds. There is a little mound where the earth has been piled up and laid with grass, and every day Mrs Leverton likes to climb this mound and have a moment to look about her.

In the afternoons, she reads or writes poems or plays a tune on a flute-like instrument. She told me, when I asked her, that it is called a tin whistle. She is very good at it. She knows many different songs, but she always comes back to the same melody, as if she cannot get it out of her mind. I wonder if that is part of her affliction? I shall make a note of it in my attendant's book, which I keep to record Mrs Leverton's bowel movements and sleeping patterns and any changes in behaviour.

She is quite like a normal person until night comes. She enjoys her dinner with the Basildons. Who wouldn't? Each night, there is a magnificent amount of food like I have never seen before, even at Eastley Manor! Mrs Leverton makes polite conversation with the doctor about the weather or something just as trivial, as might any lady of her social standing if they were not deemed mentally infirm. But when she leaves the dining room and returns to her chamber, she becomes ever so sad. She weeps silently as she changes into her nightclothes, then she gets to her knees and prays for an hour.

It is a dreadful thing to see. She lifts the mat from the floorboards so that she has no comfort for her bones, and as the minutes pass by she begins to tremble until, by the end of the hour, she is shaking so violently it almost looks like she is fitting. She is too weak to spend such a long time in one position, and I have told Mrs Thorpe about it, but she says that she has always done it and could never be broken of the habit, no matter how hard Dr Basildon Snr tried.

After her hour of prayer, Mrs Leverton gets to her feet, her joints snapping as she does so, and slides into bed. I have to lift Annie onto the bed, for the dog is too fat and too old to jump for itself, and it curls up beside its mistress and is snoring within seconds.

On the fourth night, Mrs Leverton whispered something to me as I was about to leave.

'She likes you.'

I was so tired that I couldn't fathom what she meant.

'Annie. She doesn't like everyone.'

'I've always had a soft spot for dogs,' I said, as quietly as if I were talking to a child. And Mrs Leverton did look like a child, in that huge bed, the covers up to her chin, her pale, open face poking out above the sheets.

'She's my fourth Annie.' She smiled so tenderly at her pet, like it was her own baby. 'They've all been loyal. Dogs are the only beings one can trust, don't you think? They keep all our secrets.'

I said I supposed that was true.

'Good night, Katy.' It was the first time she'd said my name, and I left her room with a little ball of happiness rolling around in my stomach.

. . .

Mrs Leverton's room is quite close to Miss York's station. All of the bedrooms have slats in the doors so that the night attendant can do the rounds every hour and check the patients are in their beds, alive and sleeping.

The closest room to Miss York's station is Rose Huxley's, Marion's patient. She is thirty-eight years old and one of the most difficult patients. I do feel rather sorry for Marion for having to deal with her. Marion is smaller than I am, though far more rounded than me, and she wears spectacles that do not suit the chubbiness of her face. Mrs Huxley is almost two heads taller than her, and when she gets into a rage, Marion cannot placate her alone. I have had to help hold her down twice this week already, and it always leaves Marion breathless and shaken.

One night, as we were getting into bed, I asked Marion what was wrong with Mrs Huxley.

'She's a poor soul,' she said.

That's another thing about Marion, she's far too nice. I wouldn't be quite so understanding with someone who had left me with so many bruises.

'She suffers from mania and hallucinations.'

I knew what hallucinations were from reading my handbook, and they struck me as one of the worst types of insanity.

'What are they?'

'She believes she can see her children.' Marion took off her glasses, set them on her bedside table, and rubbed her fingers down each side of her nose. 'Her children are dead.'

I bristled, as if there was a cold draught upon my neck.

'They are such terrible hallucinations,' Marion continued. 'She thinks the devil is torturing them. She thinks she can smell their burning flesh.'

'What do you say to her? How can you make her stop?'

Marion sighed. She was exhausted; her puffy cheeks were a waxy, grey colour, and the skin around her eyes was almost purple. 'I cannot say anything to help. She is so convinced of what she sees. The best thing I can do is to be normal, to show her that I cannot see anything and therefore there is nothing there.'

Marion opened her handbook and began to read. She reads it every night, over and over again. There is nothing in that handbook that she could not recite from heart. She is going to take her examinations as soon as she can.

I wriggled down into my bed, rubbing my feet against the sheets to warm them, and I thought of my own patient.

Mrs Leverton is said to suffer delusions. No one had told me what those delusions are, only that they are becoming less frequent, which is a positive sign, and that, if she should talk of them, I must not indulge her fantasies. I thought it difficult to not indulge a fantasy I had no idea about, so I asked Marion if she knew.

'She believes she killed someone.'

I must admit, I had been on my guard since I discovered the nature of Mrs Leverton's delusions. I had been watching her closely, wondering if I could recognise a killer if I saw one. I think I would be able to. After all, there must be something that sets them apart – like horns underneath their hair or sharp teeth or something – and I have concluded that Mrs Leverton certainly has nothing of that sort. She loves animals and is a mother-figure to another patient called Alice, a thirty-year-old epileptic whose brain has not developed since infancy. She even smiles at me nowadays.

Dr Basildon is pleased with my progress. He had me into his office today to review my first week. He said that Mrs Thorpe has spoken highly of me and that Mrs Leverton is pleased with me.

'Are you happy here?' he said.

I didn't know what to say. No employer has ever asked me the question before. But I am happy here, I decided in that moment. The house is beautiful, and I am making a good friend of Marion.

'Yes, sir.'

'You should like to stay?'

'Yes, sir.'

'Good. You understand that we value respectability here?'

I nodded.

'Attendants must set the best of standards.'

I nodded again.

'Relationships are not allowed. It does not set the moral tone we aim for.'

I nodded, but my head felt very stiff. Suddenly, Bertie's tongue was on mine, his hands were pressing into my thighs. I cleared my throat and pushed away those thoughts, for I did not want them to show on my face.

Dr Basildon stood up and wandered around his desk, trailing his finger along the spines of his books, until he came before me. He smelt of soap, as if he'd just scrubbed himself clean. I stayed in my seat, and studied his shiny black shoes.

'You have Thursday afternoon free. You may leave now, Miss Owen.'

I jumped up straight away and scarpered out of there, and then I wrote a note to Bertie and sent it off with all the other letters.

5

1956

Iris tiptoed down the centre of the ward. Some of the patients moaned at her as she did so, but she put a finger to her lips to keep them quiet. When she reached the end, she discovered Kath's bed was empty.

'Miss Lowe, you're here early.' Nurse Rattan emerged from the staff room, quickly swallowing whatever she had just stuffed into her mouth. White crumbs clung to her lips.

'I couldn't sleep. Thought I might as well come and make myself useful.' She put her bag in the staff room then joined Nurse Rattan. 'Any trouble tonight?'

Rattan shook her head and her jaw dropped open into a yawn. 'All pretty quiet.'

The light from outside was trying to get in through the gaps in the curtains. There was a beam of bright yellow on the empty bed.

'Where is Kath?'

'Took a turn, apparently. Yesterday morning.'

'What kind of turn?'

'Something to do with her chest, I'd imagine. Or her heart. Who knows with them in here? They're all at death's door.'

'She's not dead, is she?' Iris said, trying to keep her voice calm. Kath's breathing had been getting worse and worse, and she'd been hacking up great big globs of green phlegm.

'She wasn't yesterday. Haven't heard anything since.'

Iris fell quiet.

'You have to get used to it in here,' Rattan said as she stared into the gloom of the ward. 'They're all going to go at some point.'

They sat in silence, the only sound coming from Nurse Rattan sucking her teeth. It set Iris on edge. She would have started to clean the floor, but that would have woken the patients, and Rattan had no intention of getting any of them up; she was to look after them whilst they slept and nothing more.

Finally, the other staff arrived, and Nurse Rattan hauled herself to her feet. Iris hopped up and opened the curtains.

'You're very fresh this morning,' Shirley said, scowling at her.

'He still hasn't called?'

'No.' Shirley yanked the bedsheets off Flo and grappled the lady onto the commode.

'Do you know what happened to Kath?' Iris said.

Shirley squinted to where Kath should have been. 'She was fine Saturday.' She lifted Flo back onto the bed.

Flo grabbed Iris's hand and pulled her close. She had green eyes which were watery at the edges, lips that disappeared into her face, and short, fine hair as grey as a rain cloud. Who would she have been when she was Iris's age? The Kath in this life and the Katy from the diary seemed like completely different people, but of course, they weren't. Had Flo been as full of life as Katy? And what would Iris be like when she was old, with liver spots and cataracts, a burden to everyone around her?

'You're all right, Flo, just lie down for me and we'll get you dressed soon.' Iris stroked Flo's hair until the woman's grip began to weaken.

'Ready now?' Shirley waited beside Dot's bed, staring at Iris, hands on hips.

Iris hated that about Shirley; when she was in a bad mood, everyone knew it. The patients cringed away from her, Iris stepped on eggshells; nothing anyone said was right, and everything earned you a glare from her beautiful blue eyes.

Iris wouldn't speak to her whilst she was like it.

When they had finished seeing to the patients, Iris caught Nurse Carmichael as everyone made their way to the day room for breakfast.

'Excuse me, ma'am, what has happened to Kath?'

'She's been moved to the infirmary. Pneumonia, they think. Her lips were turning blue.'

'Is she any better today?'

'I haven't had the time to enquire.'

At the end of her shift, Iris paced down the corridors of Smedley. Sun slanted in through the tall windows, bleaching the white tiles on the floor. Everyone was on the move, the day shifters leaving, anxious to get home to enjoy the last rays of sun, the night shifters plodding inside, reluctant to get to work.

'Iris!' Behind, Shirley trotted up to Iris, a grin pinching her lips, her eyes glinting. 'Where are you off to so quick?' She didn't give Iris time to answer. 'What are you doing Friday night?'

'What do you want, Shirley?'

'What's stung you? Will you come to the pictures with me?'

'Does this have something to do with Dr Brown, by any chance?'

She pouted and scuffed her shoe on the floor. 'Might do.'

Iris turned to walk away. 'I shall only be in the way.'

'Don't be silly! I wouldn't be asking if I didn't want you to come.' Shirley grabbed her arm. 'Please come, Iris!'

Shirley could be a pain, but there was something about her – a giddy, childish charm – which Iris couldn't ever seem to say no to. 'Fine.'

'Fabulous! There's a late night showing at ten.'

'We might not have finished work—' Iris called, but Shirley was running down the corridor and out of the main door, where a young doctor held the door for her.

Kath was not dead. Iris found her in a bed at the far end of a ward by the window. She and the other patients around her were dozing, sunk into their beds, the flowers on their cabinets wilting in the heat.

Kath looked so small. The loose nightgown showed the protrusion of her breastbone and the stretch of thin skin across it. Propped up on top of three pillows, her mouth gaped, and her breath rattled in the quiet of the room. Her hair was a mess; she would have been upset about that. Iris would bring a brush next time.

Iris slipped her hand over Kath's. Her fingers were icy, the bones sharp under the weak muscle, but on contact, Kath opened her eyes and peered at Iris.

'Hello. How are you?' A stupid question, but Iris couldn't find any other words.

Kath's mouth opened further. She sucked in a breath, then coughed. The cough grew worse, the liquid on her lungs bubbling up her throat. Iris put an arm around her back and sat her upright so she could get the stuff up. She spat the green mucus into the dish that Iris held under her chin, then Iris wiped her mouth and made her sip some water.

Kath sagged onto her pillows. Some strands of hair stuck to her forehead, and Iris pushed them off, feeling the heat from Kath's head.

'I started your diary.'

Kath squinted at her.

'Mrs Leverton sounded quite a character.'

Kath brought her lips together as if she would say something, but no sound came out.

'It's all right, you just rest.'

In a few minutes, Kath was sleeping. A middle-aged nurse came onto the ward to distribute the tablets.

'How is she?' Iris said.

'Bad.' Nurse Okeke – as it said on her name-tag – put her hand to Kath's forehead and tutted. 'Are you her daughter?'

'No. I... She was on my ward before.'

'You work on Ward 13?' The woman's chocolate-coloured eyes widened.

Iris nodded.

'That place.' The nurse sniffed and said no more; she didn't need to. The ward was a shambles – was it any wonder Kath had fallen ill in there? Too many patients and too few staff.

'I wasn't here yesterday. Has she improved?'

'A little. She was given oxygen last night, which seemed to help.'

'Will she recover?'

The nurse shrugged. 'She is old, too skinny. The antibiotics must fight it off.' She placed the penicillin tablets on the table. 'Kath?'

Kath flinched.

'It is time for your tablets.' The nurse slipped her hand underneath Kath's head and lifted her. She put the tablet into Kath's open mouth and held the glass to her lips. Kath did as she was supposed to, and Iris saw her throat move as she struggled to swallow.

'Good girl.' The nurse placed her down, then looked at Iris. 'It is getting late.'

'I would like to stay a little longer, if that's all right?'

The nurse glanced through the door but, seeing everywhere was quiet, nodded. 'Twenty minutes.'

Iris picked up her bag off the floor and brought out the diary. Kath's eyes opened when she saw it, and she reached out for it. Iris put the book on the bed, and Kath's fingers traced its flat, leather surface.

'I thought I might read it to you, if you'd like that?'

Kath plucked at the binding, then pushed it towards Iris. Iris picked up where she had left off.

6

1900

Thursday, 4th October

I saw Bertie today. It was after lunch, and Mrs Thorpe had taken over main care of Mrs Leverton, and so I had several hours before I needed to return to get her to bed.

I had thought he wasn't coming, for I waited and waited when I got to the woods. I watched the leaves falling off the trees and I broke them between my fingers. I like it when the leaves go all crisp like that. I snapped them into tiny pieces and made orange-coloured confetti, and I threw it in the air and walked into it, imaging I was on Bertie's arm and we'd just got married.

I heard a giggle then, and I saw him striding towards me. His cheeks were as red as apples, and his breath was coming quick and sharp. He'd taken off his jacket and hat, and sweat shone on his brow.

He said nothing before he kissed me, long and slow. He was buzzing with heat, and I curled into him, for I'd got cold from sitting on the damp stump for such a while.

He asked me how I was getting on, and I told him all about Mrs Leverton and Marion, but I didn't tell him much more. I didn't want my whole time away from The Retreat to be filled with talk of it.

I asked about home. He said he'd seen my ma and da only this morning and that my little sister, May, was getting on well in Mr Roddington's house. He hadn't told them he was meeting me, of course.

He'd brought a blanket with him, and a sausage roll and a bottle of beer, so we sat on the grass beside the river and ate and drank in silence, watching the water but mainly watching each other. That's when I told him.

'I'm not supposed to have relations with you.'

'Why?'

'Dr Basildon says it's not appropriate, that it doesn't set the right morals for the patients to follow.'

'Never stopped us when you were at Cotton's.' He smiled at me, just a small smile with a glimmer of his teeth showing. 'Do you want to stop now?'

'No.'

'Well, then.' He gulped his beer.

'But I don't want to get sacked again.'

'Cotton never knew about us.'

'Then why was I let go?'

Bertie rolled up his jacket and used it like a pillow as he lay down. 'If he'd known about us, he'd have said. And I wouldn't be delivering to him now.'

I lay down beside him and put my head on his chest. He wrapped his arm around me.

'No one knows, Katy. Stop worrying.'

And I did stop worrying. Anything Bertie says, I just do.

I kissed his chin, and then his mouth, and then he rolled on top of me and kissed me some more. And then... Well, I shan't write it down, but I shall say that it was wonderful like it always is.

By the time we'd finished, it was almost dark. We lay in the twilight, looking up into the navy sky, watching the stars begin to peep out. Bertie started whistling, just gently.

'My little Bertie Blackbird. A song to send me to sleep.'

My eyes shut, and all I felt was the thrum of his breath and his heartbeat against my cheek. My feet had gone numb with cold, but Bertie had put his jacket over both of us, and I was snuggly warm on my top half.

When his song ended, I opened my eyes, and the sky was black. I said I needed to get back, and then I remembered I hadn't brought a lamp. Bertie said he would walk me to the track so that I wouldn't be alone in the dark. We held hands all the way, and I could have spat at the track when I saw it, for it had come up too fast.

We kissed again, and I clung onto him a bit too tight. He took my hands in his, kissed my fingers, told me he loved me, then disappeared into the night.

Friday, 5th October

I am dead to the world as I write this, but write it, I must.

I woke this morning like usual, had my porridge, then went to Mrs Leverton. The first thing she asked was what day it was. I told her Friday. She asked for the date. I told her the fifth.

She nodded. I took her to the closet, let her do her business, then washed her in the bathroom. I put her in a black dress, like usual – she only ever wears black – and then she said she would not be eating anything today. I told her that she must eat, and I brought her breakfast tray to her, but she would not pick anything up. I buttered a slice of toast and brought it before her lips, but she would not open them.

I had to tell Mrs Thorpe. She nodded and said Mrs Leverton does this every year on this date, that it's all connected with her delusions. She told me to find Dr Basildon and inform him.

I went to his office and knocked, but there was no reply. I was about to make my way back to the day room when Mrs Basildon emerged from one of the doors on the first floor. She was dressed all in pink, her black hair piled on top of her head like a deflated air balloon. She is not the handsomest of women; her nose is rather long, and her cheeks are flat, and there is a dark shadow across her upper lip, but the worst thing is that she never smiles.

'What are you doing here?' She stopped a few feet away from me, as if I might have had the plague.

'I was looking for Dr Basildon, ma'am.'

'He will be examining in the male wing at this time. You shall have to wait.'

'Yes, ma'am.'

'What is your name?'

I told her, and her face changed. Her previous expression had been one of boredom, at best. Now she looked at me with such disgust that I had to avert my gaze. Without another word, she flounced past me and was gone.

I waited almost ten minutes for Dr Basildon to return. As he came up the stairs, I noticed the bald patch beginning to form on his crown. He was taken aback when he saw me, and he smiled so widely that my words caught in my mouth. He's a different man when he smiles; the lines that crinkle his face soften him, and his eyes glitter instead of pierce.

'Miss Owen, for what do I have the pleasure?'

I told him, as best I could as I tried to cool my cheeks, what was wrong.

'After you.' He gestured for me to lead the way. Mrs Leverton was in her chamber, on her knees, like every other night. This time, though, she was crying as well as reciting whatever it is that she normally says to herself over and over.

'Mrs Leverton, I hear you have not eaten today.'

I thought it rather rude to interrupt someone at prayer, but then, perhaps, it doesn't count when they are insane. Mrs Leverton did not respond.

'You must eat to stay healthy, Mrs Leverton.'

No response. I could feel my toes twitching, but Dr Basildon didn't seem at all flustered.

'Mrs Leverton, you know what will happen if you do not eat.'

Mrs Leverton stopped whispering. The doctor walked in front of her, blocking her view of the cross.

'I must repent,' she said to him.

He nodded very slowly. 'You must eat.'

'I cannot. He cannot, so I must not.'

'Mrs Leverton, you are a reasonable woman, so I shall reason with you. You may repent for the rest of the day, but you must eat all of your meals.'

His eyes never left her as she considered her options. I don't wish to imagine what would have happened if she had refused.

He left then, after thanking me for my diligence. Mrs Leverton ate a slice of toast without fuss before returning to her prayers. The day continued like that. I walked Annie on my own, and I even had to do some sewing so that I didn't have to watch Mrs Leverton all the time, for I couldn't bear to see the way she quivered, as if she might collapse from exhaustion at any minute. When it came time for dinner, she could not get to her feet herself, and I had to help her up by fixing her arm around my shoulder.

When we came back from dinner, she winced as she got to her knees once more, and I saw vast yellow-brown bruises on her kneecaps. She stayed there for another hour before she let me get her into bed. Annie came up to the pillow and burrowed against her, as if she might bear some of her mistress's pain if it were possible to do so.

'Thirty years,' she said as she struggled to keep her eyes open. 'He would be fifty-one now.'

I pulled the covers up to her chin, smoothed down her hair. 'Who?'

'Edward.'

I shouldn't indulge her delusions, so I ignored her.

'Sleep well, Mrs Leverton,' I said, but tears were already sliding across her temples.

7

1956

Her mum was lingering outside Iris's door, listening for gossip; Iris could feel her presence.

'I don't like that girl,' she had grumbled when Iris had said Shirley was coming over. 'Father's a drunk, so I hear.'

'What's that got to do with Shirley?' Iris had said as she'd shovelled cold fish and chips into her mouth. The fat on them had solidified into white slime.

'They live on Brookside.' Mum blew on her cup of cocoa. 'Rough area. I don't want you going around there.'

'She's courting a doctor.' Iris had smirked as her mother's jaw dropped.

Now, Shirley was in Iris's bedroom. She had brought her own makeup bag and had sat Iris on the edge of the bed whilst she threw rouge on her cheeks. She brought out the mascara wand.

'I really don't want—'

'Don't be silly. You have lovely eyes, Iris.' She grabbed Iris's chin and held her tight as she poked the mascara at her. Iris blinked instinctively, her eyes filling with water each time she saw the black stick darting towards her. 'Hold still, will you? We'll be late if you carry on like this.'

Iris tried her best, but eventually Shirley jabbed the wand back in the pot, defeated. She pulled out an eyebrow pencil instead.

Shirley smelt divine, and Iris caught sight of the bottle of Chanel No. 5 in her makeup bag. She didn't know where Shirley had got it from; it was too expensive for a nurse's wages. But Shirley always got her hands on the latest fashions, one way or another.

She was wearing a black cocktail dress, pinched in tight at the waist, showing off her enviable figure. The black was arresting against the paleness of her skin, the sparkle of her platinum hair, the blood-red of her lipstick.

'There you are.' Shirley stepped away from Iris, her arms wide as if Iris was a prize worth presenting.

Iris found her own reflection in the mirror. She was nothing compared to Shirley, but she wasn't bad. Shirley had done a good job, combing her hair into a classy chignon, forcing her into some kitten heels to show off the slenderness of her ankles. The red lipstick was a bit garish, but the pink skirt and cream top suited her, and her eyes did sparkle.

'He'll love you,' Shirley said.

Iris whirled around. 'Who will?'

'Simon.'

'Who on earth is Simon?'

'John's friend.'

Iris ripped a tissue out of her bag and rubbed off her lipstick.

'What are you doing?' Shirley caught her hand.

'I'm not going on a date with a man I have never met before.'

'Why not? It'll be fun.'

'It might be for you, Shirley, but it won't be for me.'

'Oh, come on, Iris! You're such a bore.'

Iris chucked the tissue on her bed and faced Shirley. 'Then why do you want me to come, anyway?'

Shirley sighed. 'I didn't mean it like that. Don't get upset with me. I just think you'll like him. He's nice.'

'Is he?'

'He's tall.'

'And?'

'He must be clever; he works at a bank. Him and John have been friends since school.'

'Was this your idea or John's?'

'John just said that Simon was looking for a girl and asked if I had a friend. And, of course, I said you were my best friend and would be delighted to go out with us.' She clutched Iris's hand. 'Come on, Iris, it's only one night. Surely it's better than wiping old ladies' bottoms.'

They waited outside the picture-house next to the growing queue. Shirley kept stepping into the pavement to see if their men were coming, cigarette in hand and blowing out puffs of smoke, before slinking back to Iris's side.

'A smile wouldn't hurt,' Shirley said.

Iris glared at her. Boys in the queue were already gawping at them – at Shirley, mostly – and twisting their heads away from their sweethearts, who sent dirty looks to Iris.

'They aren't coming. Let's just get in the queue and get inside.'

'Of course they're coming. John wouldn't stand me up.'

'Wouldn't he?' Iris said under her breath, but Shirley caught it.

'Have a drag on this and shut up.' She shoved the cigarette in Iris's face, but Iris pulled away. Before Shirley had time to try again, something caught her attention. She flung the cigarette on the floor and trotted towards the pavement. 'Told you!'

She ran straight for Dr Brown. Iris hadn't seen John Brown before. He was dashingly handsome. His hair was slicked back in the way of the film stars, and he wore a tight white t-shirt and denim jeans. His skin, in the weakening light, appeared dusted with gold. Shirley draped her arms over his shoulders and pecked him on the cheek, and all the boys in the queue turned disappointedly back to their sweethearts.

Next to him, and almost a head taller, was the man who Iris assumed must have been Simon. He was meatier than John, his features soft behind his fleshy, pink cheeks, and his hair was dark and short. He wore a suit and tie that would not have looked out of place on her dad.

'This is Iris,' Shirley said as she brought the men over. John gave Iris a quick nod then got his cigarettes out of his jeans back pocket.

'Nice to meet you. I'm Simon.' His hand jerked up, as if he would have doffed his hat, had he been wearing one.

Iris forced her lips into the best smile she could muster.

'The Talbot, then?' John began to walk off with Shirley still clinging to his arm.

'I thought we were seeing a film?'

John stopped and glanced over his shoulder at Iris. 'We're having a drink first.' He walked on.

Shirley didn't even look at her, too busy whispering and giggling in John's ear. Iris hesitated by the picture-house, cursing herself for agreeing to come out at all. She hated pubs, she hated blind dates, and she was beginning to hate John and Shirley.

She could sneak away; they probably wouldn't even notice she was gone until she was home and safe, but there was Simon, halfway between his friend and Iris, turning between the two of them, waiting for Iris to catch up.

She chomped on her tongue and stalked to meet him.

The pub was full of old men. Their glassy eyes turned on the four of them as they entered, staring in awe and contempt as Shirley and John paraded to the bar.

Simon led Iris to a table in the corner of the room, as far away from the other customers as possible.

'What would you like to drink?' he asked.

'Half a shandy, please.'

Once he'd gone to the bar, Iris took the opportunity to pull the neck of her top up. She had become all too aware of how the loose cotton sagged to show more of her flesh than she was comfortable with, especially in a place like this. Her skirt felt too short as well, and her nylons were far too thin. The backs of her heels were already beginning to throb from her shoes.

Shirley scuttled over to Iris and slid onto a chair.

'So, what do you think?' She scrunched the curls in her hair tighter and glanced down at her cleavage.

'We were meant to be seeing a film.'

'We will, but John doesn't like the little one at the start, nor the news. What do you think of Simon? Handsome, isn't he?'

Iris supposed he was handsome to some, but he was too big for her. He took up so much space at the bar, a bit like her brother, and in truth, the size of him made her uneasy.

'For goodness' sake, Iris, try to cheer up. You look constipated.' There was the glint; the old Shirley that Iris knew.

'What did we miss?' Simon placed their glasses on the table.

'We were just laughing about Nurse Carmichael, what a dragon she is.'

Iris shot Shirley a look – it would do them no good if rumour spread about them laughing at the charge nurse. Shirley merely rolled her eyes.

'You work at Smedley too?' Simon said, averting his gaze from his friend, who was moving his finger down Shirley's arm and under the table.

'Yes, I'm in the same ward as Shirley.'

'I should say that's a hard job.'

'I like it.'

'I couldn't be doing with those sorts of people around me all the time.'

Iris bristled. 'Those sorts of people need help. If we didn't give it to them, they wouldn't get any at all.'

Simon gulped his beer. 'They're thinking of letting them out now, aren't they? They'll be roaming our streets doing God knows what.'

'Oh, yes, they'll all go about murdering babies, I should imagine.'

Shirley's shoe stabbed Iris in the shin.

'And what do you do, Simon?' Shirley said quickly before anyone noticed Iris's moan of pain. 'John tells me you work in a bank?'

'I'm the manager at the one on Hayward Street.'

'Manager!' Shirley widened her eyes at Iris. 'And how is it you've not got yourself a sweetheart, Simon? I'd imagine you'd be batting them off.'

Simon blushed as he laughed. Iris also couldn't believe the brass of her friend.

'He's picky. Aren't you?' John slapped him on the shoulder. 'Another pint.'

It was mercifully dark on the walk back to her house. Shirley and John had splintered off. They'd said John was going to walk Shirley home, but Iris wasn't a fool; it would be a while before Shirley was tucked up in bed, alone.

So now, Iris had to try to make conversation with Simon. The film had been a bore; unknown actors and a terrible plot line which mainly involved murdering young girls in black alleyways. The other girls in the picture-house had seemed suitably horrified, squirming into their men's arms and letting them shield them from the terror.

Shirley had buried her face in John's neck and kept it there for too long. Simon had glanced at Iris a few times, wondering, she'd imagined, whether she too was going to fall faint. Iris had kept her gaze locked on the screen, her face arranged in an expression of frosty scepticism.

Now, her heels clipped too loudly on the pavement. She feared she would wake the neighbours and hated the idea of old ladies peering out from behind net curtains at them.

'Are you cold?' Simon said, about to take off his jacket.

'I'm fine. It makes a nice change.'

'Heatwaves,' he said, and she heard the smile in his voice. 'We can never get it right in this country.'

They were one street away from Iris's house. She picked up the pace.

'You're working tomorrow?' Simon said.

'Yes. You?'

'Yes.'

She racked her brain for something to say, anything to fill the silence until she could shut the door on him, but nothing came.

'I didn't mean to upset you earlier, with what I said about your patients.'

'You didn't.'

'You're sure? It's just that I have very little experience of anybody so... afflicted. I think of them as they are in the films. And you hear things in the newspapers, dreadful stories.'

'The women on my ward are just old. They've been there most of their lives. Forgotten or turfed out by their families. It makes me angry that people could do such a thing to their own.'

She stopped outside her house. Simon walked on for a moment, then saw that she was not by his side. He looked back at her and at the cramped Victorian terrace in alarm.

'This is you?'

Iris nodded, trying to hide her smirk. He was a rich boy, no doubt about it.

'Right, good. Well, nice to meet you, Iris.'

'You too.'

He dashed in to kiss her cheek and she felt the stubble on his top lip, smelt the scent of beer and the faint mustiness of sweat as the breeze caught his jacket.

'Do you know how to get home?' she said, because he was lingering.

'I think so.'

She smiled briefly, then walked to her front door. She didn't turn around.

Her mother was in the hallway, waiting, perching on the stairs like a gargoyle.

'How did it go? He looks a very nice boy.'

'You were spying on me?'

'I heard voices. I didn't know who it was.'

Iris dropped her bag on the step and trudged into the kitchen to get herself a cup of water.

'What's his name?' Her mum came up behind her, her slippers slapping on the floor.

'Simon.'

'Simon what?'

'I don't know, I didn't ask.'

'You've been on a date with a boy, and you don't know his surname!'

'But I didn't know it was a date, did I?'

'Well, I told you I don't like that Shirley. If you will insist on going out with her...'

Iris slumped onto the kitchen chair and drank the water, concentrating on the sensation of it trickling icily into her stomach.

'What's he like?' Her mum was wide awake, though Iris was more than ready for sleep. 'What does he do?'

'Bank manager.'

'Oh, my!' She let out a giggle, then pushed her hand to her lips. She continued in a whisper. 'You keep hold of him, love. They don't come around often.'

Obviously, it didn't matter that Iris didn't like him, that she found the thought of his body against hers repulsive. Just so long as he had a bit of money!

'Good night.' She left the glass on the table and kissed her mother on the forehead. She could not have another conversation like this, not now.

She dragged her feet upstairs. In the bathroom, she splashed her face with cold water, flinching at the temperature, then wiped her makeup onto an old towel. She heard her mother creak up the stairs, and for a moment, she felt guilty for not being the daughter her mum seemed so desperate for. But then she looked at her reflection in the mirror.

She did not want to wear pink skirts and have pretty hair and totter around in high heels. Her reflection was pleasant, yes, but it wasn't Iris, not the Iris she wanted to be. She didn't care if the Johns of the world looked at her like something on the bottom of their shoe, or if the Simons of the world thought her odd – to hell with them! And apart from a handsome face and a fat bank account, what was so special about them anyway?

She pulled out Kath's diary before she slipped into bed. She had been reading little bits to Kath all this week after her shift, hoping it would rouse her, but still Kath had not improved. Iris would have to ring Albert tomorrow and tell him to prepare for the worst, but for now, all she wanted to do was disappear into Katy's world.

8

1900

Monday, 29th October

I have been here for over one month now. As with anything, I can't imagine my life as it was before. Did I really work for Reverend Cotton, cleaning the step and blacking the range and cooking all the meals and darning the socks?

It is luxurious to only attend to Mrs Leverton, for truly she seems as sane as me. Our habits are forming well. After wash and breakfast, we take a stroll around the grounds with Annie. The little dog runs along in front, sticking her nose into clumps of grass and hunting for worms and birds. Mrs Leverton takes my arm for support now, whereas at first, she would not. We wander at her pace, and we follow the same path which skirts beside the woodland until we come to the mound. Mrs Leverton walks onto that mound each time and smiles at the view, and it is like she is a goddess overlooking the earth.

'I can breathe up here,' she said to me once, by way of explanation.

I've realised she always positions herself near a window so that she may look out. She hates the woods, the closeness of the trees. I believe she does not like the thought of being trapped.

After our walk, we go to the day room, where she plays her tin whistle or writes. She does not show me her writing, but once I happened to look over her shoulder and saw that she addressed it to Edward. I told Mrs Thorpe and she just shook her head and smiled, the same kind of smile that mothers do when they talk about how useless fathers are, but love them all the same.

Alice always finds her when she is in the day room. She is a sweet girl, and it is hard to believe that she is twelve years my senior and daughter of a Laird and Lady on the Scottish borders. She holds her mouth open and often drools onto Mrs Leverton's dresses, but Mrs Leverton doesn't mind. In the afternoons, they read her favourite book, *Alice's Adventures in Wonderland*. When they have finished that, they begin the sequel, *Through the Looking Glass*, and when they have finished that, they start all over again. I asked Mrs Leverton how many times she has read the books, and she said she has lost count.

There is a tenderness between the two of them, a language that doesn't need words. Mrs Leverton is the only one who can calm Alice when she gets herself in a bother. It's a dangerous business for Alice to get in a bother, for that is when her fits begin, and they can last whole minutes. I've only seen it happen once. She fell to the floor, and her body shook and arched. The veins popped out on her neck and forehead, her eyes rolled back, and her lips went blue.

That one lasted only seconds, and she started gulping for air soon enough, but then she was all wobbly and her words didn't come out right. Miss Wade – that's her attendant, who used to be her governess, when she was a child – was no use whatsoever. She just stood beside the wall, watching, waiting for it to pass, while Mrs Leverton was down beside Alice, telling her it was going to be all right, telling her to breathe, holding her hair out of her face. I felt ever so proud of Mrs Leverton then.

When Alice had finished, Miss Wade and Mrs Thorpe bundled her up between themselves and carted her to her room while she flopped between them, still murmuring nonsense.

'She'll sleep for a day now,' Mrs Leverton said as she resumed her seat beside the fireplace. I could tell she was upset. She tried to hold her book, but her hands were trembling, so she threw it on the table.

'You're very close to Alice,' I said as I started on a piece of sewing.

'We've been here the longest. She arrived in eighty-two.'

The year I was born, I thought. I was never any good at numbers and it took me a good few minutes for me to work it out. 'She was twelve when she came?'

'She was abandoned. I can remember that day with such clarity. She was small for her age, arms as thin as twigs. She was like a deer who'd been shot, her eyes bulging as she clung to Miss Wade. She's never given that poor girl any affection, you know, not even then.'

'Does her mother visit?'

Mrs Leverton laughed, but it was a bitter laugh, and her eyes looked as hard as marbles as she stared into the fire. 'She is dead to her mother.'

'I suppose you are like a mother to her now?'

She opened her book again, and after a while, she said, 'Do you wish to be a mother, Katy?'

My needle dropped into my lap, silver against grey. I couldn't find it until it poked into my wrist and made me bleed.

'I don't know.'

'It is not easy, being a mother. One has to be selfless, to put one's child above all others. Not everyone can do it.'

I thought that I didn't want to be a mother just yet, but perhaps in a few years, when me and Bertie were more settled. It made me think of Bertie, and of lots of little Berties all running around. Our babies would have his black hair and my blue eyes. They'd have clear skin like Bertie and no silly freckles like me. They'd have my da's height, for Bertie does loath how short he is, and our sons would be strong like their father, and our daughters would be loyal, like me.

'Alice is the only female in here who is childless,' Mrs Leverton said, and I dragged my thoughts away from Bertie.

I looked about the room. The other three patients sat with their attendants against the walls, each doing their own thing.

Mrs Josephine Beckwith was playing a game of bread-and-honey with Winifred, her attendant. Wini seemed to be letting her win, for Mrs Beckwith had nearly all of the cards. Mrs Beckwith was somewhere in her forties, although she looked older than Mrs Leverton. Marion told me that was on account of her habit, the alcohol making the blood drain from her face, leaving her grey and shrivelled.

'She started drinking after her husband died,' Mrs Leverton said, when she saw me looking. 'Her brother took her daughter as his ward when he had Josephine committed.'

I then turned to Mrs Viola Milton, who was staring at the centre of the room while Nella brushed her long, grey hair. Nella was a kind woman who always talked to me if she ever found me on my own. She'd become an attendant after her husband had died, for she'd no hankering to marry again and wanted to put her Christianity to good use. She'd told me that Mrs Milton was almost eighty years old and was suffering from senile insanity, that she couldn't even remember her own children, so they'd stopped visiting.

'It is Rose you have to be careful of.'

Mrs Rose Huxley and Marion sat at the far end of the room, attempting to read.

'She twitches, do you see? There, her hand.'

Mrs Huxley's hand jerked, as if batting away a fly.

'And now look at her eyes.'

Mrs Huxley was staring at the pages of the book.

'She is not reading,' Mrs Leverton said.

'She is.'

'Watch. Her eyes are not moving, are they? She is still, so still. Don't you think it looks like she is listening to something?'

The longer I watched, the more I could see what Mrs Leverton meant. Mrs Huxley's head was slightly tilted, and a frown deep onto her forehead. Her fingernails began to dig into the leather on the back of the book. Marion, on the other hand, was busy arranging a vase of flowers on the table beside her, oblivious.

'Watch her,' Mrs Leverton whispered. 'Any moment ...'

Mrs Huxley screamed and hurled her novel into the air. It came crashing towards me, stopping just inches from my chair. She sprang to her feet and charged, pounding towards me, her arms outstretched, her fingers clawing at nothing, her face the colour of blood.

The scream turned into a low, animal wail the closer she came, glaring at me, and just as I closed my eyes and braced myself for her impact, there was the dreadful crack of bone against wood. I opened my eyes to find Wini straddling Mrs Huxley on the floor, her muscular arms pinning Mrs Huxley down as she writhed.

'Leave them alone!' Mrs Huxley screamed, again and again.

Mrs Thorpe came running into the room and told Marion to take charge of Mrs Beckwith, for she too was becoming agitated.

My heart had never beat so fast in all my life. My breath was too quick, and it was making my head dizzy. Mrs Leverton squeezed my hand until I'd got myself under control.

Mrs Huxley started to cry. Her body grew limp, and she sobbed into the floor, her tears spilling onto the wood. I wanted to lift her up and hold her in my arms and tell her that it was all in her head, that none of it was real, that not even the devil would torture a babe, that God would not allow such a thing. But Wini and Mrs Thorpe dragged her upwards, and when she would not walk herself, they dragged her out of the day room too. In the silence, we heard her shoes banging against each step as they carried her up the stairs.

'She would have been a wonderful mother,' Mrs Leverton said. 'Sometimes, death really is better than living.'

Wednesday 7th November

It has been bitter today and has not stopped raining. I do hate November. It is such a bleak month. The fog this morning never lifted, and all day we've been held in the clouds, as if we are the only people on Earth. It made Mrs Leverton odd. She paced relentlessly, not even sitting down for Alice when it came time to read the next chapter, but Mrs Leverton knows the story so well that she recited it from memory while the girl followed at her heels, like Annie.

'I have to see,' Mrs Leverton mumbled as she leant against one of the stone pillars under the veranda this afternoon, squinting at the fog. Her brown eyes absorbed the whiteness and looked ghostly. I didn't like it one bit. I begged her to come inside, to keep warm beside the fire, but she would not have it.

'It is like we have been buried,' she said.

Mrs Thorpe told me to prepare a hot toddy for Mrs Leverton, which seemed to ease her, and when the sun had gone down she returned to normal, but when she got into bed, her feet were so cold they did indeed feel as if they belonged to a corpse. I rubbed them for several minutes until the blood returned, and when I'd finished, she had already fallen to sleep.

My feet never warmed, though. Our room is full of draughts, and the grate splutters out such useless heat that it is pointless even lighting it. Marion came into my bed to try to warm me. She reminds me a little of a wood pigeon, all plump and soft, her chin tucked into her bosom because her neck is so short, and she is never cold.

I'd been moaning about the state of my hair. The weather had made it all flat and dull, and I'm meeting Bertie tomorrow afternoon, so I was desperate for it to have a curl. I'd been trying to get my hairbrush through it, but the tangles were so bad, and I was so cold and tired that tears were coming to my eyes.

'Let me do that,' Marion said, and began brushing for me, easing out the knots so I didn't feel a thing. 'I used to do this for my little sister.'

I told her about my May, how she'd never liked me to brush her hair or dress her or do anything for her – she was always so headstrong. She infuriated me at times, and I her, although I must admit that now I do rather miss seeing her sullen face. To stop me from wallowing in silly homesickness, I asked Marion what her sister was like.

'She's dead.'

I cursed myself for speaking harshly about May. Marion must have thought me so mean-hearted and selfish.

'I'm sorry, Marion. What happened?'

'Her lungs were weak. All of her was weak, really. She would sit up most nights and cough until blood came out. It was a dreadful thing to see, broke my ma's heart. I remember putting her to bed and thinking it looked as if there was no one inside the sheets. She was nothing but skin and bone, you see. But she had the sweetest heart, and she'd always want the window open so that she could hear the birds in the morning. And she was so pretty. Blonde hair and blue eyes, just like you, and the prettiest smile you ever did see.'

'How old was she when she passed?'

'Eight. She had no fear. She was the bravest little girl I've ever known.'

We were quiet for a while as Marion carried on brushing out my hair. Then she started to curl it round my ribbons.

'You've got beautiful hair. I wish I had it. I am just plain Marion.'

'You are not,' I said. I tried to think of something that was pretty about her, but by the time I'd remembered that her lips were fair and red and full, she'd laughed and moved on.

'Going to see your ma tomorrow?'

I mumbled nonsense at her, for I didn't want to lie to her, but I couldn't tell her the truth, either.

Suddenly, she nicked me in the ribs and whispered like a schoolgirl, 'You got a beau?'

I shook my head so violently that some of the ribbons tumbled out and Marion had to quickly tie them back into place.

'Surely you must have all the boys after you back home?'

'Hardly. What about you?' I said, and hoped she would not see my face.

'Oh, yes, I have all the boys.' She snorted and put her hand over her mouth. 'Have you ever kissed a boy, Katy?'

I didn't think a kiss was such a bad thing, and I didn't need to say who I'd kissed nor how many times. 'Yes.'

'What's it like?'

'Nice.'

'You have got a beau! I knew it! I can see it in your smile.'

'Don't be silly.'

She jumped out of my bed, as if there was a bright, new day ahead of her instead of a long, cold night. 'To kiss a boy's lips,' she said with a deep sigh then fell onto her own bed. 'I shan't ever find out what it's like.'

'Of course, you will. You will make a fine wife, Marion. A boy – a man – would be lucky to have you to call his own.'

'Not for me. And I've no need for your pity, Katy Owen! In all truth, I am only curious about it. I have no real yearning for it.'

'What do you yearn for?' I rolled over so we were lying on our pillows, hugging our covers, and staring at each other.

'I want to help people. I just want to do this.'

'Forever?' I said, unable to contain my horror at the prospect.

'I'll pass my exams next year, and I'll work here for a few more years, but here isn't where the real trouble is. They're all ladies, and it's really no hardship for them here, is it? Not like in the counties. That's where I want to work eventually, and I want to be a matron.'

I couldn't help smiling at her. Matron Marion amidst a sea of rocking and screaming lunatics – I could just imagine it.

'So.' She reached under her bed and found her handbook.

'It's almost midnight, Marion, can't you leave it just for tonight?'

She shook her head and started reading. She is a truly wonderful woman.

9

1900

Thursday, 8th November

The weather was kinder today. The sun was nowhere to be found, but at least the rain never came and the bitterness of yesterday did not return.

Bertie was already at our spot by the time I got there, and I could hear him whistling before I saw him. He had a small basket with him, and under three towels he'd packed two meat pies, still hot, and a jug of milk which had gone warm what with being next to the pies.

'How many children do you want, Bertie?' I said as we ate. The question almost made him choke. 'I'm being serious. How many children? I think I would be happy with two.'

Two seemed a good number to me, one boy and one girl. I don't have the hankering for any more pain than I really have to endure. You hear about women who push it too far, and on their fifth or sixth, something goes horribly wrong, and then they're dead. I don't want to die in childbirth. Can there be a worse to way to go? All the pain and blood, and then the thought that you'll never get to see your baby, never get to watch him or her grow up, never get to hold them and kiss them goodnight.

Those thoughts were making me sad, so I elbowed Bertie for an answer.

'Two would be fine, I suppose.'

'You only suppose?' He was such a man. I shook my head and laughed at him.

'You've never talked about babies before.'

'I was just thinking.' I didn't tell him about my conversation with Mrs Leverton.

'You should think a bit less.'

I was going to laugh again, but when I looked at him, he wasn't smiling. 'What's wrong with you today?'

'Nothing.' He wiped his hands on his trousers and sighed. He was looking about himself, never managing to keep his gaze still.

'Don't you want to be here?'

'It's not that.'

But he didn't meet my eye.

'You can go if you like, Bertie. I wouldn't want to keep you.' My voice was high and haughty, just a notch away from cracking. I bit into my pie again and chewed and chewed and tried to swallow the lump in my throat.

'I'm just cold,' he said.

'You sure that's all?' I turned to him, but he was blurred, what with the stupid tears that had come to my eyes.

'Eh, none of that. Don't you go crying over me, Katy. Don't ever cry over me.'

He wiped the tears off my cheeks, and he smiled and went back to his usual self. I could eat my pie again.

I leaned against his arm and we watched the stream, which was thicker and faster now, and as grey as steel. He rested his cheek on the top of my head, and I slipped my arm around his waist, and we sat like that for a good few minutes.

'I love you, Katy,' he said, and I squeezed him tighter.

He got hold of my chin and lifted my head up to his. His dark eyes were sharp as he stared at me, but his kiss was as soft as snow.

I tried to make a note of it in my head so that I could tell Marion exactly what it felt like. I closed my eyes, and it was just me and him, only ever me and him. We could have been anywhere. The cold left me. His hands came to the sides of my face, holding me close, his thumbs resting against my ear lobes as his lips pushed against mine. My hands fell down his neck and onto his chest, slipping inside his coat until I felt the heat of his skin.

He tilted my head to the side, his grip tightening as his mouth opened and in turn, opened mine. And then somehow, we'd fallen off the tree stump and were on the ground, the wet grass cold against my back but Bertie hot on top of me. I unfastened his trousers as he hitched up my skirts.

And then I stopped trying to keep track of everything, for there was no way I could tell Marion anymore.

We were both breathless at the end. The mixture of hot and cold had left me with a damp sweat under my slip, a chill developing around my breasts. Bertie helped me to my feet and rubbed one of the towels over my back to take away as much wet and mulch as possible.

'You best be getting back,' he said.

The dark was approaching fast, the clouds making an early nighttime. I didn't want to go, not even with the chill that was spreading over me, but he was already packing away the basket and brushing himself free of twigs and leaves and creases. He walked me out of the woods a little bit then stopped.

'I need to get home,' he said, meaning that he was not going to walk me to the track like usual.

We stood together for a moment, and it felt as if something had changed between us – a shift that I couldn't understand and didn't want to voice in case Bertie confirmed my fears.

He turned to leave, and I began to trudge away too, but then he strode back to me and kissed me again, as intense as before. I held him tight, breathing in his scent of butcher blood and sweat, bringing him closer and closer, tasting his tongue and swallowing so that he would be inside me again.

Then his face disappeared, my hands gripped air, and I saw his dark shadow running into the trees.

Monday, 12th November

Yesterday marked Mrs Leverton's anniversary in here. Thirty years ago, she first stepped over this threshold.

'They had to drag me in,' she said as we walked outside. 'It was a terrible day. The wind was howling, the rain was pouring. I can remember their hands on my arms, how my dress clung to my skin, the splat of my wet skirts in the hallway.'

Frost silvered the trees, and the grass looked as if

diamonds had been thrown across it. We had already stopped on the mound, and I was about to head inside when Mrs Leverton asked if we might continue walking towards the lake.

It is a fair distance to the lake. At first, it looked like a little river, but when I got closer, I could see it was just the way the land fell that made it look so big, and that actually it was quite a small lake, with a tiny island in the centre, where ducks were nesting. There was a grotto beside it, and we sat on the bench there whilst Annie moseyed around at the edge of the water.

'This is nice,' I said.

'I thought they were going to hang me.' Mrs Leverton ignored me. 'For months, I thought they were going to hang me, that this was all a ruse. I was so sure death was coming for me.'

I shouldn't have asked. I shouldn't have encouraged her to think of such bad times, but I couldn't help myself. 'Why?'

'A life for a life. In truth, I wanted it.'

'You wanted to die?'

She laughed at me, then waved to a male patient and his attendant on the other side of the lake. I recognised the patient as Mr Merryton, an old man suffering from melancholia. His young attendant, whose name I didn't know, held his arm as they walked, always keeping a few feet's distance from the water.

'I confessed everything. What was the point of denying what I had done? Then I realised that this was a different kind of prison.' Her brown eyes cut across to me, daring me to challenge her.

She was right, of course. No matter how much Marion

and I convinced ourselves that these ladies lived happy, peaceful lives, with comforts that the poor could only dream of, there was no getting away from the fact that their bedroom doors were locked, that their windows were barred, that their privileges could be given and taken away as if they were dogs, that needles could be forced into their flesh if needed.

'He's watching you,' she said.

I looked up and followed her gaze. The male attendant and his patient were closer to us now, and I met the male attendant's stare before I could gather my thoughts and drop my gaze to the floor once more.

'You have many eyes upon you, Katy, do you know that?'

'What do you mean?'

'You are a pretty girl.' She waved again, then called out, 'Nice weather today, Mr Merryton.'

'Beautiful, Mrs Leverton. How are you fairing?'

'Very well, thank you.'

Mr Merryton passed with a nod, and I caught the smirk on the attendant's face before he turned his back to us.

'It is nice, to be desired. I was like you, once. At eighteen, I could have had any man in a room.'

I felt myself blush.

'Be careful who you end up with, Katy.'

I thought of Bertie, of our odd farewell, but Bertie was the only one for me.

'Do you believe in true love, Mrs Leverton?'

'Not in the way you do.'

'What do you mean?'

'I believe we each have a notion of true love, something we mistake for being something profound and right. A love that is so intense that it is painful. A love that is so fierce, that each touch could light a fire. A longing that makes us wake in the night and weep, and we must have them, at any cost. But that is not true love, Katy. That is an obsession.'

I didn't agree with her. My heart ached for Bertie each and every day, but I was not obsessed. Our love was true and honest.

'I was obsessed with him,' she said, staring at the lake again.

'With Edward?'

She flinched. In this place, no one ever said his name, never acknowledged he might have been something more than a figment of her imagination.

'What was he like?'

It took her a few moments to answer, and I thought she was probably deciding whether she should talk to me or not, whether I had any other reason than simple curiosity in asking her to talk of him, this ghost to whom she wrote letters and for whom she prayed.

'Grey eyes, the colour of that water. Skin the shade of strong tea. Dimples when he smiled. I had never seen hair like his before, past his shoulders, lank and shiny with grease.' The tension in her shoulders slowly melted.

'He said fairies lived under the hoods of bluebells and sang at sunset. He took me into the woods one night and made me listen, and do you know' – she smiled at me, her eyes suddenly bright – 'I could hear them. I really could.

'Annie adored him – Annie the first, my best friend.

She would bite Henry.' Mrs Leverton threw her head back and laughed. 'She was a good dog.

'Edward came on a boat from Ireland, out of the fog, one early March morning. A silly little boat, smaller than this grotto, filled with everything he had ever owned. At night, I would open my chamber window and lean out so that I could see his bucket of coal smoking in the moonlight.'

She rested her head back against the stones and closed her eyes. She's there at her window, I thought, and so I let her stay there a bit longer, watching the smoke from Edward's boat, until clouds started to form in real life and threatened rain.

We walked back to the house in silence, and the rest of the day passed as every other day does, but at night, after her prayers and once she was tucked up under the covers, she reached for my hand and thanked me. I couldn't do anything but nod back at her, but I went to bed with a smile on my face.

Saturday, 24th November

Dr Basildon called me to his study today. It was half past eleven when he opened the door, and he let me walk in front of him towards the desk before he pulled the chair out for me.

I was struck again by the darkness of the room, what with the window being north-facing, and the books all being dull and leather-bound. This time, I noticed the little stand to the right of his desk, on which sat a squat wooden box, open to show the glass jars filled with medicines. The room smelt of carbolic soap like the rest of the house, but in there, the stench was even stronger. Perhaps the unusually low ceiling made it worse, but it caught at the back of my throat and made my nose sting.

Dr Basildon didn't seem at all disturbed. He sat in his big chair, and again, I couldn't make out his facial features for a while, but eventually the bright circles of his eyes shone in the gloom.

'You've been working here for two months.' He said it as if I could not count the days myself. 'I must say I am impressed with you. Mrs Thorpe says you are one of the cleanest attendants she has ever managed.'

'I like things tidy, sir.'

'You administer medicine well. Never leave a bruise.' He smiled as he tapped my notebook which was lying on the desk. 'You keep detailed notes. Very detailed. But you do not have an opinion on Mrs Leverton.'

'Should I, sir?'

'Is she improving?'

It was hard to say whether she was improving or not. From what I had come to understand from Mrs Thorpe, she'd first been sent to The Retreat because of trouble after having her daughter, and her mind had got so jumbled that she'd come up with fanciful notions to punish her lack of motherliness.

'She is very affectionate to Alice,' I said.

'What has that got to do with anything?'

My mouth went all dry, and I wished I'd kept it shut. 'I just thought that... She is like a mother to her. A very good mother.'

'But the delusions?'

'Then I should say no, sir.' I felt such a coward for

saying it, and I thanked the Lord that Mrs Leverton could not hear me.

'What do you make of her?'

I looked at him, trying to see something behind his meaning, wondering if he sought to trap me into talking negatively about my patient so that he might dismiss me.

'Speak plainly, Katy. I am asking your opinion; you are allowed to have one.'

'She is a very nice lady.'

'I've known her nearly all of my life. She was only a little younger than my mother when she came here.' He got to his feet and sauntered towards the wall where small, framed photographs and sketchings hung. He motioned for me to join him.

'This is my mother.'

'She is very beautiful,' I said, although she was quite plain. I imagined Mrs Leverton would have been infinitely more dazzling.

'This is the house in 1802, before my grandfather started taking in patients.' He pointed at a sketch on beige paper of a small manor house. 'My father had the male and female wings built in 1845, and the staff quarters. There you are.'

He pointed at another sketching. This one, I recognised as The Basildon Retreat now. His finger hovered over the building in which my room was set.

'This was taken just a month before my father's death.' He showed me a tiny photograph of him and his father, poised in front of a grand landscape which must have been a curtain. Dr Basildon stood tall beside his father, who was curled into a chair, his white hair scraped over his egg-shaped head, their stares matching each other's intensity.

'And here he is again.' His father was propped up in a soft chair this time, his eyes closed, his lips shrivelled into his face. It took me a while before I realised he was dead. Dr Basildon chuckled at my shock.

'I have a soft spot for Mrs Leverton,' he said. 'She was one of my father's favourites and I feel I inherited his tenderness for her. I am glad you are her attendant. She likes you.'

I drew away from the pictures on the wall. I didn't want to look at death any longer.

'Is she really delusional?' I had said the words before I could stop them coming out. Dr Basildon did not reply, and with the silence stretching, I continued. 'I mean; she talks so clearly of it all. Her description of Edward is very detailed.'

'Edward?'

I should not have said his name. I could feel the heat rising in me all the way from my toes, as if a fire was licking at me.

'Have you been discussing Edward with her?'

'No. She just started talking about him.'

'You did not encourage her?'

'No, sir. I just listened.' The fire crept higher as I lied.

'Very well.'

I let out the breath I had been holding.

'You must not indulge these fantasies, Katy. I am sure she is only testing you, a new person, seeing if she can bring you onto her side. It is what they do, I am afraid. But you must not be taken in, you must set an example of a sound mind, one in which they can trust and follow.'

'Yes, sir.'

He took a step closer, and I was about to step back in return, but I found a table against my backside.

'Do not get tempted by the serpent, Katy.'

I felt my head nod, but it was a jerking, stiff movement.

'You may go.'

10

1956

Her shift had run over. Dot was having another one of her outbreaks, and Iris had had to hold her down while Nurse Carmichael got the medicine ready. Shirley had been on the other side of Dot, gripping her shoulder as the woman writhed and raved.

Shirley had been grumpy all day. She hadn't worn any makeup, and she was already looking deathly pale before Dot's eruption, but as she held onto Dot, she grew whiter and whiter.

Shaking, once the injection had been administered, Shirley flopped into a chair and fanned her face with her apron. Iris brought her some water.

'You can wipe that smirk off your face,' Shirley said with her eyes closed.

Iris sat beside her. 'What time did you get in?'

'Two? Maybe three? It's his day off today.'

'At least you can have a rest tonight.'

'He's taking me out for dinner.'

Iris didn't know what kind of dinner companion

Shirley would make tonight. She was on the brink of sleep already.

'He's keen.'

Shirley opened one eye, grinned. 'He's bought me a dress to wear. It's red silk.'

'Where is he taking you, the Ritz?'

'You jealous?'

Iris just smiled at her friend. She didn't like John, and she didn't buy into his romantic gestures.

'He won't tell me, says it's a surprise. What if he... you know?'

Iris drew a blank.

'What if he asks me to marry him?'

They had only been courting for a few weeks! 'I don't think he will.'

Shirley sniffed, closed her eyes again. 'He might.'

Iris left her in the chair as she retrieved their things from the staff room.

'You'd better get going, or else you'll be late.'

Shirley squinted at the clock on the wall, gasped, grabbed her bag out of Iris's hand, and dashed out of the ward.

Dusk was brewing when Iris arrived at Kath's ward. Some of the other patients had recovered and been discharged. One had died. Kath remained in the corner next to the window overlooking the car park, still sleeping, chest rattling. But tonight, Albert was by her side.

He stood for Iris and offered her his chair while he brought over another one. They sat beside Kath, staring at the little old lady neither of them recognised.

'Thank you for doing all this.' Albert gestured at the vases of fresh flowers and the tubes of sweets that Kath had not eaten. 'The nurse told me you've been every night.'

'I should have called you before, but I thought she would be better by now. I didn't know if you'd want to see her like this.'

Albert took Kath's hand. 'They were giving her physio when I came. It seemed to help a little.'

Iris got the hairbrush out of the bedside cabinet and brushed Kath's hair as best she could. 'The nurse told me they are going to give her a bigger dosage of medicine, see if that will clear it up.'

Kath opened her eyes as Iris leant over her. 'Read to me,' she whispered.

'I've forgotten it, Kath. I left it at home. I was in a rush this morning.' Iris turned to Albert. 'I've been reading her diary to her.'

A shadow danced across his face. 'How far have you got?'

'We're a couple of months into her time at The Retreat.'

Albert nodded, the shadow passed. 'Do you remember how we met, Katy? April 1898. The twelfth, I think.'

'Tenth,' Kath breathed, her eyes lifting to Iris, glinting for the first time.

'The tenth, sorry.' Albert laughed. 'I'll never forget you, stood in that scullery doorway. It had been pouring down, a real April shower, you remember? I'd been out on my deliveries, and I was soaked. It was hammering down, and I banged on Cotton's back door, expecting to see old Mrs Cranleigh, and then there you were.' Albert stroked the back of her hand, and her smile slowly dissipated as sleep took her.

'She was the fairest girl I'd ever seen,' Albert whispered. 'Hair the colour of flax. Skin as pale as cream. She frowned at me as I stood there, waiting to be brought in from the rain. She was having none of it. She kept me out on that step until I told her exactly what my business was and showed her the delivery in my basket. She let me in to stand by the range then. I can remember the steam coming off me as she whirled around in that kitchen all by herself, up to her neck in vegetables that needed scrubbing and rabbits that needed skinning and shoes that needed polishing.'

He was back in that old kitchen, the fire warming his legs, watching Katy as she worked.

'I loved her ever since.'

'And she loved you.'

'Not at the start. It's different for boys – we fall in love like falling down holes. Katy took her time. She gave me nothing for weeks, months even, but then she started to come around. I couldn't believe my luck the first time she kissed my cheek. The most beautiful girl in the world had kissed me!'

A spot of pink bloomed on his cheeks.

'She loved you in the diary,' Iris said. 'She really loved you.'

Albert's head sunk down. 'She gave me everything in time. I had her whole heart. I didn't deserve it.' He gripped the edge of Kath's bed and used it to lever himself up. 'I need to go home.' He kissed his fingers then put them on Kath's wrist.

'Will you come again?' Iris said. 'It's nice to have you here.'

Albert looked at her sideways, nodded, then hobbled out of the ward.

She could smell beef as she changed; the fat melting, that lovely, earthy smell reserved for Sundays. She slipped off her best Sunday dress, which she had worn for church, and pulled on a thin brown skirt and white top. With the diary safely in her bag, she skipped downstairs.

'Where are you off to?' Mum sat at the kitchen table, podding peas.

'I'll be back in time for lunch.'

'That's not what I asked. You going to meet that Simon?'

'No.'

Mum's face dropped. She would have preferred Iris to be sneaking around meeting boys than going to visit an old lady.

'I'm seeing a friend.'

'This friend's name?'

'Katy.'

'Never heard you mention her before.'

'She's from Smedley.'

'Is she why you've been late getting home all this last week?'

Iris nodded, popped a pea in her mouth and grinned at its sweetness. Her mum slapped her hand away.

'When you next seeing Simon?'

Iris marched for the door. 'I'm not.'

'Eh!' Mum pushed out her chair and put one hand on

her hip. 'He seemed like a nice boy, walking you home like that. Don't look a gift horse in the mouth, my girl.' She jabbed an empty pod at Iris.

'When will you realise that I don't want a boyfriend, or a husband?'

'Don't be so daft. You really want to be a spinster all your life?'

Iris rested her head on the cool wooden door. It was hopeless trying to get through to her mother. Iris couldn't understand how a woman who had lived through the war and been an ambulance driver with independence and purpose would happily return to this kind of life.

'What time do you want me back?'

'Half past one.'

Iris left her mother squeezing the ends of the pods as if they were Iris's head. She took the bike to Smedley instead of walking, gaining an extra twenty minutes. She sprinted up the driveway, the sweat dribbling down her neck and forehead, and dumped the bike outside the main doors.

It was unusually quiet at Smedley; there was a Sunday hush to the place. The staff didn't walk as quickly, the patients were quieter, and most people offered her a smile. She turned left instead of right into the main corridor, slipping away from Ward 13. When she looked through door windows this way, she saw outpatient clinics and therapeutic rooms. The whole area seemed brighter, the breeze blowing freely through the open windows.

She neared Kath's ward. She had come to expect the worst each time she visited, sure that one time she would walk in and find Kath's bed empty, the nurses sweeping away the last traces of her. Yet today, Iris was shocked.

Kath sat up in bed, her eyes open and looking out of the window. Sunlight bathed her, blanching the blue bed clothes to white and making Kath's hair shine. When she heard Iris's footsteps, she turned with a smile.

'I didn't expect to see you today.' Despite her brightness, Kath's voice was quiet and punctuated by rasps of strained breaths. She coughed and spat bloody phlegm, and Iris was about to call the nurse for help when Kath stopped her. 'A burst blood vessel, they said. Too much coughing. Nothing serious.'

Iris put the sputum dish on the side. 'You seem better.' Placing the back of her hand against Kath's forehead, she was relieved to feel the fever had passed.

'Getting there.'

'We were worried about you. I've brought the diary today.'

Kath reached for Iris's hand. Her skin was as smooth and dry as grease paper, but when Iris met her gaze, she saw the fleeting image of young Katy – fierce, keen, tender. 'Thank you, Iris.'

'For what?'

'For listening.' Suddenly, Kath's strength ebbed. She let go of Iris's fingers and her head fell into the pillows. 'I haven't heard those words of mine since I wrote them.'

Iris opened the diary: the book of secrets. The scratched writing sprawled across the pages, Katy's messy letters unreadable at times. Ink spots flicked onto the edges of the paper. Iris could imagine Katy sat in bed with the flame of one candle flickering beside her, ferociously scribbling down her memories.

'They used it against me. When they took me away. A journal of a madwoman.'

A sudden pang of anger flared in Iris's gut. To think that foreign hands had been through these pages, ridiculing Katy's thoughts and feelings, laying her bare for men to dissect.

'I haven't seen it since. I asked for it to go to Bertie.'

'It's yours again now. No one need read it if you'd prefer.'

'I want you to. I couldn't do it by myself.'

11

1900

Wednesday, 5th December

We have been kept inside for much of the time lately. The weather is so bad; the clouds are low again, and the rain spits at us from the sides. The fires keep damping down, and we have to stoke them far too often, but even then the room is so huge that it is well past midday before it begins to grow a little warmer.

Mrs Leverton sits with her furs about her. I do even more cleaning than necessary, for scrubbing the floors on my hands and knees is one way to make sure I do not feel the cold. My hands do not thank me for it, though, and they have grown red and sore, so that I cannot sew easily, for the needle feels as if it goes straight into my flesh with each push.

Mrs Leverton is fidgety for the lack of outside excursions. She paces up and down in the day room, keeping close to the windows, though the valley below has vanished. Even the woods are hidden behind the mist.

As way of distraction, earlier today I asked her to play the tin whistle and take a seat before the fire.

She sat with a grumble but removed the instrument from the hidden pocket in her skirt. The fire set a soft glow upon her face, smoothing out the lines of old age, making her dark hair look like black treacle and the tin whistle glimmer like a stick of toffee. She put it to her lips and began. She closed her eyes as she blew, her thin fingers prancing up and down like the legs of show horses.

I wriggled into my chair, cracking out the ache in my back and letting the blood flow into my legs. I have heard this tune so often that I began to hum along and closed my eyes, but this time, for some unknown reason, I felt such sadness that when I sang the final high note a tear fell onto my cheek.

'You should not cry,' Mrs Leverton said. 'It is not a song of sorrow.'

She should not have seen my tears. I wiped my face quickly and smiled garishly at her. 'Where did you learn to play?'

'Edward taught me.'

We should not speak of him, but it was the first time in days that she had sat for so long and I didn't want her to go back to pacing and getting herself worked up.

'That was a tune he created for me. "Persephone's Melody."' She laughed, just a little. 'He would play it after we made love.'

I checked the room to make sure no one had heard her.

'You think I care what they think of me? I will die here, Katy, so I will tell my memories whether they think me insane or not. It makes no difference.'

'You will be released if your delusions cease, if Dr Basildon believes you are of sound mind.'

She tilted her head as she looked at me, her smile soft and crooked. 'You are an ignorant child.'

I set my gaze onto the fire once more, determined not to indulge her again.

'Come, let's not fall out,' she said. 'I say this in kindness to you.'

I didn't know how calling me an ignorant child could possibly be kind, but it would do me no good to sulk at my own charge. I handed her a book to read but she would not take it from me.

'Aren't you curious about what happened?'

She saw me hesitate. I should have said no and ended the conversation, but of course, I forget that it is not only me who observes Mrs Leverton; she watches me just as closely. She knows my interest.

'It was a long summer that passed too quickly. I used to watch him from the gallery as he worked. He was a gardener, you see, an outdoorsman. I would find him by the wood store, cutting logs as if he were slicing through butter.'

'What about your children?' I said, the meanness barking out of me. It brought her up short, and for a moment, I felt satisfaction. But it soon dissolved.

'James,' she sighed his name. 'He came here once. I couldn't believe the size of him. I'd last seen him in a little sailor suit, and there he was suddenly, a twin of his father.'

'What happened?'

'I will never forget how he looked at me. He sat there,

where you are now. He wouldn't call me mother. He said Clara was his mother.'

'Who was Clara?'

'A whore.' Mrs Leverton glared at the flames, then her anger burned out. 'James's governess before I... left.

'He asked me why. I told him it was a mistake, a bad accident, I never meant to hurt Edward. And then James stood up, his face cold, not at all like how it used to be when he was a boy – a sweet little boy. He said to me, "I meant, why couldn't you love us?"'

Mrs Leverton dragged in a breath. I wished I had never mentioned her children.

'Why couldn't I? Patience was the bonniest of babies. She had fat little arms and legs, a perfectly round head. Her eyes were as blue as the sky, and she never cried.'

She was beginning to crumble, her eyes wide and wet.

'I would love her now; I know I would. But then...'

'Mrs Leverton, please don't upset yourself.'

'I wished her dead.'

My hand dropped away from her, too late to hide my shock – my disgust, in all honesty.

'I wished my own child dead.'

'Why?'

She shook her head. 'I have asked myself that question so many times. She was an anchor, I suppose, to that place, to Henry. She was so small and fragile – she needed protection, and I didn't want to protect her. I wanted to run out of that valley, out of the dark, and never come back.'

'Was that when Edward arrived?'

She trailed her fingers across her brow. 'He said he'd take me with him. He said we would sail the seas. I would stand on his boat and close my eyes and pretend that we were on the ocean, that if I opened my eyes there would be water for as far as my eye could see and a sky so vast I could fall into it.'

She sighed. The memories which had blurred her eyes vanished. Her brown pupils sharpened, her face lost the soft golden glow, and she scowled at the tin whistle in her lap.

'I will not call him a liar. Edward was not a liar. He was just a man. But I'd forgotten that that was all he was.'

I've been replaying mine and Mrs Leverton's conversation in my head. I don't know how any woman could wish her child dead, and I must confess I am finding it hard to talk to her properly since she told me her feelings.

I keep imaging her in a grand old house, her white face pressed to the window, watching Edward on his boat while her family go on without her. I imagine her stuck there as Edward cuts away the rope and sails off down river. I imagine her screaming as she watches him leave. I imagine her breaking the glass and jumping from the top floor. I imagine a little boy in a blue suit wailing for his mama.

Friday, 7th December

Marion woke me last night. I found her crouching over me, her face nothing but a black shadow in the darkness of the room. She was shaking my shoulder and calling my name.

'What is it?' I said, once my tired mind allowed me to form words.

'You were crying, Katy, and talking to yourself.'

'What was I saying?'

'I don't know; I couldn't make it out.'

I breathed in deep and pressed my hands against my face to find that it was indeed wet. When I turned my cheek onto the pillow, it was cold and damp.

'Sorry.'

Marion got back into bed and blew on her hands. I could hear her rubbing her legs under the sheets to warm up. 'Bad dream?'

'I can't remember.'

We fell quiet for a while. I could have let her drift back to sleep – the longer I waited, the harder it became to say what I wanted to say. But then I heard her breath grow heavier, and I thought if I didn't say it now, I never would.

'I think Mrs Leverton is telling the truth.'

Silence. I didn't let it stretch too long.

'I think there was an Edward.'

'Why?' Marion's voice muffled against her pillow.

'The things she says. She describes him as if he were as real as you or I.'

Marion rolled over and sighed somewhat impatiently. 'Delusions do seem real, Katy. That's why they are so terrifying. Mrs Huxley can describe the devil to me, from the horns on his head to the hairs on his toes. She tells me, word for word, what he says to her. She tells me how he peels away her son's flesh on his face, how the blue veins burst and run with blood.'

I didn't want to think of devils and tortured children.

'That is different though. We know that is not true.'

'We know that Edward is not true.'

'Do we?' I said. 'How?'

'She would not be in a madhouse if Edward had been real, would she? She would have been hanged.'

Sunday, 9th December

I dreamed of Edward last night, but of Bertie as well... It was all so confusing.

I was lying in a bed on a boat – Edward's boat. I could feel it bobbing up and down in the current. I heard the tin whistle playing "Persephone's Melody". Edward was on top of me, and I turned my head to see where the sound was coming from and found Bertie sat beside us, his eyes shut as he played.

I looked up to Edward. His hair was dangling around his face, tickling my nose, his smile like a wolf. When I looked down, I saw he was naked, his body lithe and taut, unlike Bertie's. I saw I was naked also.

He kissed my lips and then my neck and breasts. He pressed into me, and the pain was sharp before the pleasure. I pulled his face up and saw that he was now Bertie, white and plump and gentle, but the tin whistle was still playing. He wouldn't look at me as we made love, and I kept dragging his face towards me, but he would not open his eyes. I shouted at him to look at me, but it was like he was deaf.

Suddenly, the walls of the boat fell away, and there was nothing but blue sea all around us, on our raft. Fearing the water, I struggled, pushing at Bertie's arms. But they would not move. He continued to pound into me. His hands came up to my neck, and his grip began to tighten, and I was writhing to get away from him, my legs kicking but meeting nothing but air. I was reaching for something that might save me but never found it, and then his hair swung back over his face and showed me Edward once more, his eyes grey and mean, his mouth twisted in effort as he pushed down on my throat.

I woke gasping, my chest violently rising and falling as I propped myself up on my elbows. I checked my face for tears but found it dry, and when I looked over at Marion, I saw I had not woken her.

The room was gloomy, the dawn still far away, but there was an unusual brightness from the window. I tiptoed over to it, shivering as the cold air raked against my sticky skin, and saw it had been snowing outside. The moon shone bright from the clear sky and bounced against the whiteness on the ground.

I ran back to bed and pulled the covers close to me. I was just beginning to drift into sleep once more when I heard something – a creak of a floorboard. I opened my eyes and squinted into the darkness, but it was as black as coal in the corner where our doorway is. I strained to see, thinking that this is how it must feel to be blind, but there was no further sound. I snapped my eyes shut and pulled the blanket over my head. I would not think such silly things. I would not scare myself. As time went on, I convinced myself it was nothing but my fevered imagination and fell asleep.

But this morning, as the dawn came piercing in through the window, I still had that sense of unease. Marion and I dressed as usual, but I couldn't help checking that doorway corner.

Once we were dressed, we made our way down the

short wooden steps, through the laundry and outside. It was a world of white, and on the ground, from the laundry door all the way back to the main house, were footsteps in the snow.

Marion saw me hesitate.

'What is it?'

I pointed at the footsteps. She frowned at me.

'They're from Miss York.'

Marion trod over the top of them and waddled towards the house, her cloak wrapped tight around her body.

I couldn't take my eyes off the footprints. Surely, they were too large to be Miss York's, who was five foot nothing? And I am convinced that it had not been snowing at the time Miss York had gone on duty yesterday evening.

12

1900

Thursday, 13th December

I must apologise for the state of my writing. I cannot stop my hand from shaking.

It was beautiful weather this morning – the worst days always start as such. The snow had all melted by yesterday, and today the sun was shining, the frost was sharp, and the view was breathtaking once more.

Mrs Leverton and I made the most of the weather and did the long walk to the lake. She has an odd relationship with the water; she never gets too close but likes to be next to it, and when Annie's little legs go under the surface, she shrieks at the dog to come away quickly.

She's been talking to me about Edward almost every day. In all honesty, I feel like she is better for it. She still prays each night but not for quite so long, and she no longer cries in her sleep. I feel that the act of talking about him lightens her burdens, makes him real and alive once more.

We sat on the bench inside the grotto.

'I want to tell you the truth, Katy. About how it ended.'

I had wondered when or if this time would come. She had been forthcoming telling me all about her and Edwards' affair, their long nights on the boat in each other's arms, the sound of crickets and owls all about them as Annie lay in the doorway, acting as lookout. She had told me of how she would spy on him, creeping from window to window, or tree trunk to tree trunk, just so she could watch his body move, the way he wiped the sweat from his neck, the way his torso rippled when he was alone and shirtless.

Edward has become my own fantasy; her stories sink into my mind like sand, so that I too have felt the callouses on his fingers as they trace my collarbone, smelt his scent of hacked pine and gin and river as he kisses me.

I didn't want him to end; I wanted that summer to live on forever, unspoilt, but I knew Mrs Leverton needed to tell me the truth, the brutal truth.

'Autumn was in the air. I remember seeing the first orange oak leaf on a branch, and it felt like a hand had grabbed my innards and pulled down hard. Then Annie died.'

I gasped at that and looked at Annie number 4, sniffing at the foot of the grotto, and suddenly wanted to bring her close and wrap her in warmth and life.

'It is silly,' Mrs Leverton said, bringing her handkerchief to her wet eyes, 'but she really had been my best friend for so many years. She was almost sixteen when she passed, and I could only be grateful that she went quickly. For a week, she had been quiet, off her food, unable to move much at all. I tried to leave her in my room when I went to see Edward, but it was like she knew where I was going. She adored Edward, did I tell you?'

I nodded.

'I carried her in a basket, a blanket over her, all the way down the river and to his boat. She was a weight, I can tell you. She lifted her head when she saw him, and her tail wagged, just slowly, but she was happy to be with both of us beside the water. Edward stoked his bucket of coal, and we laid her next to it to keep her warm. We shared his flask of gin, and I stroked her head. She closed her eyes eventually, and I think she knew that it was all right for her to go, then, that I would be happy with Edward.'

To my dismay, a tear dripped off my chin. Mrs Leverton offered me her damp handkerchief and I took it quickly, whilst Annie IV nuzzled into her mistress's skirts, as loyal as her namesake.

'Edward buried her not far from his boat. I picked a stone for her a few days later and Edward carved it. He would find me there at night, kneeling next to the stone, crying over her.

'Henry couldn't understand. He never had affinity with animals – unusual for a country boy. He hadn't liked Annie one bit; she'd never let him close. I think it was then that he thought my mind was fraying. We had an argument one night, and he said I cared more for a dog than for my own daughter. He was right.'

She cleared her throat and stuffed the wet handkerchief into her pocket. She stared at the lake, her mouth opening every now and again as if she were going to speak, but nothing came out. She swallowed her words several times before continuing:

'Two weeks later, Edward was leaving. It was the first week of October, and there was a mist over the river so that I couldn't see his boat until I was right next to it. He had not seen me either. I found him on the deck, sorting everything out. I asked what he was doing, and he looked at me like a little boy who'd been caught with his fingers in the jam. He said it was time he left, that he always moved on after summer.

'I asked him where we were going.' Her lips curled into a smile, then fell flat. 'He wouldn't look at me. I should have known what he meant, but I didn't. I got excited – our adventure beginning sooner than I had imagined. How often had we spoken of sailing away together? We had talked of Africa, Italy, even America, anywhere where the sea might take us.

'I jumped aboard, muttering to myself of things I would need to pack, mementoes that I could not leave behind, a lock of James's hair, Annie's leash, my book of Shelley's poems. I would have to be quick and not arouse suspicion. I would kiss James for the last time, and I would not think of the face he would make once he realised he would not see his mama again. I had convinced myself he would be happier without me, and Patience could not miss what she had never had.' She laughed bitterly. 'I was right about something.

'He stopped packing and looked at me. He said he was going alone. I didn't understand him. I just stood there until he said it again. The ground went from under me. He caught me and I held on to him. I was on my knees and his face was so close, I could see all the tiny veins in his eyes, the stubble on his upper lip. I kissed him and he kissed me back for a moment, and I thought, *I will die if he leaves.*'

Mrs Leverton clawed her skirts – I was sure the material would tear. She was somewhere else. She was on that boat, with Edward, and her heart was breaking right there in front of me. Breaking all over again.

'He tried letting go of me, but I grabbed him. I begged him to take me with him. All he did was tell me to be quiet, that someone would hear. I didn't care if the whole world heard me. I was sobbing and clinging to his legs like a child. He shook me off, dragged me to my feet. I lunged for him, but he pushed me away. I was screaming, and I remember how hot my eyes felt, as if my tears were acid. He slapped me then – that stopped me. I had to catch my breath. I just watched him, shocked that he could do such a thing, that he no longer seemed to care about hurting me. We remained silent for a while, and then he said I must stay and be a mother to my children. He said he did not want me to go with him. He said he did not love me.'

Her voice broke and she collapsed into herself. I wrapped my arms around her shoulders, brought her close to me, and felt her body rack with each sob, the pain just as raw now as it had been all those years ago.

'He turned away from me, and then... then his hammer was in my hand, and I just...'

Cold fingers tickled my spine. I shushed her – I didn't want to hear.

'I didn't mean it. Not really. It was just one moment...'

I didn't ask. I didn't want to know what she had done. I didn't want the image staining my mind, but terrible fantasies were already flooding in. Edward, bloodied, his brains smattered across wooden planks, his eyes blank as he stared at the sky and took his last, quivering breath.

'He didn't move. He just... lay there.' She shuddered against me. 'So much blood—'

'Please, Mrs Leverton, stop—'

'I ran. I didn't know what else to do. I ran to the house and straight to Henry. I think he put me to bed, but I can't remember much.'

She turned to me, her face blotchy and her eyes red, but the trauma was now ending. She peeled herself out of my arms, sniffed, and composed herself once more. She had aged ten years since we first sat on the bench, and minutes passed as we gazed vacantly at the lake before us.

'What did they do with him?' I whispered, for I could not leave Edward just lying on his boat, even if he were only there in my imagination.

'I don't know,' she whispered. 'That was the last time I ever saw him.'

She was beginning to shake from the cold. I took her hand and felt the iciness of it even through her glove.

'Come, we must get you inside.'

We strode back to the house, seeing Alice and Mrs Milton and Mrs Beckwith on the way, who were all out with their attendants enjoying the weather. Nella caught my arm as we passed and asked if everything was all right. I said it was, that we had just walked too far and got too cold. I'm sure she didn't believe me, but she let me go and told Alice that she must go for her walk and leave Mrs Leverton in peace for a while. I smiled my thanks at Nella and felt for Alice, who stared after Mrs Leverton like a puppy.

We found Marion and Mrs Huxley in the day room.

'There you are!' Marion bustled over to me. Her smile faltered when she saw Mrs Leverton. 'What is wrong?'

'Nothing, we are just cold.' I walked Mrs Leverton to the fire, which was thankfully burning high.

'It's a good job I've just made some tea then. All the others are out.' Marion was by my side. 'I need to... you know... relieve myself. Could you keep an eye on Mrs Huxley for me? I won't be a moment.'

I flicked my eyes to the far end of the room where Mrs Huxley sat with a cup of tea in her hands, looking remarkably calm.

'Of course.'

Marion trotted out of the room. My attention returned to Mrs Leverton, who was still shaking. I rubbed her arms and told her to hold her hands to the flames. Her teeth were beginning to chatter, and the sudden greyness of her skin and the rawness of her eyes, showed she was exhausted.

'We'll get you to bed once Marion is back.'

'Thank you, Katy.' She smiled at me, and I'm sure it took all her strength to do so.

A crash startled us both. We stared at each other for a moment, trying to work out where the noise had come from, before someone started wailing. I turned to see Mrs Huxley with her left arm stretched out in front of her, blood streaming from the wrist, her other hand holding a piece of broken china. She brought the weapon down on her wrist again, hacking at her skin, and howled.

I ran at her and hit the jagged piece of china out of her hand. She and I watched it scatter across the floor.

Then my breath was knocked out of me and I was on the ground. Mrs Huxley was over me, punching and kicking my stomach. I curled up on my side, taking each blow, hearing screams crack over my head, and trying to suck in air but getting nothing.

The room started to blacken. My head felt as if it were floating. The searing pain throughout my body began to ebb away, and calmness descended.

I wonder now, if that is what dying is like.

But it was not long until my consciousness returned – as soon as the kicks stopped and my lungs could open. I coughed, and the sting in my chest and the ache in my stomach returned with piercing clarity. I pulled myself on to my hands and knees, my body throbbing with each movement, and saw Marion and one of the housemaids struggling to hold Mrs Huxley down. I looked around for Mrs Leverton but could not see her, then there were more footsteps – I felt the vibrations through my hands – and I saw the black trousers and shiny shoes of Dr Basildon sprinting for Mrs Huxley, a needle in his hand. He jabbed it into her neck, and after a little more writhing, her body relaxed.

A cool hand brushed back my hair. I flinched as it caught a wound on my forehead.

'Katy? Katy, look at me.'

I turned towards the voice and found Mrs Leverton on her knees beside me. She reeled at the sight of my face.

'Doctor!'

Dr Basildon ran to me, his frown deep, his lips in a set

line as he turned my head from side to side and pressed my stomach. I cried out from the pain.

'Bed, Miss Owen. I will have to carry you there, and it will hurt.'

I braced myself as he put one arm under my legs and the other under my shoulders and lifted me from the ground. I whimpered from the pain but bit my teeth together and prayed the journey would be over soon.

It took a long time to get to my bed. He laid me on it, taking care to do it smoothly.

'I am going to get morphine. Then I will check for any broken bones.'

He left, and it was just me and the pain.

When I opened my eyes again, Marion was crouched beside me on the bed. She was wiping my face clean, and I could see that her bowl was filled with red water, a mixture of Mrs Huxley's blood and mine, no doubt.

'I am so sorry, Katy,' she said, when she saw my eyes open. She was crying.

I shushed her, but my mouth was so dry that I could not speak.

'Dr Basildon needs me to undress you so that he can examine you.'

Despite her gentleness, the pain was excruciating as Marion got me down to my slip. I could see for myself that fat bruises were already flourishing on my pale arms, and I dared not imagined what my abdomen looked like.

Dr Basildon returned. 'Miss Rowley, you can leave.'

I didn't want Marion to go, but it was clear Dr Basildon was in no mood to be undermined. He stood over me, assessing the situation.

'I need to check your ribs and stomach.' His fingers pushed into me. I arched away from him, but couldn't get free of his grip. He lifted my slip over my drawers to see my stomach, and I felt my skin burn. My own employer, seeing my naked flesh! I thought I might die from the shame of it. I squeezed my eyes shut so I did not have to watch his face and imagine the thoughts in his mind.

'This will be cold.'

Once again, I gasped as he pressed what felt like a disc of ice against my chest.

'Now, breathe long and slow for me.'

I tried, but it felt like a rag was stuck in my throat. I coughed, and Lord how the pain soared!

'And again. Slowly.'

I breathed in once more as best I could, and then the disc of ice came away, and I saw it was only a stethoscope.

'I don't think anything is broken, but you are very bruised.'

He opened the little wooden box full of medicine that I had seen before in his study. He brought out a jar labelled *morphine* and a syringe. I closed my eyes as he pierced my flesh.

'That will take the worst of it away, and then you shall have to rest.'

He took one last look at me, his lips still just as straight and unhappy as previously, then left the room without another word.

It only took a few minutes for the morphine to take effect. I slept for the rest of the day and woke only half an hour ago.

The pain is still intense, but I think the doctor is right

and that nothing is broken, only my pride. Marion is with me now, worrying that I should be resting and not writing, but if I do not get my thoughts down, I fear that they will be lost in this daze of morphine. She is to inject me again, any minute, so now I must sign off for the night and pray that my bruises heal quickly.

Saturday, 15th December

I must write this before Marion comes in for the night. If I thought things could not worsen, I was wrong.

Dr Basildon called me and Marion to his study today. It was the first time I had been up and dressed since the incident. Marion helped me, like the good friend she is. The pain is not quite so sharp now. It is more of an ache, a persistent throb, more annoying than anything else. But when I saw myself in the big mirrors in the main house, I hardly recognised myself. My face is blue and brown, lined with thick, red crusts of blood from my healing wounds, and when I stand, I am all hunched up, for my stomach cannot take the strain. I would look better with my corset, but the thought of squeezing myself together like that is unbearable.

Dr Basildon showed us inside and told us to sit down. He had put cushions on the chair meant for me, and I was grateful for it. Marion's leg tapped under her skirts as we waited for the doctor to take his seat, and I could see her breasts filling out her dress with each quick, short breath. I wanted to touch her arm and tell her she had nothing to worry about, that it was all my fault, but Dr Basildon spoke.

'I need an explanation, girls.' He unbuttoned his

jacket, laced his fingers together, and rested his arms on the desk. He was trying to smile, but it wasn't working.

'It was my fault, sir,' I said. 'Marion needed to go... out. She asked me if I would supervise Mrs Huxley, and I said that I would, but I was occupied with Mrs Leverton. I had my back to Mrs Huxley when she...'

I took a deep breath. My head was beginning to swirl, and it felt like my temples were in a vice and someone was screwing it shut.

'Mrs Leverton had got cold, she was shivering – my fault also, we had been outside too long. I was trying to warm her. Then there was a crash, and I didn't realise what it was for a while, and then I saw Mrs Huxley doing what she was doing, but I was all the way on the other side of the room.'

'Calm yourself, Miss Owen. I have asked Mrs Leverton her account of the incident and she confirms what you have said.'

'I shouldn't have gone,' Marion whispered, her chin in her chest.

'It wasn't Marion's fault, sir. I should have been looking after both of them.'

'There was a pot of tea not too far from Mrs Huxley,' he said.

Marion and I faltered, not understanding what he was getting at.

'Scalding tea.'

'I am sorry, sir, I did not think—'

'How long have you been here, Miss Rowley?'

'Almost eighteen months, sir.'

'Eighteen months. Long enough to know that hot

liquid of any kind should never be left within a patient's reach.'

'Yes, sir, I'm sorry sir, I didn't—'

'You didn't think, Miss Rowley. You didn't think of your charge at all. You left a vulnerable woman with the means to harm herself, and in turn, you abandoned your own colleague to deal with the fallout.'

Marion was crying.

'Sir, please, it was me—'

'Be quiet, Miss Owen!' His voice boomed. I caught my tongue before I could say any more. Marion was silent, but her shoulders were shaking.

Dr Basildon cracked each and every one of his knuckles before he spoke again. 'I am disappointed in you, Miss Rowley. I had thought you would make a fine attendant, but now I am not so sure.'

'Please, sir, it was a mistake, I shan't ever do it again. It was one moment.'

'One moment of folly can lead to a lifetime of regret, Miss Rowley. Look at your friend. Two lives could have been lost because of your one moment.'

Marion crumbled. I opened my mouth to speak but didn't know what to say.

'I admire your courage, Miss Owen.' Dr Basildon looked at me, ignoring Marion's emotions, and his eyes softened as he glanced over my face and down my body, taking in the way my arms lay awkwardly in my lap as I tried not to catch a bruise. 'You did nothing wrong at all. Mrs Leverton is your charge, and I can see that you were taking care of her to your best ability. She has been worried about you, and I think it would please her if you could visit her on your way back to your room.'

'Yes, sir, I will.'

'Now, Miss Rowley, I shall not dismiss you yet.'

Marion moaned in relief.

'But you are warned. Do you understand?'

Marion nodded.

Dr Basildon pushed out his chair and got to his feet. I was about to stand when he came to my side and put his hand under my arm and helped me up. He took hold of my chin and turned my face from side to side.

'Any sharp, stabbing pain anywhere?'

'No, sir.'

He dropped his hand. 'Very good. When do you think you shall be able to return to your duties?'

'I should like to begin tomorrow, sir. The pain improves each day.'

'You are a credit, Miss Owen.' He smiled at me, like he had that time when he'd been on the stairs.

I dipped my head and followed Marion, who had been waiting by the door for me. She had stopped crying, and when the door shut, I was about to grab her for an embrace and tell her that he was just angry, that he didn't really mean what he had said, but she turned to me with such a scowl that I stopped.

'Quite the favourite, aren't you?'

'What?'

'What happened with Mrs Leverton that morning? She wasn't just cold. What had you been doing?'

'Nothing. We'd walked too far.'

'She had been crying, Katy.'

I would not tell Marion. I had tried to confide in her before about Mrs Leverton and she hadn't wanted to know. Now, I feared she would use it against me, so we stared at each other in angry silence.

'Marion…'

She ran down the stairs, and I saw our friendship slipping away.

'Marion!'

'Get yourself to bed.'

13
1956

Iris waited in the corridor for the nurse to finish giving Kath her physio. It looked brutal on Kath's boney frame: Kath lay on her side, her arm held up in the air, wincing while the nurse rubbed and pounded on the side of her chest. When the nurse sat her up, it was a strain to breathe. Suddenly, her body convulsed, and she coughed up the poison inside her lungs and spat into the sputum dish. When she had recovered, the nurse held a glass of water to her lips, and they shared a joke.

'How is she?' Iris said when Nurse Okeke came out of the ward.

'The antibiotics seem to be working better now.'

'Does it hurt her, what you were just doing?'

'It looks worse than it is.'

'Has Albert been to see her?'

Nurse Okeke shook her head. It was obvious she didn't think he was coming back, but Iris had more faith in him than that. Perhaps he had just been busy, or perhaps he had fallen ill too.

Iris entered the ward. There was a new lady across from Kath who snored as she slept.

'Heart attack,' Kath said, seeing Iris looking. 'I find the sound comforting.'

'The nurse said you're improving. It won't be long until you're on your feet again.'

'Back in Ward 13.' Kath picked at the bed sheet, and her gaze flitted towards the window. 'I haven't seen a different view for years.'

'Sorry it's a carpark.'

Kath smirked. 'I think I prefer the oak tree. I never understood how Persey could hate trees. So much life in them.'

'Persey?'

'Mrs Leverton. Persephone. She liked me to call her Persey, in the end.'

'You became friends?'

Her smile grew sad. 'We were the only friends we had left.'

Iris left the diary in her bag and took Kath's hand instead. 'What was it like, The Basildon Retreat?'

'It was the biggest house I had ever seen. Grand. I thought it a palace – a palace with bars. Carpets – we never had carpets, see. And great long curtains, like waterfalls of solid gold. It really did feel like you were halfway to heaven.'

'You remember it well.'

'It is as clear as you are. It is everything since that is a blur. The years have all rolled into one. I had no idea it was 1956, you know. I asked the nurse and thought she was teasing me.'

It had not crossed Iris's mind that Kath could have

been so ignorant. Why hadn't she thought that the patients would like to know the date? Because every day was the same. Because they weren't going anywhere. Because no one thought it mattered.

'Fifty-five years... Persey will be dead now, and Annie long gone.'

'Do you think Marion became a matron?'

'No doubt about it.' Kath smiled before her chin began to tremble. She blinked rapidly, trying to flush away the tears. 'What happened to the rest of them?'

'I'll find out,' Iris said. 'I promise.'

Elvis sang to her as she lay in bed, watching the sun slide behind the row of houses across the street. The sky was flaring in pinks, the clouds whispering across the expanse of blue and disappearing. The air smelt dry and hot, no hint of rain to feed the dying plants, all shedding their petals as they slumped in their pots. Even with her window as wide as it would go, there was no breeze to cool her sticky skin.

Her back sweat as she lay on her sheets. She went to the bathroom and splashed her face, then filled the basin and rested her hands in the cold water. Downstairs, she could hear the wireless and the soft murmur of her dad as he read out the crossword clues.

Someone knocked on the front door.

Mum got in a fluster – Iris could hear her scrabbling for her shoes, imagined her checking her reflection in the narrow mirror in the hallway. The door clicked open, her mother squealed, and there was the low rumble of a man's voice, someone she seemed to recognise.

'Iris!' her mother called. 'Come here.'

Iris pulled the plug out of the basin, shook the water off her skin, and plodded down the stairs. Mum was at the bottom, holding the door open, though not enough so that whoever was on the other side could see into the hallway. She glowered at Iris, pushed the tips of Iris's shoulders back, and licked her thumb to scrub something off Iris's cheek.

'Smile,' Mum hissed, then opened the door.

'Hello.' Simon stood on the step. His hands were thrust deep into his trouser pockets, and he swung a little from side to side as he talked. 'How are you, Iris?'

'Fine, thank you.'

Mum crouched behind the front door. She flicked Iris's hand as it rested on the doorknob.

'And you?' Iris added begrudgingly.

'Fine, thank you.'

She didn't want to talk to him. What kind of man called on a girl he had only met once, at half past nine on a Thursday night? He twisted round so that he faced the sunset.

'Beautiful night.'

'It's too hot for me.'

'Ask him in,' Mum whispered.

Iris stepped outside and shut the door on her mother. 'Is there something you wanted, Simon?'

'Just to see if you were all right and if you enjoyed the other night?'

'It was pleasant.'

'Good.' A smile broke across his face. 'I thought it was. I wondered if you would like to do it again some time?'

She was too hot to think of an excuse. 'I'll ask Shirley when I see her.'

'I didn't mean with John and Shirley.'

'Oh.' Iris plucked the head off a shrivelled daisy. 'I'm busy at the moment. I visit someone after work so I'm not back until late.'

'Right, I see. Another time, then.' Reluctantly, Simon strolled for the gate.

She followed him out, making sure that he did indeed leave, but she couldn't help but feel a stab of guilt at the way he hung his head like a scolded puppy. Still, she would not relent. Not with her mother peeking at them through the letter box. She folded her arms and pursed her lips until she saw the little red car parked on the pavement.

'Is that yours?'

'Pride and joy.'

'I'm surprised you can fit into it.'

He laughed, and his face brightened. 'It's getting out that's the trouble.'

She couldn't help but laugh as Simon folded himself awkwardly into the car, banging his head and scraping his knee in the process and yelping when something sharp stabbed him in the side.

'Right, well… Good night, Iris.'

He shut the door and started the engine.

'Wait,' she said just before he pulled away. 'What are you doing this Sunday?'

Branches scraped the sides of the car. The track was not well used, and grass was growing in the middle of it. The car spluttered as the road wound higher and higher up the hillside, jerking them backward and forward.

After another five minutes, they reached a set of open iron gates. Luckily, the ground had levelled out, so Simon could stop the car without fear of rolling backward.

Iris walked through the gates.

'This it?' Simon called through the window.

There were too many trees lining the driveway to see the house. 'Let's go up and find out.'

'We can't just drive onto someone's private property.'

'The gates are open; we can always say we got lost.'

Simon frowned. She should have known he would be a stickler for the rules. She rolled her eyes, then jumped back in the car.

'Go on, hurry up.'

Huffing, Simon shunted the car into gear, and they lurched forward. They followed the gravelled drive until the house came into view. It was a mighty house, just as Kath had said. It was Georgian, with pillars and long windows. The white paintwork was peeling, however, and the closer they came, the more cracks Iris saw in the plaster.

They parked on the driveway at the foot of the steps leading to the front door, beside several other cars. Behind them, the landscape rolled for miles, a chequerboard of green and yellow fields.

'Can I help you?'

A man's voice came from somewhere near the house, and he appeared through the front door. He skipped down the steps towards them, his grey hair flopping over his eyes.

'Sorry to bother you,' Iris said. 'We were looking for The Basildon Retreat?'

The man laughed. 'It hasn't been called that in years. It's Highfields now. Suits it, don't you think?' He spread him arms towards the view. 'I'm Edgar Farrington.' He put his arm out for a handshake.

'Simon Raybould.'

'Iris Lowe. We've just come on the off chance, really. I know somebody who used to work here. She's been telling me all about the place, and I was wondering what had happened to it.' Iris smiled, trying to do it the way Shirley did when she wanted something. 'Did you know Katherine Owen?'

'Afraid not. I'm Mrs Basildon's nephew, you see, so I don't have much of a connection with this place.' Iris gazed past him to the house. 'Would you like to come in? I'm packing everything up, so it's a bit of a mess, but you're welcome to have a look around, see how it's changed.'

'That would be wonderful, thank you!' Perhaps she should smile more often.

Edgar led the way. Iris had to prod Simon to follow. She hadn't told him about Kath until they were well into the journey. When she'd said they were going to an old madhouse, his cheeks had paled. But to be fair to him, he hadn't protested too much, even though it wasn't the secluded picnic he'd probably been hoping for.

The great oak door slid open to reveal a grand entrance hall where large clumps of furniture were hidden underneath old sheets. Male voices, shouting at each other to take hold of one end of something or to put something down, echoed from the rooms upstairs.

'I'm trying to get everything in order for the sale. There's so much stuff, you wouldn't believe.'

'You're selling it?'

'It's too much upkeep just for me. Everything is falling to pieces. What did you say the lady's name was who worked here?'

'Katherine. She was known as Katy, though.'

'When was she here?'

'1900.'

'Blimey.' Edgar brushed away the mop of his grey hair. 'She saw it in its heyday. Was she a domestic?'

'An attendant.'

Edgar nodded. 'She'd have been working through here.' He ushered them down a long, bare corridor. Through the far door, a bright hall was revealed, which was clearly being used as a storeroom. A few of the windowpanes were smashed, and the metal bars were rusting. A black smoke stain smudged the inside of the fireplace, and she imagined how Katy might have once sat before it, a little white dog by her feet.

'The day room.'

'That's right,' Edgar said. 'To be honest, I hate the thought of it, all those women locked up in here.' His eyes darted around uneasily.

How her own patients would have loved the space, the peace, the freshness, Iris thought.

'I won't show you upstairs, if that's all right? The dust gets on my lungs, and the damp.'

'Of course.' She glanced longingly at the ceiling before Simon put his hand on the small of her back and made her return to the main hallway.

'Outside has remained pretty much the same—'

'Is that Dr Basildon?' She pointed at the top of the staircase. Amidst all the other smaller frames hung one huge painting of a man in a fine Edwardian suit with slicked blonde hair and keen blue eyes. He sat on a great armchair in front of a large window, through which one could see the Shropshire hills. He held a book, and there was a skull on a table beside him.

'Yes. Ernest Basildon II. My uncle. He would have been in charge here in 1900.'

'May I ask what happened to him and his wife?'

'Ernest died just after the first war, not much older than I am now. Heart failure apparently, all very sudden. There were a handful of patients still here at the time. My aunt couldn't look after them herself, of course, so they were shipped out to some other place.'

'And you don't know who those patients would have been?'

'I don't. I would imagine it would be in the files.'

'Files?'

'I found them all in the attic only the other day. Great big chests of books and papers. Aunt never told me about them.'

'What happened to your aunt?'

'She lived here on her own for over thirty years. Just her and one maid. She was steely, old Aunt Harriet. Not one to get on the wrong side of, if you know what I mean?'

'Didn't they have any children?'

Simon coughed too loudly. He widened his eyes at Iris, but Edgar didn't seem to take offence at her question.

'No, unfortunately. It was a blow to her, so I believe. That's why I inherited this place. Uncle Ernest was an only child, his father an only child before him. My mother was Harriet's one sister, so it all came to me. I can't say that I was best pleased with the prospect, but here I am.'

'Well then, we should let you get back to packing. We don't want to take up anymore of your time,' Simon said, cutting in before Iris could ask anything else.

Iris scowled at him. She would never have got him involved if she'd known he was going to be such a pain. When he tried to manoeuvre her towards the exit, she jerked away from his touch. Edgar studied his shoes and cleared his throat, waiting for the tension to pass.

'Those files,' Iris said, forcing her voice to be light as she fixed Edgar with a smile and ignored Simon. 'I would love to have a look at them, if you wouldn't mind? My friend really wanted to find out what happened to the lady she cared for.'

'Of course. I was only going to burn them anyway. I don't know what else to do with them, otherwise. I wouldn't want you going into the attic, the floorboards aren't safe. I shall get a man to bring them down. Would you mind coming back?'

Reluctantly, she turned to Simon, swallowing down her anger and her pride. She needed him, after all; she needed his car, at least.

'Would we?'

Simon sighed. He was uncomfortable here, Iris knew, but she also knew he would not lose his chance for another day with her. The power of that realisation sent a tiny thrill through her body.

'I suppose not.'

14

1956

The mercury was over eighty by midday. Iris's uniform stuck to her sweaty skin, making her cringe. The patients were languid because of the heat, grumbling that they wanted to go back to bed and lie down. Rules were rules, though, and Nurse Carmichael would not permit a change in the routine.

The smell was getting worse. The old women didn't usually perspire, but it was impossible not to now. Their nightgowns were changed daily, their dresses and skirts and blouses all taken away to the laundry as soon as possible, but still the stench clung to the walls and mattresses.

Iris and Shirley prepared the lunch meal. Minced meat and potatoes, again, slopping out of the pans and splashing onto the plates. It was beginning to make Iris feel nauseous.

Iris had rolled up her sleeves as much as possible and unfastened the collar of her blouse, but Shirley remained buttoned up. A sheen of sweat sparkled on her forehead and top lip as she ladled out the food. She had been distant lately too. Her smiles and her snide comments had both been lacking.

'Any news?' Iris said.

Shirley shook her head.

'Seeing much of the doctor?'

'John and I are very happy.' The side of her mouth twitched; she knew Iris's eyes were on her. 'It's just this heat. I wish it would rain.' She rubbed the back of her wrist across her forehead.

They finished the last plateful, then rolled the trolley out and served the ladies who sat at the dining tables. Most of them could eat by themselves, the spoonfuls of mash shaking as they brought it to their lips, dripping gravy onto their skirts, but some could be tricky. Shirley fed Dot, while Iris helped Flo.

Flo was too weak now to do much at all. She opened her lips for the food and did her best to swallow, but after a few mouthfuls she was beginning to droop, her eyelids falling. Iris held the side of her face.

'Flo? Can you finish your lunch for me?'

Flo's eyelids fluttered a little, and she squinted at Iris. She opened her mouth again.

'That's it, good girl. We've got to keep up your strength.'

Iris hovered the next spoon in front of Flo's lips. Flo's fingers, as skinny as a bird's claw, wrapped around Iris's wrist and gently tugged her hand away. No one else would have seen, so slight was the movement, but Flo shook her head a little. She was saying no to all of this, her life being strung out, kept alive on bland mince and weak tea and a stranger's kindness.

Iris put the spoon on the plate and let Flo's head drop in sleep. Some of the other women on the table looked over, knowing another one of their own would soon be gone. She wheeled Flo out of the day room and into the ward. Nurse Carmichael might not like it, but Iris didn't care. A dying old woman should be allowed to go to bed at midday if she was falling asleep in her dinner.

Flo was light to lift, though her frailness made Iris careful not to hurt her. She laid the old woman on her clean bed, unhooked her shoes, and rolled off her socks. Flo's feet were as cold as metal, the skin so thin that the blueness of her veins was startling.

Iris sat on the bed, holding Flo's hand. It was strange being alone, just the two of them in a ward that usually held the bodies of over thirty women. With the sunlight falling across the white sheets, it looked almost nice. A few vases of flowers sat on the windowsills – after Nurses Shaw and Diya had finally taken it upon themselves to cut some bouquets from the hospital gardens – but now the roses were beginning to brown at the edges, the sun searing them dry. It was blissfully quiet, though; the usual groans and moans and shrieks safely down the corridor, so that Flo's breath and the creaking of the curtains as they caught in the breeze were the only sounds.

Flo. Why was she in here? Iris's notes were useless. Patients' mental health mattered little in Ward 13; they were considered merely old and demented and unable to care for themselves. All Iris had to do was keep them clean and fed and watered and safe. It was not what she had been hoping for. She wanted to help them, learn from them, study their minds. The women here were just shells, the years of incarceration breaking them down from the inside out. What had happened to Flo? She imagined abandonment; that would explain why she tried to cling on to everybody – she was scared to be left alone.

The door burst open. Flo stirred as Shirley came crashing through, her hands to her face. She hadn't seen Iris, who caught her arm as she ran through the ward.

'What's wrong?'

Shirley dropped her hands, shocked. Her face was blotchy, and tears were thick in her eyes.

'What's happened?'

'I can't do this. Look at me!' She gestured at her uniform. Bits of brown mince and mashed potato were splattered across her body.

'Dot?'

'Stupid old bitch.'

'Hush!' Iris pulled her out of Flo's earshot. 'No point getting yourself so worked up, is there? We can clean it off.'

'I hate her,' Shirley snarled. 'I hate this place and these stupid old hags.'

Iris pulled her close, even as she tried to squirm away. She hugged Shirley until her anger fizzled into tears. Tiredness and heat, that's what Iris put it down to. She lifted Shirley's face and straightened her cap, then felt Shirley's forehead.

'You're too hot. Crying like this will only make it worse.' She sat Shirley on the nearest bed. 'Why don't you undo your collar a bit?'

'No!' Shirley hit Iris's hand away. The room stilled. Shirley tensed, as if she were going to run.

'What is going on, Shirley?'

'Nothing.' Shirley sniffed and scratched the tears off her cheeks. 'I'm fine now.'

'Why don't you come round to mine later? I'll make some lemonade, and we can have a gossip.'

'I can't, I'm seeing John.'

'All right. Tomorrow, then. We can have a girl's night.'

Shirley shook her head and pushed her hair out of her face. 'I'm busy.' She stood up. 'I need to change.'

There was a hush in the hospital ward. The patients were sleeping, Kath too, though the curtains had not yet been drawn and the weak sunlight was still slanting in. Iris tiptoed to Kath, placed her bag gently on the floor, and put a hand on the woman's arm.

Kath didn't stir. She heaved in a breath; the sound of tight airways and full lungs. Her skin was grey again, the blood drained out of her cheeks. Dark purple patches made her look as if she had two black eyes.

Something wasn't right.

'What's happened? I only saw Kath on Saturday.'

Nurse Okeke ushered Iris into a quiet corner. 'A sudden slump. We see it sometimes in older patients. They look as if they are recovering but their body can't fight it off.'

'Is she still on antibiotics?'

The nurse nodded. 'But the longer she is on them, the less affect they can have. We are monitoring her.' She squeezed Iris's arm. 'We're doing what we can.'

Iris tried to smile. 'Has Albert been?'

'Not yet.'

Iris returned to Kath, hating the way she sounded as if she were drowning.

'I went to see it yesterday. It's called Highfields now. It's a good name for it.'

Iris poured herself a glass of water, spilling some as she trembled. She should be stronger than this. She had been warned: patients in Ward 13 get ill all the time, they die. But today had been hard – first Flo, then Shirley, and now Kath. And Kath had been doing so well.

'There was a really nice man there. He said I can go back to look at the files. I can find out what happened to Mrs Leverton.'

Kath's eyelids slid open. A shadow of a smile passed over her lips when she saw Iris beside her.

'How long have you been here?'

'Not long. How are you?'

'Where's Bertie?' She craned her neck to look for him.

'He can't make it, not tonight.'

'I was dreaming about him.'

Iris rummaged in her handbag. She was sure the piece of paper she had scribbled his number onto was in there. Underneath the diary and her purse and packs of tissues and a fresh pair of stockings, she finally found the scrunched bit of paper. She asked Nurse Okeke if she could use the phone. His voice was small on the other end of the line.

'Is everything all right, Albert? You haven't been to see Kath for a while.'

'No.' The line crackled, as if he were pulling on the cord.

'Is something wrong?'

'No.'

She imagined him bent over in the hallway, studying his shoes as he spoke, wishing he hadn't answered.

'I think Kath would really like to see you. She's not as good as she was.'

'Is she dying?'

She had been dying for years, a slow death of loneliness.

'I think you should visit her.'

'Yes. I will. I've been busy.'

'Would you like me to call for you, and we can visit her together?'

'No, dear, don't worry about that, I can sort myself out. Are you still reading the diary?'

'Yes.'

He paused. 'I'm glad you are with her. Goodbye, Iris.'

He put the phone down.

Nurse Okeke glanced at Iris. 'He's not coming, is he?'

But why? It had been Albert who had started this whole thing. He had come looking for Kath. He had given Iris the diary. He had promised Kath he would come back.

Iris slumped on the hard chair. Kath had fallen asleep again, but Iris got out the diary anyway. They didn't need Albert; she would stay with Kath and she would find out the truth.

15

1900

Wednesday, 19th December

It was my afternoon off today, and I'd sent a letter to Bertie on Monday to tell him to meet me in our usual place. I'd found Dr Basildon in the hallway where the letter bag is, and he'd asked me again how I was fairing as he eyed my letter, but he didn't ask who Mr A. Jones was. I'd said that I was coming on well. Indeed, the pain has gone to almost nothing, although the bruises look worse than ever; they've turned yellow and brown, with veiny patches of red dotted amidst them. I tried to cover them with some powder, but it was useless. All I did was make myself look even paler and even more like a ghoul. Bertie was horrified when he saw me. I told him what happened, keeping my composure until I got to Marion. She is ever so cold. She barely speaks to me, and when we go to bed, she rolls onto her other side so that her back is to me.

'Don't you go worrying yourself over her. It isn't fair she's taking it out on you.'

'But it's not her fault. Goodness, if we cannot go to the closet in peace we might as well be patients ourselves!'

'Don't talk so daft.'

'I'm not talking daft, Bertie. I'm just saying that it was one big accident, none of us could have seen it coming, and Marion's got the rough end of it.'

'Well, you know what to do if you don't like it. Leave.'

He'd gone in a huff with me, I could tell by the way his one eyebrow was raised. But this was not his time to get offended; it was me who had the bruises and me who had to deal with Marion's cold shoulder.

'I'm not asking for your opinion, Bertie. I just want to talk to someone, don't you understand? I wanted to tell you everything that had happened, and I wanted a cuddle. Why must we argue?'

'I'm not arguing with you.'

His brow was still raised.

'And how can I just leave? I'm doing this for us.'

'You shouldn't stay if you don't like it.'

'Do any of us like working?' I laughed, trying to lighten the mood, but he didn't join in with me. 'It's good money too, better than at Cotton's. I reckon another year and we'll be there.'

He sniffed and watched the water.

'What do you think? One year before we can get married, get our own place.' I snuggled into his arm, trying to ease the tension that had developed. He pulled himself free to get out a pie.

'I don't want that,' I said as he tried to hand it to me. I kissed his nose, then his lips.

'We shouldn't.'

'Why not?'

'I don't want to hurt you.'

'I think it would do me good.'

'No.' He put his hand on my shoulder and held me away from him. He wouldn't look at me, and I thought of that nightmare I'd had, and it was all too much.

'Fine.' I stood up and flung my coat about me, liking the pain that rippled down my ribs. 'Suit yourself.'

I strode away, hoping he'd call out for me, say he was sorry, and I'd run back to him, and we'd make love. But he didn't say anything until I was almost out of sight. Then I heard him shout my name, but it was too late, and I was already weeping, and there was no way I was going to let him see me like that.

Saturday, 22nd December

It was the Christmas Ball tonight. We've all been excited about it – Marion even forgot her anger for a moment as we dressed ourselves in our best gowns, but she went back to ignoring me once I'd fixed her hair. I didn't ask her to do mine, so I left it in its usual boring bun and went to ready Mrs Leverton.

Annie ran up to me, sniffing at my legs, trying to work out why I smelt different. Mrs Leverton was in her day gown but was brushing out her hair before the looking glass. She saw me in the reflection.

'You look beautiful, Katy.'

I could see myself better in Mrs Leverton's mirror. It was an old dress, one of my ma's, but the light blue colour was pretty and brought out my eyes. The next moment, Mrs Leverton got up from her seat and forced me into it instead.

'Your hair will not do for a ball.'

We are not allowed curling irons for fear the patients will burn themselves, and my hair was as flat as a fluke, but Mrs Leverton began to brush it until it looked like liquid honey, and then she used her own pins from the locked drawer to fasten it on top of my head, curling it round into pretty patterns.

'No one will notice your bruises now,' she said, smiling at me in the looking glass.

She had ordered a new dress for the ball. It was black like usual, but instead of her normal taffeta or silk, this one was made of velvet. It hugged her small frame, still enviably slim even at her age, and shimmered under the light as she moved. She had also bought a new fur, which was brilliant white, and draped it elegantly over her shoulders. We both slipped on our satin gloves.

'I think we shall be the belles of the ball,' she said as we stood side by side in front of the mirror. Mischievousness glinted in her eye, and I couldn't help but giggle.

We made our way to the dining room, passing through the hallway which had been hung with fir garlands, making the air stink of pine forests. Candles were everywhere, and the light was quite dazzling as we entered the room, which had been transformed: the carpets had been rolled back to reveal a polished wooden floor; at the front was a makeshift stage, where a small, hired orchestra waited to play; and just through the door, to our left beside the raging fire, was a magnificent tree, the angel at its tip touching the ceiling. Glass and painted baubles hung from its branches beside cloved oranges, cinnamon sticks, and red ribbons tied in bows.

We joined the female patients and attendants in the

corner, who sat on the soft chairs and sofas that had been brought in from the day rooms.

'It's wonderful, isn't it?' Nella said to me, for I couldn't take my eyes off the decorations.

'I've never seen anything like it.'

'They do this every year. Dr Basildon is such a marvellous man.'

'Mulled wine?' Marion offered me a steaming cup. She had the kink of a smile on her lips, and I took the drink gladly, hoping we were some way to making amends. She gave another glass to Mrs Leverton then sat down beside Mrs Huxley.

Mrs Huxley wore long sleeves, but a bandage bulged at her wrist. She looked terrible, her eyes red-rimmed and her skin ashen. I had heard that her sheets were being fitted in at night, to stop her wriggling and to keep her arms by her sides so that she would not pick and open the wounds. She was under constant surveillance, and Marion hardly ever took her eyes off her. Marion was twitchy because of it, and each movement from Mrs Huxley made Marion start into action.

'Wini was cursing about missing it,' Nella continued to talk to me.

'Why?'

'She has to be with Miss Beckwith, you know. What with her habit, she can't be around alcohol like this.'

It was a pity Wini was missing out, and I thought I might steal some Christmas cake and take it to her a little later on. Wini would have been the life of the party, swinging the men around when it came time to dance.

'Oh, my!'

I followed Nella's gaze.

Dr Basildon and his wife entered the room and stood beside the fire. The doctor was as handsome as ever in a formal dinner suit, his hair slicked into place and his moustache twirled into crispness. His wife wore a crimson velvet gown with a sash of gold across one shoulder. The neckline was low, her waist painfully small, and her hair curled into loose, cloud-like waves on top of her head. Her throat and ears glittered with diamonds.

Dr Basildon nodded, and the orchestra began. Music broke across the room, startling some of the patients, who hadn't realised what was going to happen.

Mrs Leverton and I escaped to the library next door, where the dining table had been moved, and found ourselves some food. We took small plates of cold sandwiches, tongue, and fowl, but neither of us seemed able to stomach much of it, despite its fineness. I was too eager to return to the ballroom, and we soon put down our plates and made our way back to the music.

My stomach felt like the ocean, roiling with excitement as the room murmured with well-dressed ladies and gentlemen, their feet tapping and threatening to break into dance. It was impossible to tell who was a patient and who was not.

Dr Basildon took his wife's hand and led her to the centre of the room. Everyone stepped to the side as he bowed to her and brought her into hold. The orchestra started a new tune, and the Basildons flew across the floor, their steps timed perfectly in a fast polka.

Soon, some of the men were asking the women to dance. I turned my head away from the crowd, concentrating on my drink.

'Excuse me,' Mr Merryton addressed Mrs Leverton. 'Would you care to dance?'

The old man offered her his hand, and she took it with ease. They moved so elegantly across the floor, their fine breeding evident in the way they held their heads high and their arms up. My palms stung from all my clapping, and as the music ended, Mr Merryton returned Mrs Leverton to her seat with a salute. Her cheeks were flushed, her dark eyes shone, and her smile was as radiant as I have ever seen.

'Well done!' I gushed.

'Excuse me,' a voice said. I thought it was Mr Merryton back for a second round, but I found his young attendant looking at me instead. He is a handsome man, a few years older than me, with light chestnut hair and a firm and chiselled face; he knows it too. 'Could I have this dance?'

I stared at his hand for a moment until Mrs Leverton spoke for me. 'She would be delighted.'

I hadn't held any man's hand but Bertie's before, and even through my gloves I was aware how different his felt; bigger and stronger. He led me with a firm grip so that I could not let go.

Thankfully, the orchestra was now playing a waltz; the waltz is the only dance I know. He bowed to me, and I curtseyed to him before he gripped my waist and pulled me close. He smirked at my surprise.

'I'm Daniel,' he said as we began to spin.

'Katy.'

'That is a very pretty dress, Katy.'

We danced round and round. I was too busy concentrating on my steps to make conversation, praying that I would not put my feet in the wrong place and trip, but Daniel manoeuvred me effortlessly, much to my annoyance. I found myself looking at his smug face and actually wishing that we might go careering to the floor, just so he might stop grinning.

'I am the envy of every man.'

'What do you mean?'

He gripped me tighter until my stomach was only an inch from his.

'Have you seen the stars tonight?'

I didn't catch the change of direction.

'The sky is clear, and the stars are very bright. Perhaps I might show you them, later?'

I did not like what he was implying and would not speak to him for the rest of the dance. He walked me to my seat and saluted, and as I turned my head away, he dared to wink at me.

Mrs Leverton giggled. I feared she had drunk too much wine, and so I took her cup away, saying she might prefer a cool glass of water instead. She didn't argue but rather looked at me as if I were her mother and rolled her eyes.

'Good evening, ladies.' Dr Basildon sauntered over to our small gathering, bending from the waist to give us all a bow. 'Are you enjoying yourselves?'

We all muttered how we were having such a wonderful time, except for Mrs Milton, who stared into space, like she had been doing all evening. Alice nodded her head so viciously that I thought it might fall off her neck.

'Mrs Leverton, would you like to dance?'

She agreed demurely, and as she gently placed her hand on top of his and let him guide her to the floor, I saw the look of glee in his eye; perhaps he thought her sanity was finally beginning to show. She was no longer the dull old woman she had been when I had first arrived, who either cried or chided and smiled only at her pet. Dr Basildon swept her into a slow waltz, and they smiled and talked as they danced, looking rather like mother and son.

Alice drew my attention, for she was beginning to wherrit, her lips starting to wobble as if she might cry or burst out in a fury. Miss Wade was taking no notice of her and wouldn't take her eyes off Dr Basildon's butler, who she had managed to get the ear of.

'Alice, should you like something to eat?'

Alice pulled her bottom lip and shook her head.

'There are biscuits, and a great big fruit cake.'

Her sloppy eyes looked up at me, and she grinned wickedly.

'Come on!'

I let her hold my hand as we went into the library. Mrs Basildon was at the end of the food table, right next to the fruit cake, with her lady's maid. They were talking in hushed tones, gossiping, I suspected. I tried to interest Alice in a slice of tongue, but her heart was set on sugar. She yanked me over to the cake and began to bang my arm in excitement, right where some of my worst bruises were.

'Sorry, Mrs Basildon, may I just cut some cake for Alice?'

Mrs Basildon's back had been towards us, and now she turned to me as if I had asked her to jump from the roof, but she stepped out of the way all the same.

'Thank you.' I gestured for the kitchen maid to get me a knife – she had them all on her person with strict instructions that no patient be allowed to take one – and began to cut Alice a slice.

I was determined not to look at Mrs Basildon, but then I heard Alice, her voice too far away, and found her beside Mrs Basildon, ogling the woman's diamonds. Mrs Basildon was doing her best to ignore her. She held her head away from the girl, but Alice's hand began to slither closer.

I was too late to stop it. Alice grabbed Mrs Basildon's necklace and pulled hard, and Mrs Basildon slapped her, shrieking to get her away.

I ran for Alice and prised her hands off the jewellery. 'Now Alice, those aren't yours, are they?'

Her eyes remained focused on the diamonds, struggling against me. She was getting in a bother, I could tell, and her mouth was hanging wide, saliva dribbling down her chin.

'Disgusting imbecile,' Mrs Basildon said.

I let go of Alice in shock. Alice started to cry.

'Get her away from me,' Mrs Basildon said.

I could have hit her.

'Come along, Alice.' I took the girl by the waist and guided her to the door, and was quite surprised when she put up no resistance. I grabbed a slice of cake as we left.

Once inside the ballroom, I led her to a quiet corner and made her sit. Her tears were petering out into little sniffs. I wiped my handkerchief over her face and hoped the volume of my dress would conceal her from prying eyes.

'Let's not cry at Christmas, Alice. It is the happiest time of the year.'

Snot ran into her mouth and I wiped that away as well.

'You are prettier than the angel on the tree.'

'Really?'

I nodded, and she beamed at me. I smoothed back some stray strands of hair from her sticky forehead. 'Now, you'd better eat your cake before I gobble it all.'

She snatched her plate from my hands and shovelled the cake through her lips, dropping plump raisins down her dress as she did so. I took the seat next to her, glad of a little peace and quiet away from the main group, as the number came to an end and Dr Basildon brought Mrs Leverton to her seat. I was about to return to her, taking Alice with me, when Dr Basildon whispered to Miss Wade; I could tell by the colour in her cheeks that he had been an unwelcome and uncompromising interruption. He pointed her towards Alice.

'Miss Owen, I wondered if you would like to dance with me?'

I hesitated. 'Mrs Leverton is—'

'Miss Wade will keep her eye on Mrs Leverton, won't you, Miss Wade? And, of course, her own charge as well.'

Miss Wade nodded, keeping her gaze on the floor, her cheeks scarlet.

I couldn't refuse my employer.

His hand was gentler than Daniel's but just as big. I felt all eyes on us as we arrived on the floor, so I kept my gaze trained on his collar.

The music began. It was an unfortunately quick waltz. Dr Basildon tensed just before he took the first step, charging up for the dance, and in that short second, I forgot all the moves. I was certain I would fall, but Dr Basildon whisked me around, keeping me close, leading me like an expert. Finally, I found the breeze from our quick pace a welcome relief, cooling the heat on my neck, making tendrils of my hair flow freely behind me. I was actually enjoying myself! The people at the sides of the room whirled past us in a blur and, unable to see their stares, I felt a giggle rising from my gut. I couldn't stop it – it trickled out of me, and I thought Dr Basildon might tell me off, but when I glanced at him I found he was smiling too.

'Mrs Leverton is much improved,' he said over the music.

'Yes,' I said breathlessly.

'I think it is you we must thank for it. What is your secret, Katy?'

My smile faltered only for a second. 'I just listen to her.'

'And she tells you what?'

'Anything and everything.'

When I looked at him again, he had become serious.

'You know, there was never any trace of an Edward Blake.'

'I didn't mean...'

'None of the staff had ever known an Irish gardener, no relatives were ever traced. They searched the whole of the river for the boat and found nothing.'

I swallowed. The spinning was suddenly making me feel sick.

'Do not be taken in, Katy.'

Finally, the music stopped. He bowed to me, and when he came up, his smile had returned. He walked me back to Mrs Leverton. 'She is a fine dancer, is she not, Mrs Leverton?'

'As graceful as a swan.'

They looked at me like appraising parents.

Heels clipped closer to us. Mrs Basildon joined her husband's side. She had a glass of punch in her hand, and the red liquid was sloshing from the movement, about to spill onto her white gloves.

'Mrs Basildon, that dress is sublime,' Mrs Leverton said. Mrs Basildon pushed her lips into a smile.

'The diamonds were Ernest's grandmother's.'

'I thought I recognised them. They suit you perfectly.'

'Shall we dance, my dear?' Dr Basildon shifted on his feet.

'Where did you get your dress, Katy?'

'I… It was my mother's.'

Mrs Basildon nodded as her gaze slid down my body. 'She is a charwoman, is she not?'

'Yes, ma'am.'

'Did she work in that dress?'

My breath caught. My cheeks stinging, my gaze fell, and I saw all the faults in the dress. The bodice was not as tight as it should have been – it gaped to show my mother had been thicker in the waist than me. The skirt material had some bobbles where it lay across my thighs, and patches of it were discoloured.

'Harriet.' It was a warning, but Mrs Basildon took no notice of her husband.

'There must be some cupboards for you to clean. A front step to polish.' She laughed, a shrill, piercing sound. 'And anyway, your face is putting people off their food. Did you have no powder?'

Dr Basildon gripped her arm and whispered something in her ear which made her stand up straighter. She glared at me, then stormed away.

'I must apologise for my wife. Might I—?'

'I am tired, Doctor.' Mrs Leverton stood and smiled as if nothing had happened. 'Thank you for this delightful party, but I should like to go to bed now.'

'Of course.' Dr Basildon bowed at us again.

Mrs Leverton held out her arm so that she could put it through mine for support, and we left the room.

It was eerily quiet as we entered the female wing and the empty day room, the thick walls keeping the noise from the orchestra trapped in the main house. Mrs Leverton's voice echoed as she spoke.

'She is a vile woman, as jealous as a snake.'

I bit my tongue as we made our way upstairs and found Annie curled up in her blankets. The dog stiffly got to her feet and shuffled over to us, her tail wagging.

'You shall have to bite her, Annie. We shall train you to be our little fighting dog.'

'Would you like a bed pan, Mrs Leverton?'

'I'm not going to bed, Katy! I am not tired at all.'

'But you said…'

She cocked her head to the side and looked at me as if I were stupid. Finally, I realised she had done it for me, to save me. I had been keeping myself together until then, but Mrs Leverton's kindness made my tears fall. She came to me and hugged me, rocking me from side to side.

'Hush now. You must not let her upset you.'

'She was right, the dress is old, my face is—'

'Exquisite. And that is why she was so cruel. Katy' – she shook her head, as if bemused – 'no man has been able to keep his eyes off you tonight. Could you not see that? I told you, you are like me when I was your age.'

'Did you go to many dances?'

'All of them.' She settled herself onto the bed and patted it so that I would sit beside her. I picked Annie up so us three girls could be cosy together.

'What were they like?'

'Grander than this. Hundreds of people. You can get away with so much more in a crowded room.' She winked. 'There was one boy... It was my first season, and I was fresh-faced and new. He had the fluff of a moustache and the greenest eyes I had ever seen, truly the colour of an apple. He was my first love.'

'What happened?'

'We danced all night. We kept meeting each other at balls all season long. He took me out to Regent's Park one day, and we kissed under the shade of a tree.'

'Then what?'

'Then the season was over, and I never met him again.' She saw my face fall and laughed at me. 'There are plenty of boys out there, Katy. Someone else always comes along.'

'Mrs Leverton—'

'Won't you call me Persey? My sister used to call me Persey. I should like it if you did now.'

I wasn't supposed to, but in the quiet of the night I thought it could not hurt, especially when I was going to tell her about Bertie.

'Persey, I have... I have a boy that I have set my heart on.'

'It is not Daniel, is it?'

'What? Goodness, no!'

'Good. He is devilishly handsome, but I do not trust him.'

'No, a boy from home.'

She raised her eyebrows, encouraging.

'His name is Bertie. He is the butcher's son. We are… going to get married.'

'When?' she said urgently, as if I might be leaving her at any minute.

'Not for a while. We have to save money first. His father wouldn't allow it, you see. He wants Bertie to make a better match. He is an ambitious man.'

'So that is why you are here.' There was a sadness in her voice.

'That is why I came, yes, although now I think I should like to stay, even when we are married.'

'You know you cannot.'

'But Mrs Thorpe is married to Mr Thorpe. Why might it not be the same for me and Bertie?'

'It is different for matrons. But perhaps you are right. Dr Basildon is a reasonable man.'

'I have told no one but you about this, not even Marion.'

Mrs Leverton – Persey – smiled again. 'And I think we should keep it that way.' She yawned. 'I should get some rest now.'

I undressed her and unfastened her hair. I let mine out at the same time and locked all of the pins in the dressing table. She crept into bed, returning to the old lady she had been before the party.

'Are you not praying?'

'I think God will forgive me this once. Good night, Katy.'

I pulled the covers up to her chin and patted Annie on the head. 'Good night, Persey.'

. . .

I found Wini slumped over the night desk, her chin resting in her hands, her eyes half shut. My footsteps roused her.

'How is the party?'

'Find out for yourself. I'll stay here for an hour.'

She hesitated, but she was wide awake now. 'I shouldn't. Mrs Thorpe says it's my duty tonight.'

'Mrs Thorpe is too busy with Mr Thorpe to notice. Go on, the cake is delicious.'

She pushed out her chair, making it screech on the floorboards. 'Doctor gave Mrs Beckwith an opiate, so she'll be quiet. Thank you, Katy.' She ran to the stairs, her heavy steps clomping all the way down.

I sat behind the desk, staring into the empty corridor. I tried not to think about Mrs Basildon and what she'd said, but it kept turning over in my mind. She was a mean woman, but jealous? I couldn't believe Mrs Leverton's theory of someone like Mrs Basildon being envious of someone like me. The woman lives in a mansion, is married to a doctor, and has the finest gowns I've ever seen.

I hoped she choked on her punch.

Night duty is always such a bore. The hands on the clock slow down so that a minute becomes two. The wooden chair is hard and uncomfortable, so I stretched my legs and looked in on Mrs Beckwith. I opened the latch on her door to see she was fast asleep, lying on her back, her mouth open and quivering with each breath. I shut the latch again and tiptoed to Mrs Leverton's room. She too was asleep, curled onto her side like a child, Annie snuggled against her stomach.

I thought about mine and Mrs Leverton's conversation,

then about Bertie. It is hard to keep my thoughts away from Bertie since our last meeting. I have never seen him so distant. It makes me sick with worry. All I want is to see him again, to put my fears to rest. Perhaps he'd just had a bad day? I hadn't asked about him at all, I had only talked about myself. Perhaps his father had been difficult. Perhaps the cold weather was getting to him; Bertie much prefers the warmth of summer. Or perhaps he was coming down with the flu and didn't want to pass it on to me, like last year, when he had refused to kiss me for three whole weeks so I remained healthy, although love-sick and frustrated.

It could be any of those reasons – I hope it is any of those reasons. If I could only speak to him and apologise for my sharp tongue! I hadn't meant to ruin our afternoon. Why did I have to be so hard on him? If I'd have just said, *Yes, you're right Bertie, Marion is being unreasonable*. Or, *Yes, Bertie, I'll leave if it happens again*. Or better still, if I'd have never started talking about it at all – then our argument wouldn't ever have happened.

'Not coming back to the party?'

I'd been leaning against Mrs Leverton's door and suddenly found Daniel behind me.

'You shouldn't be in the women's wing.'

'No one will know.' His hands were in his pockets, and his hair had fallen out of its hold so that it flopped over his forehead. He was grinning. Did he ever stop grinning?

'I'll know.' I strode past him to the desk. 'I am on duty.'

'Winifred is technically on duty.' He sauntered towards me. 'I told you I wanted to show you the stars.'

'And I never agreed to that.'

'I heard about Mrs Basildon, what she said to you.' He leant over the desk, putting his hands on it. If the wood hadn't been there, he would have been gripping my thighs. 'Rumour has it that Doctor has no taste for his wife. I should say her mood would be improved by a good fuck.'

I stood up. 'You will not say such things in front of me.'

'I am on your side. She's a stuck-up bitch who is as ugly as a pig.'

'You should not talk about the mistress like that.'

He laughed. 'You are a good little girl, aren't you?' He folded his arms, his smirk growing.

I would not rise for his bait. I would not give him the satisfaction. I held my ground; this was my ward, and he was not welcome.

'Wini will be back soon.'

'Good, then I can show you the stars after all.'

'Do you never give up?'

'Never.'

And I knew that he would not. I just wanted him to go away. I didn't want his handsome face and his poisoned tongue anywhere near me.

There is a danger from Daniel I can't explain. He is like a cat, lurking, waiting in the shadows, and I am scared he sees me as a mouse. I was sure the punch had emboldened him, even though Dr Basildon had drowned it in water, and I recalled tales of men coming home from public houses, unsteady on their feet, a menace to any woman in their path.

'Daniel, I am tired. You might show me some other time.'

He considered this for a moment, and I thought he was trying to see if I was playing him, but in the end, he accepted it.

'Another night, then.' He slipped away as silently as he had arrived.

I only had to wait a few more minutes before Wini returned with red cheeks, beaming with pleasure. She held a napkin full of Christmas cake, and I left her stuffing it into her mouth as she swayed from side to side, a tune from the orchestra still playing in her mind.

Outside, the cobbles were already slippery with frost, glistening like water under the moonlight. I looked up at the stars – a vast, black sky filled with them, just as Daniel had promised.

I scuttled to my room before the cat had time to pounce.

16

1900

Sunday, 23rd December

Nobody wanted to get up this morning. I even had to wake Marion and prod her out of bed. The patients were just as reluctant, but we rounded them up for their baths and made them eat whatever breakfast they could stomach.

I wasn't sure the change in routine suited all the patients. Mrs Huxley was on edge once again, and Alice was rather lively, charging about the day room, coming close to knocking the vases off the tables. But it is Christmas, so allowances can be made.

I asked Mrs Leverton if she will be having any visitors. I had expected some to come before now, what with them having to travel from Wales, but Mrs Leverton told me she doesn't have any visitors at all.

'The last time I saw Henry was from the carriage window when they took me away,' she said as we stood on the mound in the grounds.

'He has never been to see you?'

She shook her head.

'Why?'

'Because of what I did.'

'You told me you had a sister, though?'

'Alexandra.'

'Surely she visits from time to time?'

'She sent me a letter almost a year into my time here. In it, she said she'd had a baby and must put her son before her own feelings. She said she would not be as selfish as our mother, or me.'

Perhaps the letter had some effect when it was first received, but now Mrs Leverton looked nothing but bored as she informed me of her abandonment.

'What about James or Patience? Do you think they might agree to it now? They are adults, after all. They might like to get to know their mother, and what better time to make amends than at Christmas?'

At last, a change came upon her face. Was she daring to imagine it?

'I do not believe they would wish to see me.'

'You don't know that. When did you say James visited you that time?'

'1883. He had just turned eighteen.'

'There you are, then. He is a man now; he might be more reasonable.'

She nodded a little, regarding the silver landscape that stretched out beyond our feet.

'Why don't you write to them?' She was forever writing letters; they were just always to the wrong person. 'Tell them how sorry you are, how much you would love to see them, convince them you are…'

'Sane?'

'Yes, to put it bluntly.'

She laughed at me and cupped her hand against my cheek. 'Forever hopeful. But where would I send the letters? I have no idea if Argoed is still standing, let alone if James still lives there. And if James is there, where is Patience? She will be married now, she will likely have children of her own.' She was quiet for a moment, her face scrunching in the low sunlight. 'I could be a grandmother, Katy. I have never thought of it before now.'

I could see her sinking. I took her hand. 'Come on, let's go and write those letters.'

At three o'clock, I knocked on Dr Basildon's door. It took a few moments for him to answer, and when he did, his tie was loose, his collar undone, his hair unwaxed. When he saw me, he turned and tidied himself, but crusts of sleep remained in the corners of his eyes.

'What do you want, Miss Owen?'

'I have two letters here.'

'You know where the mail bag is.'

'Yes, but they are not from me, they are from Mrs Leverton. She would like to send them to her children.'

Dr Basildon tugged his gaze up from the floor, then stepped aside so I might take a seat.

'Why?'

'She wants to put things right.'

'Did you have something to do with this?'

'Not really, sir, but I said I thought it was a good idea.'

Dr Basildon shoved his fingers into the dark sockets of

his eyes, and breathed a long, low sigh. 'She cannot write to them.'

'Why?'

'Mr Leverton has forbade it.'

'He can't stop her.'

'He can do whatever he likes. He is paying for her to be here.'

I stalled, taken aback by his ferocity. 'I don't understand. I thought the problem was her lack of interest in the children. Pue ... pueper...'

'Puerperal insanity. Leading to delusions.'

'Surely the root cause has been fixed? She wants to see her children now, begin a relationship with them. It shows she has recovered.'

'And her delusions? She still prays for salvation?'

'She did not last night.'

He paused for a moment, as if considering. 'It is still no use. Mr Leverton will not have his children contacted.'

'But why?'

'It is not your place to question!'

I hoped his irritability was only from lack of sleep. I must remember, men do not like to be irritated, or questioned. I continued in a more soothing tone.

'I am sorry, sir. I am only trying to do what is best for Mrs Leverton.'

'I know you are.' He softened, although his brow remained furrowed, as if in pain.

'Can I get you some water, sir?' I didn't wait for him to answer before I poured him a drink from the glass decanters on the side of his desk. 'I do think it odd of Mr Leverton.' I kept my voice gentle, although I could not help but probe. 'His wife's recovery would only be a benefit to the family. Perhaps there is more to it than we know.' I set the glass before him and did not chance to see his expression; I kept my gaze on the floor.

He gulped down the water and eased back in his chair. Only then did I look up, hoping I might have persuaded him about Mrs Leverton, but his eyes, though dull with fatigue, chilled me.

'You must stop this, Katy. Your obsession with Mrs Leverton and her stories is… concerning.'

It was a warning. Fear made gooseflesh of my skin. I nodded and said nothing more.

'Those letters will not be sent. You will stop indulging her fantasies. And you will tell her that no one is visiting.'

Monday, 24th December

I shall not see the morning. I will not wake, for I am in a nightmare.

I visited my parents for a couple of hours this afternoon. It had been three whole months since I last saw them. My heart was glad for it. Da has started to look old, the lines around his eyes are as thick as tree trunks, but Ma is ever youthful. May couldn't make it because of work.

'Working her like a mule,' Da said, as he spat black phlegm on the fire.

I didn't tell them about everything that has happened. They cannot understand why I should want to be at a place filled with mad folk. Ma was telling me there is work come up in the village and she is run off her feet. She is trying to tempt me back, I know, but I cannot leave Mrs Leverton.

It was so odd to be back at home. All my memories of the house are of when I was just a little'un. Hiding in the cupboard under the stairs when May hunted me. Snuggled under blankets and coats in the winter when the frost came on the inside of the glass. My ma on her knees, her face blackened from the soot of the old range as she cleaned it. Bacon fat on bread, sat at the table with the wobbly leg. All these things came upon me at once, memories that felt like they were from another child. I didn't seem to belong there anymore. I'd been gone for too long, almost half of my life working away from those childhood walls.

It made me think of Mrs Leverton, how she was no longer the mistress of a grand house, though we had to pretend she was. She had lived longer in a madhouse than she had free.

I was eager to get back to The Retreat in the end, but not before I'd seen Bertie.

It was fading to dusk as I walked out of the village. I passed Jones and Sons Butchers, saw old Mr Jones behind the counter, surrounded by massive fowls and hunks of beef and pork. Customers were coming to get their Christmas meat, and I could smell cooking wafting down the streets – people preparing their feasts for tomorrow.

I walked over the bridge slowly; Bertie would be busy for a while by the looks of it, stuck somewhere in the backroom slicing up dead animals.

I followed the path by the stream. It had been another fine day for winter. There was no snow, but the ground was hard, the November mud solidified into dips and ridges which made walking difficult. I tripped twice, catching myself, checking over my shoulder to ensure no one had seen me.

A low, white mist smoked above the water, making the heads of the trees look as if they were floating on a cloud. The bare branches scratched against a sky that was no longer blue but rather a vibrant clementine, stretching into fuchsia pink. There was no sound but the thump of my footsteps and the cry of a blackbird rustling in the stiff leaves, trying to get its supper.

I wondered if Mrs Leverton was by her window watching the sun set too. She would have enjoyed the spectacle, and a part of me wished I was there with her. But it was nice to be alone too – alone but not lonely.

What would Dr Basildon be doing? His wife? I imagined them in their drawing room, their fire raging, both reading something and ignoring each other. My own isolation was physical, unlike theirs, and for a second, I had a pang of pity for Mrs Basildon. To be unloved, undesired, by your own husband must be the worst kind of loneliness. I thought I too would be bitter if Bertie had so deserted me, and I remembered how it had stung when he had pushed me away.

I would not let that happen again.

I sat on our usual stump in our usual place as the last of the orange light faded and the world turned silver. I leant back against a tree and watched the stars sparkle, thinking how different tonight was compared to the party and how much I preferred to be out here, though my feet were numb and my hands were stuffed under my armpits to warm them. I pulled my cloak closer. Mrs Leverton had leant me an old brown fur stole, and I tightened that about my neck, thanking her again under my breath.

I waited for Bertie. The silence was broken every now and again by a small creature shuffling in the undergrowth, and my heart started in fright when a ghostly spectre of a barn owl swooped nearby. I knocked on wood to prevent any bad luck. The longer I waited, the more I felt as if I had a hundred eyes trained upon me, faint dots in the darkness all around. I kept turning to peer past tree trunks, certain I would find a shadowed figure.

Then there was a yellow light in the distance, swaying from side to side, as if it were on a ship on the rolling sea. I heard the crunching of hoarfrost, the swishing of woollen trousers, the rapid breathing of someone walking too fast in the cold. For one awful second, I thought it might have been someone else, and I crouched against the tree, hoping whoever it was would not see me, but then the light stopped swaying.

'Katy?' Bertie whispered in the silence.

'I'm here. Watch yourself.'

Bertie found me. He put the lamp on the stump and blew into his hands, his breath coming out in white puffs against the light.

'It's freezing. We shouldn't be long tonight.'

'I'm sorry, Bertie, for last time. I can't stop thinking about how we left it. It has given me bad dreams. I shouldn't have gone off like that.'

'It's all right.' His dark eyes darted towards mine. He opened his mouth to say something, shut it again, then said, 'You been well? No more attacks?'

'Fine. Everyone is too happy for Christmas.'

'That's good... And Mrs Leverton? You still think she's telling the truth?'

I smiled at him for asking and picked up his hand. It was colder than mine, and I wrapped it in my skirts, bringing him closer as I did so. 'What she says is just so detailed. Her first dog dying, the birth of Patience. She admits her faults as a mother and as a wife. Why would she tell the truth about that and then lie about murdering someone?'

Bertie shrugged.

'Dr Basildon says she has created a false guilt. It makes more sense to be guilty of murder, something she can understand, than to know why she could not love her own child.'

'And you don't think that's it?'

'I think it is a good explanation – a convenient explanation that fits with what her husband said. People are put into madhouses and forgotten. A reputation of a murderer in the family is not so easily swept away.'

'But you like her?'

'Oh yes. She is not how I expect a murderer to be at all.'

'Does it really matter?'

I looked at him, at the dark side of his face, at his profile outlined in yellow light. 'What do you mean?'

'Well, she's mad, or she's a murderer. Either way, she should be locked up. I don't understand why you're pushing for it to be true when that truth would mean the noose for her.'

The realisation silenced me. I hadn't ever thought of it like that. What a dreadfully miserable notion! I kicked my heels against the stump.

'I just want to know what really happened. It is like a scab I must pick until it bleeds.'

'Don't.' He turned to me, his face now in total shadow, and pulled his hand free. 'Can't you see how it looks? You're obsessed with her and soon you'll have—'

'I'll have what?'

'You'll have gone mad too.'

I could have argued, but there was fear in his words; he was scared for me. He searched my face as if I might already be lost.

'Yes. Yes, all right,' I said and looked away before his fear infected me too. 'I understand.' I didn't want another row. I didn't want Christmas Eve to be like that. 'Let's talk about something else.'

'It's getting late.'

'It's just dark. Tell me how your day has been.'

'Busy.'

'Yes, I saw the shop on my way from Ma's.'

He was too quiet. He pulled back some skin next to his thumb nail, his spine curled inward and his eyes intent on the action. He pulled and pulled until the skin ripped off. The blood pooled against his nail, trickling down over his thumb in tiny veins as thin as spider's silk.

'Our wedding will be—'

'I am engaged.'

I blinked.

He had not moved, I had not seen his lips move, had I?

'I am engaged to Mabel Robins.' He stuck his bleeding thumb in his mouth and sucked.

'Mabel Robins?' I forced the words out. It was all I could do to repeat the name, as if by repeating it I might understand. *Mabel Robins... Mabel Robins...* I dug through my mind, trying to match a face to the name, and then it came, a person appearing through the fog. Black hair, a thick jawline, a firm and hardy body bound tight in a dress clogged with mud. 'The farmer's daughter?'

He nodded.

'Engaged?'

He took his thumb out of his mouth and the saliva on it glistened. 'Da wanted it. She's got money and land. We'll be set up.'

I couldn't speak. Mabel Robins? How? And why? He couldn't love her, could he? He couldn't love her whilst he loved me.

A noise echoed through the trees. It sounded like a wounded animal, and then I realised it was coming from me.

'Don't cry,' he said, as tears fell from his own eyes. 'Don't cry, Katy.'

It didn't feel like I was crying. It felt like I was dying, like I was suffocating, like there was a rope slicing into my throat. I dragged in air and heard the rush of it against my closing airways. My chest burned as if I were being sawn open.

'I couldn't do anything!' Bertie stood up, started jabbing his feet into the ground as he walked in circles, grabbing at his face and hair. 'There was nothing I could do! It was done before I knew it was ever a thought.'

'Don't marry her, Bertie,' I managed to choke out, my voice cutting off into sobs.

'It's done, Katy. My word is given, it's out there, it's hers! And you know Da wouldn't have allowed me and you.'

'We were saving.'

'I never asked you to save, Katy. That was your idea.'

'You said we would be married!'

He stopped pacing, and his shoulders crumpled in. He stood in front of me, my Bertie, my little Bertie Blackbird. I would have hugged him, pulled him close, kissed those big, soft lips of his, kissed the tears away from his cheeks, like I had done before because I could, because he was mine, but I couldn't move.

I wanted him to tell me he could get out of it, that it had been a mistake, that he would stand up to his father, but he just stood there crying, his fist pressed into his cheek, and I knew he was not going to do anything.

'How could you?' I breathed.

'I had no choice!' His leg jerked up and he kicked the lamp, smashing the glass, spilling oil on the mulch. For a moment, the ground blazed blue and yellow, then all was dark. 'Shit!'

As my eyes adjusted to the light from the moon, a sudden calmness came over me. My tears stopped; my breathing returned to normal. I stood, but my legs buckled and I grabbed hold of the tree trunk just in time. He ran for me, his hand out to catch me, but I pushed him away. My feet felt like they belonged to someone else as they started to move.

'Katy. Katy, I should walk with you.'

He had not bothered before when it had been dark. I continued to stagger, my head feeling like tissue paper was stuffed underneath my skull.

'Katy,' he called, but I did not turn. Then I heard his feet plodding towards me, his voice high pitched like a little boy. 'Katy. Katy, I should walk with you.' He grabbed my arm. 'Katy.'

'Go away!'

My scream reverberated all around us. Animals scuttled away. Bertie's eyes widened as he stared at me. I had creased over, digging my nails into my arms and ripping the material, bruising my flesh once more as I wailed dementedly.

'Go away!' I screamed over and over and over again until I heard his footsteps retreating. When I next opened my eyes, he had gone.

I fell to my knees and sobbed until I was sick.

I don't know how long I was slumped on the grass. My eyes burned with each blink, my mouth was dry and sour from the vomit. When I finally moved, my arm and leg joints cracked and creaked. I put my hand to my face but felt nothing. I was numb.

I forgot where I was. Something moved out of the corner of my eye, startling me, before I realised that it was only a cow walking under the moonlight, that there were more cows behind that one too. The animals gave me a strange sense of comfort and focused my mind. The river was to my left. The thick clump of trees where Bertie and I had met was in the distance in front of me.

I turned my back on the woods and made my way along the riverside until I found the familiar track that wound up the hill to the The Retreat.

I slipped around the back of the house to the women's wing, for I wanted to clean myself up before I checked in on Mrs Leverton.

'There you are.' I knew the voice, though I couldn't see

the face until it came out from the doorway to the dairy. 'Been anywhere nice?'

'Have you been following me?'

'Just having a smoke before I went looking for you.' Daniel took a cigarette from his top pocket and struck a match against the stone wall. The flame flickered as he brought it before his face.

'I have to see Mrs Leverton.'

His head tilted to the side. 'Do you know what time it is?' My silence was his answer. 'A search party is about to go looking for you.'

I ran past him straight into the female wing, not bothering to check myself. I took the stairs two at a time and found Miss York at her desk.

'There you are! You'll have to go to Mrs Thorpe. Where have you been?'

'I lost track of time.'

'You'll have to think of something better than that if you don't want a hammering off her.' Miss York sniffed, pushed her spectacles up her nose, and brought her attention back to her book.

I scurried to Mrs Leverton's door and yanked down the latch. She was sleeping, Annie beside her, as usual. I had said I would be back to share late night ghost stories over some hot milk.

'She was worried about you,' Miss York said, making me feel even worse.

'Will you tell her I am safe if she wakes? And that I'm sorry.'

Miss York nodded. I closed the latch as gently as possible.

'Mrs Thorpe's gone to Doctor about you, so I wouldn't hang about.'

I cursed and ran down the stairs, into the main house. I met Mrs Thorpe in the hallway.

'Where on earth have you been? Do you have any idea what time it is?'

'I'm sorry, Mrs Thorpe. My... My da is ill, and I was nursing him. I lost track of time, and then it was dark, and I got lost.'

'We thought something dreadful had happened. Dr Basildon was just going to look for you himself.'

And then he appeared on the landing, swinging his coat over his shoulders, rushing down the stairs.

'Very sorry, sir, Miss Owen has just returned.'

He slowed, but his face remained stern. 'Where have you been?'

'Her father was taken ill, and she forgot to check the time.'

'Can she not speak for herself?'

Mrs Thorpe blushed at that but said nothing.

'I'm sorry, sir. I shouldn't have stayed so long; I didn't mean to.' I studied the patterns on the carpet.

'Go to bed, Mrs Thorpe, we have a big day tomorrow.' He sighed. 'And thank you for letting me know about this.'

'Thank you, sir.' Mrs Thorpe bobbed into a curtsey. I tried to smile at her, but she turned away.

Dr Basildon had been standing on the last step. Now he approached me. 'What has happened to your cheek?'

My fingers found dents in my skin, but from what, I did not know. 'I got lost in the woods and tripped.'

He grabbed my chin and lifted my face, like he had

done after Mrs Huxley had attacked me, but he was not so gentle this time. 'You have been crying.'

I tried to swallow, but my mouth was too parched. 'Just upset for my da, sir.'

'Twenty years I have been a doctor, Miss Owen. I know when someone is lying to me.' He dropped my chin. 'I will not tolerate lies. You must tell me the truth, always.'

'Yes, sir,' I whispered.

He waited.

I waited.

He was simmering with rage, I could tell. I didn't want to be in that confined space with him a second longer.

'Go to bed.'

I gladly left him there.

Outside, the cold took my breath away. It was a wonder I hadn't caught my death earlier.

My bed called to me. I ached all down my left side from how I had been lying on the ground, and exhaustion was making me shiver. I couldn't wait to slide under my covers, rest my head on my pillow, and slip into welcome oblivion.

As I opened the door to the laundry, I found the smoking end of a cigarette on the threshold. I peered over the courtyard, squinting, trying to focus on any movement in the shadows, but everything was too dark. I stomped on the cigarette end then spat on it. I thought I heard Daniel's chuckle as I shut the door, but I could not be certain.

17
1956

Iris closed the diary. Her hands shook. She pushed them between her knees and forced herself to look at Kath.

Tears trickled over the old woman's lined cheeks, her eyes partly closed, her mouth gaping like usual as she struggled for breath.

'Kath?'

'It still hurts.' She lifted one trembling hand to her cheek.

Iris pulled a fresh tissue out of the box on the bedside table and gave it to her.

'You don't die of a broken heart, Iris. That's the worst thing.'

Iris could not imagine the pain. She had never been in love. She tried to equate it with something else – being torn from her dreams of a successful career, hope extinguished, despair looming. The ache was as fresh for Kath now as it had been back then. If she had been allowed to get on with her life, find another man who she could have loved, who would have cherished her, Iris wondered, would the pain be as acute now?

Iris felt the sting of anger in her stomach but swallowed it down for Kath's sake. She stayed by the bed and waited for Kath's eyes to shut, for sleep to ease her sorrow.

It was a long journey on the bus, which made unnecessary stops and turns down narrow country lanes. A couple of young lads hopped aboard at one point and sat opposite her. Out of the corner of her eye, she noticed their heads flicking her way. A cigarette fell by her feet, and one of them came over to retrieve it and crouched beside her, taking a long look at her legs as he did so. When she glared down at him, his round, freckled face seemed almost angelic in the evening light, but his smirk was devilish. She crossed her legs, nearly catching him with the toe of her shoe, and turned to gaze out of the window.

After an hour, the bus stopped outside the Sandhill estate. Iris marched to Albert's door.

Through the glass, she watched him hobbling, and a twinge of sympathy struck her; it was difficult to think of this frail old man as a young heartbreaker. But when he twisted his head to see who was at the door, his face fell – he'd been found out, and he knew it.

'You've read it.'

'Yes.' Now that she was here, her words, which she had imagined spitting at him, were locked in her throat.

'It was a wretched thing to do to her.' He kneaded his hands together. 'I was young; we were both so young.'

He was still making excuses for himself. Anger flared inside her. 'You were a coward, Albert. A horrible coward.'

'I know.'

'And you still are. You can't face her even now.'

'I didn't think it would feel like this. I thought she would be... different.'

'How?'

He shook his head. 'It's like the years have never passed. It's still Katy in there.'

'You thought she really was mad, didn't you?' Iris swayed and steadied herself against the wall. 'That would have made everything you did acceptable, wouldn't it?'

He couldn't look at her.

Footsteps echoed – an old woman walked along the pavement, straining to see what was happening. She stopped at the foot of the drive. Iris glared at her.

'Everything all right, Albert?'

Albert held up his hand. 'Fine, Mary, thank you.'

Mary regarded Iris warily but scampered away.

'Would you like to come in?' Albert said.

'No.' She couldn't bring herself to be in the same room as him. Her sympathy had evaporated. 'She's dying, Albert. You promised you would see her again. Or do you break every promise you make?'

He flinched. 'I thought I could face it, what I had done. I needed someone to know; that's why I gave you the diary. Fifty-five years I have had to live with myself.'

She did not soften when his voice broke.

'Fifty-five years Kath has been locked up in Smedley,' she said. 'Fifty-five years of being woken up at seven in the morning, stripped naked in front of strangers, forced to eat the same food every day, staring at the same four walls, listening to women scream. She'd have scrubbed floors at the beginning, you know. Done the laundry, maybe. Piles and piles of shit-stained sheets to scrub by hand. We don't make them do that now, you'll be pleased to hear. They have the luxury of sitting around all day, doing nothing, losing the last bits of their minds to boredom. Only occasionally, we stab them with needles to make them sleep better.'

She shoved her trembling hands into the pockets of her skirt. She didn't know who she was upsetting more, Albert or herself.

How could she work at such a place? How could she keep these pathetic old women locked in this deathly cycle? She wanted more for them, she wanted better for them, but she was only a nurse. She could do nothing but offer kindness and a smile and treat them as more than just lost, irritating souls.

Albert sagged like she had kicked him in the stomach. She had said enough. She didn't like the way her words had come out, laced with sarcasm and spite. He was an old man, after all.

'I guess I won't see you again, then.'

He sniffed. He might have been crying, but Iris couldn't see his face.

'She still loves you.'

He sobbed and brought a handkerchief to his face.

Iris walked away.

The sun had disappeared by the time she trudged onto her street. The sky was changing from baby blue to navy, and the birds were singing their final songs before they went to roost. Her feet ached – the backs of her heels would be raw when she removed her shoes. Her stomach growled, although she didn't think she'd be able to eat more than a dry slice of toast.

She slipped into the back alley. Fred, next door's ginger tomcat, jumped off the wall and prowled towards her, meowing until she stroked him. His silky body snaked around her legs, cool and gentle, and his pink tongue scraped against her palm, licking off the sweat of the day. She picked him up, carried him into the kitchen, found a saucer, and poured him a little milk. She dropped into a chair and watched him lap it up. Milk splashed on his whiskers, frosting them white.

'Where in God's name have you been?'

Fred jumped off the table and ran out of the door. The milk in the saucer quivered.

'Do you know what time it is?' Mum shuffled to the other side of the table and faced Iris, her hands crushing into the softness of her hips.

'Sorry.'

'Where have you been?'

'With Katy.'

'Your father's been worried sick. Your tea's gone cold; I had to chuck it in the bin.'

'Sorry.'

Her mum sat down and resentfully began to soften. 'You look awful. What's happened?'

'It's been a long day. One of the patients isn't well.'

'I thought that was the point of working in a hospital. You're in for a shock if you think they'll all come out dancing.'

Iris glowered at her.

'Who is this Katy anyway? What do you do together until half past nine on a weeknight?'

She couldn't be bothered lying anymore. Nothing would ever be right for her mother, so what did it matter anyway?

'She's a patient. She's got pneumonia. I read to her.'

'I thought you said she was a friend? Don't you see enough of that lot as it is?'

'She is my friend,' Iris said, crunching her teeth together, trying to remain calm.

Her mum rolled her eyes. 'You've been putting Simon off for a mad old woman. Honestly, I just don't understand you sometimes. He's been round tonight, you know, asking for you. He looked ever so sad when I said you weren't home. I offered him in for a cuppa, we sat in the living room. He looked ever so big in there, so big and handsome, like our Alan.'

'Be quiet, Mum.' Iris's head felt like it was splitting.

'I beg your pardon? Don't you speak to me like that in my own house.'

'Stop talking about Simon.' She clawed her nails into the table. 'I don't like Simon. I will not court him, I will not love him, and I will not marry him.'

'You should think yourself lucky that a man like him would be interested in you, my girl. Look at us.' Her mother threw her hands in the air and stomped to her feet. 'A bank manager, Iris! You wouldn't have to work another day in your life.'

'For God's sake, when will you get it into your head that I actually want to work? I don't want Simon! Why would I? So I can clean his clothes and darn his socks and cook his meals and look pretty for him so he can impress his colleagues? So I can have the privilege of being a bank manager's wife?'

'You could do a hell of a lot worse. Do you want to end up like me?'

'That is my point. I don't want to be anything like you!'

Her mum reeled back, her hands grasping for the edge of the cupboards. Her skin paled. She swallowed then staggered out of the kitchen.

Iris sat at the table, her chin in her hands, watching the sky blacken through the window. She let the tears drip off her face and splash on the wood.

The clock chimed eleven. Her dad crept in, his slippers whispering against the floor, his cotton pyjamas smelling of soap. He poured himself a cup of water out of the tap.

'How is she?' Iris said.

'Sleeping.' He drank. 'You've upset her, love.'

Iris nodded. More tears fell. 'I just can't get through to her, Dad. I don't want a husband.'

He walked towards her, and his soft fingers brushed her cheek. 'We're not all bad, love.'

Of course, she didn't mean him; she didn't mean to ridicule the life he had given her mother and her and Alan. She didn't mean any of it to come out like it had.

'Give her time. Then a bunch of flowers.'

They laughed quietly.

'I'm sorry, Dad.'

'It's all right, love.' He kissed the top of her head then crept out as carefully as he had come in.

18

1956

Iris concentrated on the sound of her footsteps as she made her way to Kath's ward. She would not think about Flo, how she had lain shrivelled in the bed, how her hand had finally released its grip; she tried so hard to push the image away. The terrible sound of someone's last breath, deep and long, a sigh that carries them into somewhere or nowhere. Iris heard that sound now, in the swish of her nylons, in the wind through the windows, in the opening and closing of doors.

'Iris.'

She stopped. Shirley whirled in front of her, blonde curls wisping across her forehead, her breath coming quickly.

'Where are you going?'

'To see Kath.'

No recognition passed across Shirley's face. Instead, a smile pulled at her lips. 'Are you working this Sunday?'

Iris tried to recall what day it was. Everything had become blurred.

'Come for a picnic, won't you? It's Simon's birthday, and John thought it would be nice if we went for a drive and stopped along the river.'

'No.'

'What? But Simon likes you. It will make his day for you to be there.'

Iris cleared her throat. 'I don't like Simon.'

'Don't do it for him, then. Do it for me. I don't want to be all on my own with those two. What would I have to talk about?'

Shirley was brighter than she had been. Her sparkle had returned; the wiggle in her walk was as provocative as ever.

'You'll be fine without me.'

'Please, Iris. John wants you to come. I need you to come.' Her smile faltered.

A doctor walked past them, staring because of the intensity of their conversation. Shirley flicked her eyes at him, and he fixed his gaze on the floor.

'Fine.'

Shirley squealed. 'Thank you! John will be so happy.' She skipped away, and other nurses smiled at her happiness; some scowled.

'What time?' Iris called.

'Be ready for two.'

Iris and her mum hadn't spoken since their row. The house was unusually quiet. Whenever Iris entered a room, her mother stopped talking, rammed her knitting needles into a ball of wool, and left. Iris's dinners had been kept in the range, lukewarm and congealing, but she ate them anyway and washed up her own plate, not wanting to create any more fuss.

The church service was the longest time they'd spent in each other's company for days. Her dad sat between them, acting as a human barrier, unsure if either of the women in his life would behave themselves. Mum hadn't spoken on the walk there, but once the hymns started, her alto voice boomed louder than anybody else's, just like normal.

The vicar let them sit then stepped into the pulpit and began to read a section from Corinthians. Iris's attention wandered to the stained-glass windows, to the light filtering through them, casting rainbows of colour over the congregation.

It was easy to believe in God whilst sat in a church with the vicar's voice reverberating around her. She imagined the cracked hands of Christians building this place, precisely placing stone upon stone, perching on the beams of the roof as sunshine warmed their backs, imagining it was God's own hand cradling them as they created His house. The stone floor beside her had a groove running through the middle of it from centuries of shoes shuffling up to take communion. She thought of the countless souls being christened and married and buried here, anticipating their riches in heaven.

Was Flo in heaven? She hoped she was. She hoped her skin was smooth once more, her eyes clear, her hands free of age spots. She hoped Flo was bounding through those famous gates, free at last and scared of nothing.

'Love,' the vicar said, bringing Iris back to the present, 'is kind. It does not envy, it does not boast, it is not proud.'

She sneaked a sideways glance at her mother. Her chin was raised, her jaw working.

'It does not dishonour others, it is not self-seeking, it is not easily angered, it keeps no record of wrongs.'

Her mum might not be easily softened, but after Flo's death, Iris did not want to fight anymore. She tried to catch her attention, but Mum would not take her gaze off the vicar.

'Love does not delight in evil but rejoices with the truth. It always protects, always trusts, always hopes, always perseveres.'

Iris put her arm through her dad's as they walked out of the service. Her mum mingled with the other women, trying to catch the ear of the vicar to talk about the church flower show they were arranging for August. They waited for her under the lichgate whilst sleepy bumblebees buzzed around the rose arch.

It was swelteringly hot on this last day of June, and the air was still, the clouds building and blocking out the full force of the sun. The promise of a storm lingered on the horizon.

Finally, Mum joined them, cackling with the neighbours about something that neither Iris nor her father managed to hear.

'Lovely service, wasn't it?' Dad said.

Mum remained silent as she walked on ahead.

'Looking forward to your picnic?'

Iris smiled and nodded. She watched her mother's calves wobble as she stamped on the pavement.

'Is Alan coming tonight?' Iris said. They were the first

words she had directed to her mother for so long. She waited for a response, but there was nothing. She didn't try again, and the three of them marched home in silence, sighing at the heat and themselves.

When they turned onto their street, they found a shining red car parked outside their house. Simon leant on the bonnet, his long legs stretching into the pavement in light grey trousers, his black leather shoes gleaming. He stood up straight when he saw them, uncrossed his arms, and rolled on the balls of his feet.

Iris hoped her face did not look as hot as it felt. She faltered for a moment, before her dad pulled her along.

'Good morning, Mrs Lowe, Mr Lowe.'

'Hello, Simon.' Her mum melted at the sight of him. 'What are you doing here?'

'I've come to take Iris out for the picnic.'

Iris's dad patted her arm and nudged her forward.

'Where are Shirley and John?'

'I said we'd meet them later.'

All three of them stared at her.

'It's too early, I'm not ready.' She gestured at her clothes. She was going to wear something dark and frumpy, not the nice, cool and light-yellow dress reserved for best.

'You look perfect for a picnic.' Simon held open the passenger door for her.

She glanced at her mum, whose face had darkened again; Iris imagined the eruption if she refused to go with Simon, so she slid into the car.

'I need her back for six,' Mum called, grinning. She and Dad stood on the front step waving them off.

'You really do look lovely,' Simon said once he'd

driven around the corner. His face was slippery with sweat, and he dabbed it with a hanky from his shirt pocket. He tried to put it back into his pocket, but he was too clumsy, and the hanky tumbled onto his leg. Iris shoved it in his shirt.

'I wish you wouldn't do that, you know,' she said.

'Do what?'

'Just turn up. It's rude.'

'I wanted to surprise you.'

'I don't like surprises.'

He pushed his hair off his face, but it blew back in the breeze from the open window. 'Sorry.'

She turned her face to the view and let her arm rest on the hot metal of the car, feeling the vibrations rumble into her shoulder. She closed her eyes as the wind put cold kisses on her clammy skin, and smelt the sharp zing of petrol and muck spreading. Something smacked into her neck and she opened her eyes to find a honeybee tumbling into the back of the car. There was an oblong leather case on the back seat.

'What's that?'

Simon glanced over his shoulder. 'My new camera. Thought I'd test it out.'

She'd forgotten it was his birthday and felt silly congratulating him on it now. 'How old are you?'

'How old do you think?'

She tutted; she didn't want to play games. 'Forty.'

He winced. 'Twenty-nine.'

'So...' She scratched her neck and her fingertips came away damp. 'Have you had a nice morning?'

'It's getting better.'

He didn't see her roll her eyes. 'Where are we going?'

He looked at her nervously, hopefully. 'I thought you said you wanted to go back to Highfields?'

Above them, the sky was bruising, casting the scorched grasses of the fields below an unusual dull grey. Highfields was the colour of soured milk in this light, and its windows reflected the roils of bulging clouds like ghosts.

They parked on the driveway. Simon's was the only car this time. Perhaps no one was in. Perhaps Edgar had already sold it off.

Simon led the way up the steps. He knocked on the door. No one came.

'Want to go for a look around while we're here?' he said.

She didn't think he would be so bold – he'd certainly changed since their last visit. He strode off, walking past what used to be the female wing, straining on his tiptoes to peer through the windows.

Following him, they rounded the side of the house. In front of them was a long, low building, at the end of which was a courtyard, where thick weeds had sprouted up through the cobbles, making the open space look like a miniature forest.

She traced her fingers across the rough outer walls. Fat spider webs laced the windowpanes and clung to the arches of the old wooden doorways. Peeking through the glass, she saw slate troughs for milk and a huge butter churn crouching in the corner of the room like an instrument of medieval torture.

The next door creaked as she opened it. Inside, it was stingingly cold; she shivered for the first time in weeks.

Wooden benches had been pushed against the walls and were littered with old irons. At one end, a fire grate was dusted with ashes, and to the left of it, there was a door.

The handle was worn and scratchy, the few steep steps leading upwards were dented and shiny. Then came another door. She pushed it open.

In the attic room, three narrow beds lay in a row, stripped of mattresses. A tiny dressing table sat before the one small window in the room. She crept towards it, looked down on the courtyard, and saw Simon pointing the camera at her. She jumped backward, then his footsteps banged up the stairs towards her.

'Thought I'd take some photographs and you could show them to your friend?' He entered the room, stooping from the lowness of the ceiling.

'This was where she slept.' Iris touched the knob of the bed post. 'I know it.'

He gawped, open-mouthed, taking in his surroundings.

Iris stared at the bed, imagining Katy lying in it, heartbroken.

A faint rumbling sound – the distant crunch of wheels on gravel. They ran downstairs, keen not to be seen as busy-bodies, and across the cobbles to the front of the house.

Edgar pulled onto the drive in his cream-coloured sports car. 'What a lovely surprise,' he said as he gently pushed the door shut. 'Just in time, too. The new owners are arriving a week Saturday. It's going to be a country hotel. Come in.'

He sprang up the steps and opened the door with an iron key the size of his palm. In the hallway, the sheet-covered furniture had disappeared. The paintings too had vanished, and now the yellowing walls held only square after square of white space.

'Everything is almost gone now, just some old nicknacks that I'll be taking with me.' He ushered them into the library, where the bookshelves were bare. Only the curtains and a handful of fraying chairs remained, along with two monstrous chests, which had been pushed into one corner. 'The files are all in there. It's a bit of a jumble, I'm afraid. I should have asked you the name of the patient, and I could have sorted it out for you.'

'Not to worry.' Iris put her fingers on the cold oak wood, eager to open it. 'May I?'

'Of course, go for it. Will you take tea?'

'That's very kind of you,' Simon said.

Iris heaved the lid open. Dust rose in a dense cloud, and she fanned it out of her face. The chest was full of old books, all curling at the edges and splitting on the spines. It smelt musty. She picked up one book and flicked through the pages, feeling the grit of age and attic grime under her fingertips.

This one was about a patient called Paul Roberts. There was a picture of him stuck inside the front page, a tiny black-and-white headshot showing a man with small, beady features and a blurred mouth. His malady was named as mania, brought on by bankruptcy. His brother had had him committed in January 1912. There were several scrawled pages of notes about Paul, dating until May 1913, which detailed aspects of his behaviour and treatment and how he was finding life in The Retreat (not very well, it seemed). Then the notes abruptly ended with, *Discharged, unable to pay for treatment.*

Simon sifted through some of the other notebooks, grimacing at what he saw. 'I think these are the male patients. How about you try the other chest?'

He was right; she flicked through several books in this chest to find only women in the photographs. She lifted handfuls of them out at a time, checking the dates and names. It would be some time before she found Persephone Leverton.

'Any luck?' Edgar returned with a tea tray rattling in his hands.

'Not yet,' Simon said as he helped Iris trawl through the female trunk.

Edgar put the tray on the single table in the room and poured black tea into cracked china cups. 'I was always scared of him, you know, my uncle. Both of them, actually – Harriet and Ernest. They weren't the sort who liked children.' He sauntered towards the window and gazed at the view. 'I was fifteen when he died. The funeral was a grand affair. I remember him laid out in the hallway and you know, he didn't look dead at all. I stared at his eyes and was sure they'd open and he'd find something to tell me off about.'

Simon stood, his knees cracking as he straightened, and sipped his tea. 'My grandfather was the same. He was an officer in the great war. I think he was rather disappointed I was too young to fight the Nazis, and even more disappointed when I went into the bank.'

'Families. I've never understood mine. Ernest's funeral was the last time I saw Aunt Harriet alive. I remember the black veil across her face, the Victorian dress she insisted on wearing. She never cried for him, you know. I watched her the whole day, certain there must be something soft

inside her, but nothing. I don't think she loved him at all.'
Edgar gulped the last of his tea. 'Top up?'

Iris lifted out another handful of books and wiped the dust-induced drip off the end of her nose with her wrist – there was no time to find a tissue. She opened the book on top of the pile and turned over the first page.

The woman who stared back at her had high cheekbones, small, plump lips, and eyes as sharp as a ferret's. Her dark hair was parted in the centre and pulled neatly back from her face. Her dress had a high collar with black lace trimming against her neck, and her waist was waspishly thin.

Persephone Leverton.

'Found her.'

She sat in one of the lumpy chairs. Simon and Edgar followed suit, waiting for her to speak.

'What does it say?'

The writing was thin and heavily slanted. She could make it out more clearly if she squinted. She read aloud.

'12th November 1870. Persephone Patience Leverton. Female, 25 years. Married. Gentlewoman. Church of England. Previous residence: Argoed, Gwynedd, Wales. First attack at 25 years. No previous care or treatment. Admitted by Mr Henry Leverton, husband. Suffering Puerperal Insanity and Delusions.'

Iris flicked the page.

'12th November 1870. Hysterical on arrival. Two attendants had to restrain her. After an hour, she calmed herself and took a little food at dinner. Sat in her room and cried for two hours. When asked why, would not answer. Miss Reed to remain outside her door.'

'Who is writing this?' Simon said.

'I imagine it would be my great uncle, Ernest I.'

Iris continued. '*3rd January 1871. Her moods change rapidly. She is averse to the routine of The Retreat. Has tried to escape several times and is now under constant supervision. Is forming a bond with Miss Reed and now trusts her to bathe her. Says she will be hanged.*

'*13th June 1871. The fine weather suits her. Spends many hours outdoors, reading or sewing, or walking her new little dog. She has called it Annie, and it has helped to calm her. The dog was a suggestion by her husband, who believes the death of her last dog worsened her depression. Asks when "they" are coming for her.*'

'What's all that about?' Edgar said.

Iris sipped her tea. She felt like she was betraying Kath and Persephone to talk of their secret conversations, but Edgar had let her into his house, after all, had let her nose around in business that was not hers.

'She believed she killed someone.'

'My God.' Edgar rolled his shoulders back and glanced around the room as if the dead were watching him. 'I've never liked this place. I can't imagine the sorrow held in these walls. I would see them wandering in the grounds when I visited as a child. They didn't look like humans, most of them. Wretched souls. Ernest could scream until he was blue that he had their best intentions at heart, but...' Edgar shook his head.

Iris flicked over the pages, watching the years tumble by. The notes became less frequent, less detailed. Over three quarters of the way through, the pages stopped at another photograph, which had been stuck into the binding. Persephone, older now, stood in front of The Retreat dressed in black, her face scrunched against the brightness of the sun. She held the arm of a girl, only a little taller than her, wearing a grey dress, who was very thin and had hair that looked silver in the black-and-white shading. Between them was the blur of a white dog who had not managed to keep still. The writing on the back read:

Mrs Persephone Leverton and her attendant, Miss Katherine Owen, enjoying the autumn sunshine. October 1900.

'Iris?' Simon touched her knee. 'Are you feeling all right?'

She showed him the picture.

He frowned at it. When his eyes met hers again, there was a sad smile on his face; finally, an understanding of why this was so important to her.

'Does it say what happened to Persephone?' Edgar prompted her to continue reading.

She skimmed the scant amount of words scattered across each page. Nothing new to note for months. Once or twice, the mention of slight improvement, the reduction of time in penitence, but then a downward spiral. Melancholy… Required supervision… Violence towards attendant… New delusions.

5th April 1903. Annie died two nights previously. Mrs Leverton has taken it badly. Bromides to aid sleep.

Iris's gut twisted. She did not want to turn to the last page, didn't want to see the final words. She held her breath as she flipped the paper – and gasped.

'Iris?' Simon grabbed her hand. She did not pull away.

'*1st May 1903. Mrs Leverton discovered dead in the lake. Suicide by drowning as a result of melancholia over dog's death. Investigation into attendant's neglect to commence forthwith.*'

'Thank you for this.' Iris clutched the book to her chest as the three of them stood beside Simon's car.

'I'm sorry it was such bad news.' Edgar pushed his hands into his pockets and stared up at the house. 'I could never keep it. As beautiful as it is, there's just something about it...'

He didn't have to explain. The souls were still inside Highfields. Iris could feel them watching her. Did Ernest linger in the window of his study? Did Persephone walk the corridors? Had Iris heard the tap of dog-claws on the wooden floor, the sound of a door being locked? The past had not released Highfields; the past was all that remained of it.

'I suppose we shan't see you again,' Simon said.

'I expect not. We live in Warwickshire, my wife and I.'

'It was lovely to meet you,' Iris said, feeling the sudden urge to embrace him.

'And you. And please give my regards to your friend.'

Simon slunk his camera out of its case. 'Would you mind me taking your picture to show Kath?'

'You don't want my ugly face, do you?' Edgar laughed, but shuffled beside Iris nevertheless. Both of them smiled as best they could.

'I hope it gives her some comfort, knowing what happened to Persephone. It must have been a dreadful end for her but... Well, at least it was an end.'

'You're doing the right thing, letting this place go.' Iris did not want this sweet man caught up in the horrors of the place. She kissed him on the cheek before Simon opened the car door and they drove away. She watched Edgar waving them goodbye in the wing mirror, growing smaller and smaller as Highfields towered behind him.

· · ·

They drove in silence all the way to the meeting spot and parked next to John's car. The last thing Iris felt like doing was going for a picnic, but she trudged along beside Simon, who carried a rolled-up blanket and a basket of plates, cutlery, and glasses.

The air was growing heavier, the clouds lowering, as dense as cotton wool. The birdsong was too loud as it shot across the water in the stillness. Iris's thin dress clung too closely, and the grass on the riverbank buzzed around her bare legs uncomfortably.

Simon took the lead, stomping down the long grass so that Iris could follow in his footsteps. Cow parsley and meadow buttercups reached to their waists, and disturbed butterflies fluttered between their legs.

It was a fair distance to where Shirley and John sat under a tree. The ground was parched, the pale roots sticking out of the dry earth like raised veins. Shirley had laid out a yellow blanket and covered it with plates of food: sandwiches, salads, fruit, small pies, a birthday cake, a bottle of champagne.

Shirley leapt to her feet, her pink skirt swirling around her legs, a puff of perfume wafting from her, and kissed Iris and Simon on the cheek. She handed Simon a card.

'Happy birthday, old man.' John stood and patted his old friend on the back.

'Less of the old. You're not far behind.'

'Hello, Iris.' John pecked her cheek. He was looking as handsome as ever in his signature white t-shirt and jeans. 'Champagne!' He ripped the foil off with his teeth, twisted the metal, and popped the cork. Shirley screamed in delight.

Pretty glass flutes overflowed with foam. Iris rushed

one to her lips, not letting a drop of the expensive champagne go to waste. The bubbles stung the back of her nose, the liquid dried her tongue.

'Happy birthday!' The three of them chimed in unison and clinked Simon's glass.

Simon fumbled with his camera. 'Shirley, Iris.' He motioned them together. 'Must get a picture of the prettiest girls I know.'

Shirley giggled in Iris's ear as she draped her arm over Iris's shoulder and posed for the photograph.

'Let me take one of you and Iris.' Shirley lunged for the camera and elbowed Iris towards Simon.

Simon's palm was sticky as he rested it on Iris's arm, but for the moment, Iris didn't care. She smiled as the camera snapped. Shirley took another photo of Simon and John. Side by side, the differences between the two of them were almost comical.

'So?' Shirley said, picking up her champagne and plopping herself down on the blanket. 'What have you two been getting up to this morning?'

Simon dived for the sandwiches. He stuffed his mouth before he could say anything. John tapped his plate into Shirley's arm as he lay back on the blanket, propped up on one elbow. Shirley arranged a selection of food for him. He took the plate back without a 'thank you'.

'Where have you been?'

'Shirley can't keep her nose out of other people's business,' John said.

Shirley blushed and got herself one triangular ham sandwich. 'Sorry, ignore me.'

Iris laughed. She couldn't believe Shirley would let the

subject drop so easily. She usually pestered and pestered until she'd wrung any and all gossip dry.

Iris had planned on keeping quiet – she wanted as few people to know about Kath's secrets as possible – but the silence was stretching, and Iris couldn't bear to see Shirley nibble the corner of her sandwich like that, gaze dropped to the blanket.

'We've been to a place called Highfields.'

Simon jerked his head up, surprised.

'It's past Clun, quite a distance actually.'

'Why did you go there?' Shirley said quietly, but the sparkle had returned to her eyes.

'It's where Kath used to work. It was an old madhouse.'

'I thought you'd be wanting a break from mad people, Iris,' John scoffed as he bit into a pork pie.

'Kath?' Shirley said. 'Kath from the ward?'

Iris nodded.

'What on earth have you got yourself tangled up in now?'

'I haven't got myself tangled up in anything. She's very ill, and she was telling me a bit about her old life. I thought it would be nice if I could find out what had happened to the place.'

'So,' John said, 'she was a patient at this Highfields place?'

'No.' Iris sipped her drink. 'She was an attendant.'

'Christ.' John shook his head. 'We'll have to watch out, Simon, seems like this madness must be catching.'

Simon tried to smile, but it didn't quite reach his eyes.

'You get too attached,' Shirley said, her nose sticking in the air as it did whenever she disapproved of something. 'It's no good for them or for you. She'll probably be dead by next week.'

Iris dropped the sandwich she was eating on her plate. No matter how much Iris tried to convince herself otherwise, Kath was worsening. And Shirley was right – Iris did get attached. Even her dreams had been filled with cartwheeling images of Flo's last breath and Kath's frail body. Maybe it did make her sad at times, but what made her sadder and angrier was to think of those old women being left in the hands of people who didn't care a jot about them, who had to check the tags on their wrists to know their names.

John cleared his throat in the silence.

'Sorry, Iris,' Shirley said, as if prompted. 'I didn't mean to upset you.'

'Shirley has the unfortunate habit of speaking before she thinks,' John said. 'Pass me an apple.'

Shirley did as she was told.

'Mind if I have a top-up?' Simon reached for the champagne as thunder rumbled. 'The storm's coming.'

'Thank goodness.' Shirley fanned her face with her hand. 'It is far too hot.' As she lifted her arm, Iris saw the small patches of sweat on her shirtsleeves. Her white shirt was buttoned up all the way, the pretty collar tight around her slender neck. It was no wonder she was too warm, and it wasn't like Shirley to cover up so much; even in winter, the only thing that came close to her throat was jewellery.

'As long as it holds until we're finished.' John grabbed the bottle off Simon and refilled his glass. He didn't give any to Shirley or Iris.

A few fat spots of rain splattered around them, making the dust on the ground fly. They stuffed as much food into their mouths as they could, eyes flicking at the sky as it grew blacker and blacker. Then, the clouds opened. Rain pelted down, slicing through the thick covering of leaves above them, soaking the sandwiches and splashing into the champagne.

'Shit!' John threw the food into their baskets, ordering Shirley to hurry.

It was such an unusual sensation, rain. It had been weeks since they'd had even a slight shower. Now, the breeze was strengthening, growing cooler, making Iris shudder. The rain was bitter as it stabbed her hot skin, seeping through her dress, tickling her spine as she bent over to help Simon roll up the blankets.

A burst of giggles escaped her lips as she looked at Simon, his dark hair sticking to his big, round face, water already dripping off his nose. He laughed with her, and she knew her own hair was beginning to lie in unattractive dark streaks across her forehead.

'Hurry up, will you!' John shouted at them as he chucked the final few plates into the basket, which only made her and Simon laugh harder.

The four of them raced across the open fields of the riverbank. Overhead, flashes of fork lightning split across the sky. John and Simon galloped awkwardly as they tried not to smash the plates and glasses in their baskets. Iris clutched the blankets and champagne bottle to her chest as she skipped over the grass. Shirley, some feet behind, gripped the cake.

It was so absurd! The one time they had chosen to have a picnic in this summer heatwave, and they had got caught in a storm!

Iris glanced back at Shirley to find her face as dark as

the sky, her hair unusually messy and flat. In front, Simon gaped at the storm spectacle and tripped on lumps in the grass.

It took an age to reach the cars. John and Simon dropped the baskets on the floor as they grappled the keys out of their wet pockets. Once the car was unlocked, John chucked the basket in the back then jumped onto his seat and shut the door.

Simon opened his boot and let Iris put the blankets in. They were both still laughing breathlessly by the time Shirley joined them, and Iris was not paying any attention to Shirley until Simon's face suddenly fell.

'Shirley?'

Tears melded with the rain on Shirley's face. Her skin was blotchy, her eyes red, her brows furrowed tightly.

'What's wrong?' Iris stepped around Simon and pulled Shirley under the roof of the boot and out of the rain.

'It's ruined.' Shirley stared at the cake in her hands. The white icing had begun to melt and was slipping off the side of the stand. The black lettering had smeared like Shirley's mascara.

'Not to worry.' Iris put her arm around Shirley's shoulders and felt her shivering. 'Don't go crying over cake, now. We saw how beautiful it was.'

'I made it specially.'

'I know, and it was beautiful. Simon loved it, didn't you, Simon?'

'Absolutely! It was a wonderful cake, Shirley, you did a marvellous job.'

Shirley grimaced and wiped her wet hand across her wet cheek.

'It can't be helped.' She rolled out one of the blankets

and searched for some dry patches, then she rubbed those dry patches against Shirley's wet skin. 'Don't go getting upset over it.'

'It should have been perfect.'

'It was.' Iris lifted her face and made Shirley look at her. 'It was perfect.'

'Shirley!' John shouted from inside the car. Shirley jumped, thrust the cake into Iris's hands, and ran to him.

John wound down the window a crack. 'Sorry about this, old boy, but it is your fault for being born on such a wretched day.'

Simon opened his passenger door for Iris and let her slip inside. He remained in the rain and leant against John's car. 'My fault, as always. Thanks for the picnic, I was really enjoying it.'

John nodded sharply, then started his engine.

'Safe trip back.' Simon patted the car roof and waved them off. Iris couldn't see Shirley for the condensation on the windscreen as they pulled away.

Simon slumped into his seat. Water dripped from his hair and off the tip of his nose. The sound of the rain was deafening as it struck against the metal and glass.

'Well,' Simon shouted. 'That went well.'

19

1900

Tuesday, 25th December

Mrs Leverton – Persey, as she now insists – asked me where I had been last night. I couldn't tell her. Not because I did not trust her, but because I could not bring myself to describe what had happened. I didn't know how to begin. It all seemed too big and horrific to put into stupid little words. She didn't press me on it. I said I was sorry about missing the ghost stories, but she said there would be plenty of other nights when we could scare ourselves.

After Christmas service in the chapel, we took Annie for a short walk. We didn't stay out long – the weather was cold drizzle, the kind of skinny rain that finds all your hidden nooks and crannies. We had to towel ourselves and the dog dry when we got inside.

Instead of a light lunch in the day room, all patients were to go to the dining room for a Christmas feast. And so, as Annie slept in her blankets, we crept out of Mrs

Leverton's chamber and made our way to the main house. The decorations were still fantastic, their leafy scent a welcome change from pungent carbolic. The dining room had been put back in order after the party. The carpet had been rolled out again, and the table was in the centre of the room, loaded with fine china and silverware and vast centrepieces of fresh Christmas flowers and candelabras. The tree was as splendid as ever beside the fire, and pristinely wrapped gift boxes lay underneath it.

The male patients were already in their seats but stood on our arrival. Mrs Leverton took her place near the top of table with Dr Basildon to her right and Mr Merryton to her left. Mrs Basildon sat at the foot of the table, and I felt the woman's eyes as sharp as a blade on me as I made sure Mrs Leverton was comfortable. The rest of us attendants took our seats at the side of the room like we do at dinner, to be out of sight but on hand if any trouble arises.

I had to sit near Daniel. I kept my gaze fixed on Mrs Leverton as the domestic staff entered. A bowl of steaming soup, followed by huge silver platters of food were offered to each diner. Gasps of wonder and joy rippled through the room.

I hadn't been able to face breakfast, but this food smelt so good that my stomach began to groan. I pushed my arms into myself, hoping the noise would not travel. Daniel sniggered.

The diners talked about dull things, avoiding topics that might prove too much of an excitement. They recalled previous Christmases at The Retreat, Dr Basildon amusing everyone with tales of how his father always hacked the turkey into tiny pieces.

It was both odd and comforting to see such a happy table of lunatics.

'Sleep well?' Daniel whispered to me as the cheese, nuts, and fruit bowls were brought in. I dared one quick glance at him and hated his handsomeness. 'I don't know why you look at me so. I am only being friendly.'

'How many other girls have you been friendly with?'

He smirked. 'None as pretty as you, though.'

'I suppose I should be grateful for the compliment?'

'It was not meant to offend.'

I ignored him and found Mrs Basildon eyeing me as she popped one purple grape in her mouth. I held her gaze as her jaw circled up and down like a cow.

'Did Father Christmas put anything in your stocking last night?' Daniel said, and I heard the joke in his voice.

It was a silly, crude thing to say, but for some reason it made me laugh.

'What is so funny over there?' Mrs Basildon said.

I had a moment of sheer panic when I could not stop myself laughing. It was like someone had turned a tap and all this laughter came pouring out of me and I could not turn the handle back again. Daniel had straightened his face, and I tried to do the same, but the more she looked at me, her face slackening in shock at my rudeness, the more I couldn't control myself.

The patients were gawping at me too, wondering what was wrong, if there was anything that they needed to get concerned about. But thank goodness for Persey, who smiled at me.

'Tell us,' Dr Basildon said, 'what is the joke?'

For a split second, I imagined repeating what Daniel

had said and laughed harder. How they would balk at those words coming from my lips!

'It's from a cracker, sir, that I opened earlier,' Daniel intervened. 'It is just something silly.'

'Come on, stand up.'

It was the first time I had seen Daniel nervous. He rummaged in his pocket. It was a lie – the cracker excuse had to be a lie. I wondered how he would save himself, save both of us, but he pulled out a tiny piece of paper and cleared his throat before he began.

'He says, "Do you still love me as much as you did last evening, my darling?" She says, "Why, yes, no one else has been here since then."'

Daniel put the paper back in his pocket and sat down, blushing as he did so.

It was a bad joke, but the patients nodded and muttered in good spirits. Dr Basildon laughed once, plucked a grape from its vine, and shook his head slightly as if disappointed.

'You found that amusing, Miss Owen?' Mrs Basildon said.

'Yes, ma'am.' I had managed to stop my laughter.

'A joke about a woman with loose morals. I could see why that might resonate with you.'

The room fell silent. I held my head up, blinking as water filled my eyes, biting the soft flesh of my cheek. Perhaps on another day, it might not have meant so much, but today it almost crippled me.

Mrs Basildon's knife clinked against her plate as she cut into a slice of cheese.

'I thought it a good one. Well done, Daniel,' Mr

Merryton said, turning in his chair to wink at his attendant. 'Mrs Leverton, have you anything in your cracker?'

Persey read her joke and laughed too hard, doing her best to keep the attention from me. Daniel whispered an apology and asked if I was all right. I nodded stiffly, keeping as still as possible. If I could remain still, I could remain in control.

I sat like one of the stuffed animals in the day room's glass cabinets until the macaroons had been eaten and the coffee had been drunk. Dr Basildon made a closing speech whilst his wife gathered the boxes from under the tree and handed them out to the patients.

Finally, I pulled myself to my feet and helped Mrs Leverton out of her chair. She took my arm, but I don't know who needed the support more, me or her. We were the last out of the room, with only Dr Basildon behind us.

'Miss Owen,' he said quietly, though his wife had already left the room. 'A word in my study, when you have seen to Mrs Leverton.'

'Come in.'

His study had no Christmas decorations; the scent of soap was as strong as ever. I waited just inside the door.

'Have a seat.'

He poured two glasses of brandy and put one before me on the desk. I took a sip of it, the first brandy I had ever tasted. It burned my tongue and stung my throat, like lemon juice on an open wound.

'Is everything all right, Miss Owen?'

I nodded. I didn't trust myself to speak.

'Are you worried about your father?'

I swallowed the last sticky traces of brandy, nodded again.

'Perhaps we could arrange for you to take some time off to care for him?'

'It is only the influenza, sir.'

I shouldn't have lied about Da like that. It was chancing fate – say too much, and it will all come true in the end.

'You seem... different, Miss Owen, like there is something on your mind?'

I should have liked to tell him what was on my mind. I got the feeling that I wanted to startle him, as if I could stab him with my confession, for he was looking at me like I was something to be pitied. I did not want pity. 'I didn't like the way your wife spoke to me, sir.'

There it was. A flinch, the truth punching him in the guts.

'I must apologise for Mrs Basildon.'

I waited for him to say more, but he didn't.

'She was implying I am a loose woman.'

For the first time ever, I saw a fleeting hint of colour flood his face.

'Why would she do that, sir?'

'You must not worry yourself.'

'I have a right to know why someone is accusing me of being a whore.' My voice had grown louder than I had wanted it to. The last word rung out, refusing to leave the atmosphere.

Dr Basildon snatched at his bow tie, pulled it out of his collar, and dropped it on the desk.

'My wife gets these... notions in her head.'

It was not a good enough explanation, and I could feel

myself bubbling up inside. I should have left before I said anything else.

'Then I suppose she is in the right place, at least.'

I had said the words out loud. I had said his wife was mad – my employer's wife; my better! I wondered how I might get the words back into my mouth, locked into my head once more. I was sure he would sack me there and then. And if he sacked me, I would have to abandon Mrs Leverton after I had promised never to do so. I would have to go home, shamed once more, and I would end up like my mother, scrubbing my neighbours' floors for a pittance, and I would be forced to watch Mabel living a life that was supposed to be mine.

'Forgive me, sir. I didn't mean to say that.'

'You are forgiven.'

I watched him, certain he would change his mind, that his calm exterior would break at some point. But insulting his wife would not do it, so it seemed.

I sighed the tension out of myself, and as the anger trickled away, the heartache returned. I was sick of crying. How many tears could one person shed before they ended up like the hard and shrivelled shell of a walnut? But tears came, nevertheless, and I was unable to stop them.

'Katy, what is wrong?'

It was an ugly cry. Tears poured off my cheeks, splattering onto my skirt, and snot slipped over my mouth. Dr Basildon came to my side and crouched down into my line of vision. I shielded my face with my handkerchief, inhaling the perfumed scent of potpourri.

'Katy, you must tell me, and I can help you.'

I no longer wanted to confess. The horror of Mrs Basildon's accusation was that it was true. I had given myself to Bertie, so in love with him that I had been blinded by his promises. I was tainted, dirty. I remembered the times when I had kissed him, pressed into him, purring for him like a kitten. I had been a fool, and Mrs Basildon was the only one who could see my sin written on my face.

My sobs worsened the more I tried to contain them. But then arms came around me, and a warm body embraced me and rocked me back and forth.

Ma had done this when I was little, when a rough play had left me with bruises, when I had burned myself against the fire, when Da had shouted at me for not being quick enough with my letters. It was Ma now, holding me close, whispering into my hair that everything was all right. I was in our tiny kitchen again, the range warming my legs through my skirt. If I were to open my eyes, I would find the kettle on the hot plate, steam oozing from its spout. I would see the palm-sized photograph of our queen on the mantlepiece beside the jar where we kept the tallow candles. There would be a bowl of green beans, ready for cutting, in a basket on the table, the table with the wobbly leg.

My tears began to slow. The sopping handkerchief fell into my lap as I let my head flop against Ma's chest. I was so tired. I was beginning to drift into sleep, hoping nightmares would not be able to find me whilst Ma was protecting me.

Ma stroked my hair. Her palm swept over my ear and around to my neck and lifted my face up towards her. I opened my sleepy eyes.

Dr Basildon was inches away, his blue eyes as bright as I'd ever seen them. His thumb came to my cheek, slipping over my wet skin. His mouth opened a touch, and I could feel his breath on my lips.

And then my mind caught up.

I jumped up, and the warmth of my ma bled away, as if I'd been stripped naked. Dr Basildon and I stared at each other for one dreadful moment. He perched on the arm of my chair, his hands hooked as if he were still holding onto me, his face blanched.

I bolted for the door.

Marion was supervising Mrs Leverton in the day room. I thanked her, then took Persey to change her clothes.

Annie lifted her head from the blankets as we entered the chamber, wagged her tail, but didn't get up. Persey patted her head after placing the unopened Christmas present on the table.

'Don't you want to see what it is?'

She looked at the present, then at me. I made myself busy preparing her clothes and heard her untie the ribbon, the wrapping paper fall open.

'A book.'

'That's nice.'

'It's the same every year. Some sort of moral drivel.' The book thumped onto the table. 'What did Dr Basildon want with you?'

'I... I can't discuss that with you.'

'It was about me?'

'Mmh.'

She sat on her easy chair and lifted Annie onto her lap.

'You'll ruin your dress.'

'I can get another one. Henry spares no expense to

keep me well attired in here. Sit down, Katy. You look exhausted.'

After a moment's hesitation, I slumped on her bed. How I could have lay back on it – it was so much softer than my own – and closed my eyes!

'You are heartbroken.'

I could not deny.

'What happened?'

I told her as much as I could remember about what happened with Bertie. I told her all that mattered.

'I am sorry for you, Katy.' She ran her hand from Annie's head, along her spine, to the tip of the dog's tail. 'I always question why they call it heartbreak. I never felt like only my heart was breaking, never just one part of me. It is an all-consuming pain. It begins in the brain, in the memories, the realisation of it each day, opening the wound again and again. And it sinks down into the stomach somewhere, as if someone is reaching a hand into you and is beating your insides like cake batter.'

'Does it get better?'

Persey considered the question as she gazed at Annie. 'It changes over time. The pain is not so sharp, but you will not think that now. At the start it is so agonising you believe you will die from it.'

'I cannot stop thinking about it.'

'These tears will stop. Then a rage will come upon you. We become demons when we are denied the thing we most desire in life.'

We were both lost in our thoughts for a while. Piano music began to drift up from the day room below, then someone's voice singing. It was a sweet sound, so I thought it must be Nella entertaining the patients with a

Christmas carol. We were due to play games later. Alice had requested charades, Mrs Beckwith had suggested Pass the Slipper.

I rallied myself and Persey to our feet and unfastened her Christmas gown, slipping on her usual black dress, which was more comfortable for the informal evening. I knew she had been looking forward to the games, and I did not want to spoil them for her with talk of heartache. I arranged my face into a smile.

'Let's enjoy Christmas.'

20

1956

Iris closed the diary. Kath's eyes had shut, and her breath trickled in, as weak as a stream in summer.

'It was the best Christmas night.' Kath poked her dry tongue over her cracked lips. Iris gave her some water. 'Persey won charades. She laughed the whole time.'

Persephone Leverton's record book was like a magnet, drawing Iris to her handbag, calling for her to tell Kath the truth. But how could she? How could she tell Kath that her dear friend had drowned? It was happening to Kath too, her lungs filling with liquid, the oxygen being squeezed out of her.

'Sleep now.' Iris tucked the quilt close to Kath's chin. After the storm, the days had been cooler, the breeze through the window chilling rather than comforting. Iris kissed Kath's cold forehead and tiptoed out of the ward.

She stopped to look back at Kath through the glass. The ward lights were low, all the patients settled in for the night.

'Here.' Nurse Okeke handed her a cup of steaming tea.

They stood together and watched the beds.

'She hasn't got long, has she?'

The nurse blew across her tea. She didn't need to answer.

'Does it affect you? When they go?' Iris said.

'I would not be human if it didn't.'

There was some comfort in knowing Kath would be mourned by more than just Iris.

She drank the tea, keenly aware of how her handbag, weighted with Persey's record book, strained her shoulder. 'I'm lying to her.'

Out of the corner of her eye, she saw the nurse turn her way.

'At least, I'm not telling her the whole truth. Her friend died. Suicide. Years ago, but… I don't want her to think of Persey like that. I want her to remember her how she was when she knew her. I don't want everything to be tainted.' She met Nurse Okeke's gaze. 'But if I do that, I'm just like everyone else, aren't I? Keeping the truth from her, when that is all she wants.'

Miss Okeke placed her cup down on the desk. She looked at Kath, her head tilted slightly to one side. 'She needed the truth once, a long time ago, I believe.' She smiled at Iris. 'She's not mad.'

Iris pressed her head against the window and sighed with relief. She had known it, but to have someone else confirm it made her feel faint. Not that it mattered now; they were both too late to help Kath.

'Let her have her last days in peace,' Nurse Okeke said. 'She will know what happened to her friend soon enough.'

Kath's pale eyelids, as thin as moths' wings, trembled as dreams fluttered in her mind. Iris hoped she was reliving that special Christmas night, sitting beside the fire as Persey's laughter harmonised with the piano music.

'You must rest.' Nurse Okeke took Iris's cup. 'Rest for her sake. I will take care of her tonight.'

Shirley had not been at work since the picnic. Nurse Carmichael groaned at the lack of reliable staff as she helped Iris strip the soiled bed sheets with a face as sour as the smell.

On Thursday, Shirley returned. She looked awful, the effects of a stomach bug showing in the gauntness of her face, the gingerly manner in which she performed all tasks. She was unusually quiet and flinched at any noise.

Nurse Carmichael asked Iris to keep an eye on her and to keep her away from the patients as much as possible. The last thing they needed was a bout of diarrhoea and sickness sweeping through the ward, but they were so short-staffed that Shirley was not sent home.

Shirley avoided everybody for most of the day. At lunch time, she took one bite of a cheese sandwich then threw it in the bin. She sipped from a glass of water, kept her gaze locked on the tabletop, as if the room around her were spinning, then staggered to her feet and ran out of the ward.

Iris found her in the staff toilets, heaving and spitting. Iris checked the other cubicles to make sure they were alone.

'Shirley?'

She heard the creak of a toilet seat, the heavy slump as someone sat on it.

'Shirley?' She pushed open the door.

Shirley was hunched over, her arms wrapped tightly around herself.

'You shouldn't be here.'

'You're only scared for the patients,' Shirley grumbled, snatching some toilet paper and pressing it to her mouth.

'I'm worried about you. You're far too ill.'

Shirley rolled backward, blowing up into her face and displacing some loose strands of hair. Her skin shone with sweat and her cheeks were as red as a teething toddler's. Iris would have no more of this. Before Shirley could say anything, Iris had unfastened her top buttons and pushed down her collar, flapping the shirt to get some air onto Shirley's sticky skin.

Shirley winced and pulled away, but Iris saw it – one vibrant bruise on the top of Shirley's left shoulder.

Shirley pulled her collar together. Her fingers shook as she tried and failed to fasten the buttons.

'Who did that to you?' Iris said, though she knew.

Why had she not questioned Shirley before? The doubts had been scratching at the back of her mind for so long. And now Shirley was like this.

'I fell.'

'What else has he done?'

Shirley shook her head. 'It was me. I tripped.'

Iris grabbed her arm. Shirley wriggled as violently as she could but the sickness had weakened her, and Iris managed to shove her sleeve up as far it would go. At the very top of her arm was another bruise, older by the yellowness of it.

Iris fell to her knees before her friend. When she saw Shirley crying, Iris couldn't stop herself from doing the same. She pulled Shirley into a hug and let Shirley's tears drip onto her uniform. They stayed like that for minutes, until Iris's kneecaps had stopped aching and had turned numb.

'You have to leave him, Shirley.'

'I can't.'

'Of course, you can. It's not too late. It's good, really, that you know this now.' Iris took her hands. 'This isn't how love is supposed to be.'

'Dad does it to Mum.' Shirley wiped the back of her hand across her nose.

Iris swallowed the sickness she felt rising. 'That is not normal, Shirley, trust me.'

'He loves me, though. He doesn't mean to do it. I wind him up. I'm stupid—'

'Don't you ever believe that!' She cupped Shirley's cheek. 'This is not your fault. You are beautiful and intelligent.'

Shirley scoffed and rolled her eyes. 'You're the clever one, Iris.'

Where had she gone? Shirley, who turned every man's head, who only had to smile to get anything she wanted? The girl sat before Iris was a wreck of her former self.

'You'll stay with me tonight.'

'What?'

Iris jumped to her feet, ignoring the searing pain in her knee joints as bone ground against bone. 'You're not going home. You'll stay with me and have a good night's sleep and get yourself thinking straight.'

'But John will be expecting me.'

Iris balled her fists and felt her nails slice into the skin of her palm. She must remain calm, or she would be no better than John.

'Then he will be disappointed.'

They had to stop several times on the walk home, leaning against brick walls so that Shirley could catch her breath. The illness had left her shivery, and the fever had turned to aches and pains. Iris led her inside the house. As they reached the stairs, Mum emerged from the living room.

'What's going on?'

'Shirley's staying here for a few days. She's not feeling too well.'

'What's wrong with her own house?'

Iris shot her mother a warning look.

'I hope it's not catching,' her mum muttered and turned her back on them both.

Iris helped Shirley up the stairs and placed her on the bed.

'I don't mean to get you into trouble.'

Iris pulled off Shirley's shoes. 'You've got me into plenty of trouble before. What's new?' She rolled down Shirley's stockings. 'Let's get you into something comfy.'

She found an old, thin nightgown at the back of one of her drawers. For a moment, Shirley hesitated, but then let Iris strip her uniform away. Iris tried not to gasp at the marks on Shirley's body; swathes of purple, brown, and yellow bruises crossed her ribs and back.

'How long has this been going on?'

'Not long. I really did trip... after he pushed me.'

'Has he hit you?'

Shirley's reluctance to answer said enough.

Iris clamped her teeth together as she imagined Shirley cowering in a corner of a strange bedroom, thinking this was love. She eased the cotton gown over Shirley's head. 'Lie down.' Iris put Elvis on the record player and turned the volume low, hoping it would act as a lullaby. 'I'll get you some water and bring up a little supper for you later.'

She crept downstairs and into the kitchen where she found her mother and Simon at the kitchen table. Simon beamed at her, but the edges of his smile faltered as she glared back at him.

'Everything all right?'

'What is he doing in here?'

'I let him in. I'll have who I like in my house.'

She had no time for her mother's pettiness. 'Get out.'

Simon opened his mouth to speak but shut it again.

'I said, get out.'

'You will not be so rude, young lady.' Mum got to her feet and slammed her chair into the table. The two cups of tea rippled.

'It's fine. I'll go. Thank you for the tea, Mrs Lowe,' Simon whispered before slinking out through the back door.

'What on earth has gotten into you?'

Her heartbeat pulsed in her ears. She grabbed hold of the back of the chair, trying to hold herself together, to push the anger down... push it down.

But she couldn't.

She flew out into the yard, shoving open the door so hard that it whacked against the wall. Her mind did not have the space to worry about a cracked handle.

'How could you?' She charged at Simon. He spun round just in time.

'How could I what?'

'Shirley. She's black and blue in there.'

'I don't know what you mean, Iris. Slow down.'

'Don't fucking touch me!' She smacked his hand away. He pushed his fingers into his pockets.

She fell back against the wall. She was so tired, so tired of everything! Hot tears scorched her cheeks. She stared at Simon's face, seeing something sinister in the softness of his cheeks; there was nothing but a lifetime of privilege for boys like him, boys like John, who felt entitled to everything, who got anything they wanted any way they could.

'He's a sick bastard.'

Simon regarded her warily. 'I don't know who you're talking about.'

'John. Dr John Brown. Such a nice young man.'

'John's hurt Shirley?'

She bit her bottom lip and tasted the metal tang of blood on the tip of her tongue. 'Don't pretend you don't know.'

'Iris…' He took a step towards her. She stepped back. 'I had no idea about this. What has he done? Iris, please. Please tell me what has happened. I can't believe John would—'

'Well, believe it.' She folded her arms and straightened up. She would not be weak in front of him. 'Your best friend is a woman-beater.' He tried to speak but she cut him off. 'You can tell John from me, that if he comes near Shirley again, I'll kill him.'

It was an empty threat, and they both knew it. Iris couldn't do a thing to John. She stalked towards the kitchen and didn't look back at Simon.

'Stay away from me.'

21

1901

Wednesday, 2nd January

Everyone is so excited for a new year, all talking about what marvellous inventions and discoveries might be made in the next century. They have asked my opinion on it, but I have none to give. In truth, my mind has not been able to focus on it. It is like Mrs Leverton warned; the rage has come upon me. I remember my night with Bertie, and I am as angry with myself as I am with him.

I imagine Mabel Robins. I have only seen her a handful of times, their farm being on the outskirts of the village. It is their fields that I walk over to get here, their cows that I found comfort in that night.

I could slash the cows' necks, kill all of them, leave their bloated carcasses for precious Mabel Robins to find one fine morning and ruin her day. Would she cry over killed cattle? She is a hard woman, from what I have seen of her, as strong as any man on the farm; her father's daughter. I doubt she would cry over anything.

I could not kill the cows, though. I could not set fire to her crops before the harvest. I could not do any of the twisted ideas that have found me in the middle of the night. I think I must soon join Mrs Leverton on my knees and pray for forgiveness for my wicked thoughts.

I have not seen Dr Basildon properly since Christmas, only when he is on his rounds. Sometimes I think he is looking at me, but I cannot be certain.

I start to question the memory of Christmas afternoon. Did I think too much of it? I can only remember the closeness of his eyes and know that I cannot bear to look at them again.

Daniel still haunts me. I hear him in the night, his footsteps on the cobbles as he paces outside the laundry door. I will not go to the window and look down at him. He will not see my bare face and loose hair in the moonlight, like Bertie used to. No man will see me like that until I have a wedding band on my finger.

Tuesday, 8th January

I have burned myself out with rage. It does nothing, it is useless and exhausting, and I will not do it any longer. I must see Bertie. I must see him in the light of a new year, and I must fight for him. I gave up too easily last time.

She will not have him.

I have written him a letter, only two lines long. It reads:

Bertie Blackbird,
    If you care for me at all, you will meet me this Friday night at ten o'clock, in our spot. I shall wait for you for one hour, and if

you do not come, I will walk to the village and tell Mabel what we have done.

Yours,
Katy

I put it in the mail bag in the main house before I had time to change my mind. It has gone now, and I imagine him recognising my writing and sneaking it to his room. He will curse me, no doubt, but I had to ensure he would come.

22

1956

Shirley stayed with Iris for two nights. Iris liked to have her close, to feel the warmth of her body as the cold air from the open window blew across their faces in the dark of the night, to hear the quiet, rhythmical sound of her sleeping breath.

Shirley was so tired that she didn't want to gossip, and that suited Iris fine. It was possible to see the soft side of Shirley when she was quieter; it was possible to believe Shirley actually cared for more than just boys and makeup.

She spoke a little of her family. Despite their years of friendship, Iris had never been to Shirley's house. Shirley had never said much about her parents, and Iris had known better than to ask, but over those two nights she had recounted stories of hiding in the cupboard under the stairs when her dad came home from the pub, of her mother locking Shirley's bedroom door and never giving her dad the key, even when he hit her.

The violence was less frequent now. Her father was too fat to run about after them both, and her mother kept feeding him to make sure he couldn't get out of his chair easily.

'He's the best dad when he hasn't had a drink.' Shirley stared up at Iris like a little girl.

Iris brushed out her curls and felt the weight of Shirley's head as it relaxed against her thighs. She bathed Shirley's scabs with salt water and patted them dry with clean paper. She told Shirley a fairy tale each night to send her to sleep.

'I always wanted to be Cinderella,' Shirley said, her voice muffled by the pillow she was hugging. 'I thought John was my prince.'

'You'll find him soon.'

'What about you? What about Simon?'

Iris stiffened. 'There's nothing between us. There never was.'

'He really likes you.'

Something flipped in Iris's stomach. She did not want to be proud or happy because of Simon's attention. It meant nothing, after all; he was as bad as John. But there was a twitch when she thought of him, like a stab of nausea, which she could not hide from herself.

'I won't be seeing him again.'

'Why not?'

'Because I'm looking after you.' Iris kissed Shirley's cheek.

'You're looking after me and Kath and thirty other patients. Who is looking after you?'

Before Iris woke on Saturday, Shirley had washed and sorted out her things. She nudged Iris awake.

'What are you doing?' Iris rubbed the sleep out of the corners of her eyes.

'Going home. You've taken care of me for long enough, and I'm better now.' She was wearing one of Iris's dresses, a muddy brown colour which didn't flatter anybody. She had no makeup on, and her hair rippled messily to her shoulders. She was beautiful again.

'Are you coming in today?'

Nurse Carmichael had let Shirley have the rest of the week off; the risk of sickness to the patients was too high. Now, Iris thought Shirley could probably return to work.

Shirley pursed her lips and pretended to heave. 'Think I best stay away until Monday.' She winked; back to her old self.

Iris waved her goodbye from the front step and watched her skip down the pavement in the early morning light.

Her mum came behind Iris, dressing gown fastened tight around her waist, and handed Iris a cup of sweet tea. The two of them stood in the doorway, watching the sky brighten from pale blue to the deep azure of midsummer. They didn't speak; the atmosphere would have been ruined if they had. They sipped in comfortable silence, both of them happy to be close again.

The morning was rather lovely after that. Most of the patients were in good moods, happier now that the oppressive heatwave had turned into a quintessential English summer. A dragonfly came through one of the windows, its wings snapping like clapper boards, and the old women stared at it in awe. When was the last time they had seen a dragonfly? They watched it zoom across the day room, its green-gold back glinting in the light, bringing a slice of colour to the place, and giggled as Nurse Shaw flapped around after it, trying to usher it back outside.

There were more family visitors on Saturdays, which helped the nurses out. Saturday afternoon was a time of cleaning: extra mopping and dusting and moving beds around whilst daughters cared for their own mothers. Only a handful of patients had no visitors, so Iris collected them all at one dining table and read to them, taking advantage of the absence of Nurse Carmichael, who would have made Iris do something far more useful than entertain the patients.

At three o'clock, her little group were growing tired. She let them sit in the soft chairs around the wireless whilst she did the tea round, then she sneaked to the phone at the top of the room. It should only be used for emergencies, but Iris would be quick.

'Shirley? Is that you?'

'Iris?'

'I thought I'd give you a quick ring to see how you are.'

'You didn't need to do that,' Shirley whispered into the line. Iris wondered if her father was in earshot.

'How do you fancy going to the picture-house tonight? It's been so long since we went, just you and me. The film is probably awful but that doesn't—'

'I can't.'

'Oh. Why not?'

'I'm not as well as I thought I was... I've been sick again this afternoon.'

'Oh dear.' Iris tried not to be too disappointed. She

scratched the craving for sweets and lemonade out of her mind. 'Right, not to worry. Do you want to come back to mine tonight if you're still unwell?'

'No, no. I'm sure you've had enough of me.'

'Don't be silly.'

'I have to go now, Iris. I need a sit-down.'

'Yes, of course.' She tried to hear any background sounds on the end of the line, but the murmur of patients and visitors was too loud. 'Goodbye, then.'

'Goodbye.' Shirley put the phone down.

After church on Sunday, Iris strolled through the woods. The spring flowers were long gone, and the area was now a lush landscape of thick greenery. She picked handfuls of ferns and bunches of honeysuckle and tried to arrange them into something resembling a bouquet. Then she tied it all together with a strip of yellow ribbon from her hair.

It wasn't too far to Shirley's. She came out of the woodland near Smedley and continued walking for another twenty minutes, until the streets became narrower and the houses turned a dirty grey, as if they needed a good clean.

A loose dog trotted towards her, its eyes red and itchy-looking, slowly wagging its tail. She offered a hand to it, only for it to shy away and lope off.

She found number thirty-three. Next-door's children played in the front yard, seeing who could chuck a stick the farthest. They stared at Iris as she pushed against the little gate with one hand and awkwardly held the bouquet with the other. The gate was so rusted and slanted that she had to pick it up so it didn't stick on the ground. It made a dreadful screech as it opened.

She smiled at the children. She had never been good with children; they either smiled too much or never at all. These children didn't offer even the slightest smirk. She felt them scrutinising her as she rapped on the wooden door.

'He'll be in the back,' the tallest boy said, swinging off the handle of his front door.

'Is Shirley in?' she said, hoping they would suddenly become friendly. But they ignored her and started throwing their sticks again.

She called to say that she was coming in, then pushed the door open. It butted into a pile of letters on the floor. She picked them up but, seeing no table on which to put them, placed them back on the floor.

The air around her seemed grainy and unclear, as if years of cigarette smoke was choking the place. As she looked up the stairs, she saw how the corners of the wallpaper were peeling, their underside a sickly yellow.

She peeked through the door on the right of the hallway to discover a small living room, empty but for a few hard chairs and a dusty coffee table.

There was only one other door. The first thing she noticed was the smoke curling against the ceiling. Next, an old table in the centre of the room, followed by a stove which must have been cooking a joint of beef, for she could smell the familiar scent of it, and finally, one great big chair in the corner, where Shirley's dad sat.

'Who are you?' he said, a little too nonchalantly, considering he had never seen Iris before. He tapped the end of his cigarette into the arm of the chair, and Iris saw how the material was black and singed from years of the habit.

'Mr Temperton. I'm Iris, Shirley's friend.'

'What did you say your name was?'

'Iris,' she repeated, louder this time, and Mr Temperton nodded.

'You're not as pretty as your namesake.' He raised the cigarette to his wet lips. His shirt was loose at the top, and his great belly spread out over his thighs, bulging into the arms of the chair. 'What do you want?'

'Is Shirley in?'

His eyes rolled towards the ceiling. 'Don't think so.'

'How is she today?'

'Was there something wrong with her?'

Iris hugged the bouquet closer and breathed in the scent of sweet honeysuckle. 'I brought her these. Shall I take them up to her room?'

He opened his palm, granting her permission. She turned her back on him and shut the door. Her shoulders relaxed once she was free.

The stairs gave a little under her weight. She doubted Mr Temperton would be able to get to bed up here; he would fall through the floorboards if he tried. Indeed, it was clear he hadn't been up there in years; she could have been in a completely different house. The windows were pushed open and a cleansing breeze meandered between the airy rooms.

The first room she tried must have belonged to Shirley's mother, for it was plain and neat, with a simple cream coverlet over the small double bed. A dark blue dressing gown hung from the back of a narrow wardrobe, a pair of slippers placed carefully underneath, ready for the wearer.

The other room was, no doubt, Shirley's. The walls were littered with posters of Elvis Presley, James Dean, Marylin Monroe, Diana Dors, and Marlon Brando. Her makeup sprawled over a table, and brushes and lipsticks sat perilously close to the edge. Her bed was not made, the sheets thrust in a heap beside a frilly pink nightgown. At the foot of the bed, a stack of dresses lay piled on top of each other, their coat hangers scattered everywhere. The faint hint of perfume clung to the air.

There was no vase in which to put the flowers, and Iris was not about to go into the back room again in search of one, so she lay the bouquet on Shirley's pillow and scampered out of the house as quickly as she could.

Shirley didn't mention the flowers the next day until Iris asked if she liked them.

'Oh. Yes. The flowers,' Shirley said as she ladled out stew. 'The flowers were lovely, thank you.'

Iris didn't press the matter. 'Are you feeling better now?'

'Yes, much. A walk yesterday afternoon did me the world of good.'

Shirley handed out the dinner plates to the ladies, then gently placed napkins on their laps or tucked them into their blouses. She sat beside Dot and fed her with a spoon and didn't even flinch when Dot spat it out. She wiped the glob of gravy and potato off the old woman's top, picked up the spoon, and tried again until Dot's plate was clean.

Shirley smiled for the rest of the afternoon. Nothing

was too much trouble. When she was like that, she made everyone else happy, and the patients watched her as she skipped around the day room, imagining, Iris thought, of themselves at Shirley's age.

Shirley had gone by the time Iris had sorted Maeve out for the evening, giving her clean clothes after she had wet herself. Iris grabbed her handbag and jogged down the corridor, straining on her tiptoes until she saw Shirley's blonde head bobbing in the distance.

She followed as quickly as she could, but Shirley was striding away. She tripped down the hospital steps and out into the sunshine, but Shirley was not walking down the main driveway. Iris looked right, then left, and finally saw Shirley marching down the side of the building, her heels teetering with each step.

Iris followed. She wanted to ask about going to the picture-house this Friday, seeing as Shirley was too ill to go last weekend. She was growing itchy sitting inside at night, watching the world go by. She was growing morbid with only Kath to worry about. She needed a distraction from reality.

Shirley rounded the corner of the hospital and disappeared from sight. Iris began to run, her handbag with Kath's diary in it punching into her side. Over the sound of her shoes she heard the purring of an engine, growing louder, revving as it sped around the bend. A flash of baby-blue metal hit her eyes as she jumped out of the way of the car, blinding her for an instant. Through the rear window, she made out Shirley's distinctive platinum curls next to John.

· · ·

Iris plonked herself on the seat next to Kath and cursed God for the way of the world.

A little worm wound its way through her tummy as she thought of Shirley going back to John. After everything they had said last week, how could Shirley be so stupid? How could Iris be so stupid to think that Shirley would simply move on?

'Iris?' Kath whispered, her voice hoarse and dry.

'I'm here.'

'Is something wrong?'

Iris smiled as Kath peered at her through tired eyes. 'No, nothing.' She unzipped her handbag and retrieved the diary. 'Shall I begin?'

23

1901

Saturday, 12th January

The dawn light is far off yet. My candle burns low. Marion is on night duty, I think – is that what she said? But she is not here, so she must be.

I can hear Miss York beyond her black curtain. I don't think she sleeps yet. I woke her when I stumbled through the door. I saw her face, two of her faces, both scowling as she came out of her section, then her mouth making shapes and a noise coming out which I could not understand. She sat me on the bed, and it felt like it was on the side of the wall; it felt as if I were sliding off it. I fell on the floor. She put me back onto the bed, made me lie down. She brought water to my lips, but I almost choked on it. I couldn't grasp how to swallow.

At some point, she went back to bed. That must have been some time ago, for now the room is still, and I can swallow once more. I was as thirsty as a dog, and I drank the whole glassful of water and still wanted more, but I did not trust my legs to take me to the tap downstairs.

My hands can move on command now, but I apologise for my wobbly letters.

I must write what I can. In the writing, perhaps the memory will return, for it is all a great fog.

Last night...

Dinner. The usual, in the dining room. I think Daniel was beside me again. Did he speak to me? I cannot remember. All I see is the back of Mrs Leverton's head next to Mr Merryton's, how it nods every now and again so that her hair tickles her neck. Dr Basildon to her right, the outline of his profile, the slant of his forehead, the sheen on it. Not looking at me. Mrs Basildon, staring.

And then after dinner... The same as always, the slow parade to the bedrooms. Undressing Mrs Leverton. Persey. On her knees but no tears. Putting her to bed. She asked if I was all right, and now I remember the sensation in my stomach, the churning of hands, my insides like the slimy gloop of cake batter.

Annie barked. Yes, that's it, Annie barked, just once, as I was about to leave – I can see their faces watching me go, their dark, round eyes. I shut the door on them and darted to the laundry.

I needed my cloak. I'd come down the stairs and into the courtyard when I remembered I needed a lamp too.

My time was running out. Ten minutes past nine. There was a face at the window as I ran from the courtyard. I think it was Marion's. Was it? What window?

I remember running, the crunching and scattering of gravel. I remember feeling as if I would trip as I gained speed down the track, tumbling like a snowball, my legs working before my mind had time to catch up.

I couldn't get my breath at the bottom. I wished the corset was looser. I doubled over, my hands on my knees, the material shockingly cold and damp against my hot palms.

There was a noise, I think. I jerked my head backward, felt the sinews snap in my neck, but there was nothing there.

I must have walked on. I remember only the white spots of cows, and a stab of shame over my threats of murder. Innocent animals, as much a victim of anything as me.

My lamp on our tree stump, shining light onto the smashed glass that still lay on the ground from our last meeting, poking out between fresh, dead leaves, green sludge clinging to the jagged edges.

The stars. My breath blowing out before me. My teeth beginning to chatter.

The watch face reading half past ten.

I thought he would not come. I imagined walking all the way to the village and searching for Mabel. Which was the road to her farm? I would find it; if I had to walk all night, I would find it. My promises would not be empty.

Then the tiny globe of yellow light, swinging on the horizon.

Eleven o'clock.

Bertie's face, so achingly lovely and familiar, though its softness looked mean in the dim glow, his brown eyes almost black.

What are you doing?
What is wrong with you?

His words cracked against the tree trunks. Insults hurled like stones. My rage boiling over. And I remember thinking, *this is how Persey did it*. I could understand, that fire, that agony, making insides roil, making fists shake, making voices shriek. I wanted to hurt him. If I'd had a knife I could have stabbed him in the belly, slashed his fat cheeks, blinded his eyes. If I'd had a gun I could have shot him clear through the head. If I'd had a rope I could have wound it round his neck and heaved on it until his legs stopped twitching, until his mouth stopped saying he didn't love me.

But I didn't have a knife or a gun or a rope.

I pelted him with my fists, I think – I remember the scratch of his old coat against my hands, the squeeze of his arms, holding mine to my sides until I stopped screaming.

I remember our bodies close again, his heat on my back, his breath panting against my neck. We had grown limp, worn-out, both as sad as each other. We dropped to the floor, a pile of skirts and trousers and coats and cloaks, not knowing where one of us ended and the other of us began.

I remember his lips. I would know Bertie's lips from anyone's. Soft on mine, how they used to be, before he kissed me with anger and deception. We were gentle to each other again. I held his cheek in my hand as if it were a bird's egg. He caressed me as he brought his lips in, again and again. There was a saltiness, his tears or mine, I didn't know.

The ground was somewhere. Him on top of me. Me on top of him. Swirling over and over, like currents in the river.

Then it stopped.

I think.

He was slipping from me, as fluid and uncatchable as water. A black shape fumbling to his feet, his back to me. One last look over his shoulder, the white moon of his face, words hidden behind his coat. Then merging with the night, his light swinging away once more.

And then what?

Did I get up?

I remember a scream, a shriek – a vixen or myself – in the silence. My head on the earth, the leaves sticking to my skin.

I got up. I was going to follow him. Yes, that's it! Because I twisted my ankle as my foot fell down a rabbit hole. I remember the pain shoot up my shin. And it made me stop and lift up my skirt and bend over to rub it better. I remember my stocking on my hand, the leather of my boot. Then…

I don't know.

It is there, the memory, right at the base of my mind.

My stocking. The cold leather. The twinge in my ankle bone…

Something snapped. Too loud. Behind me.

Another snap, louder still. My face turning to see…

Whiteness. Something sharp – a pinch somewhere?

Blackness.

Then the stars again. As bright as fires but so far away. A bend in my back. I lifted my head to see my feet a mile away, to the right. My hands grappling on the floor until I managed to sit upright. The trees dancing in a circle, their crooked arms pointing at me, their faces laughing as they sang. I followed their fingers and found my skirt up to my knees, leaves on my stockings. I brushed off the leaves, leaning over, and I was sick. Yes, I remember the burn as it came up my throat.

I had to wait until my legs could move whilst the trees still laughed and danced.

I think I crawled some way, out of the woods, at least. My hands are cut now, scratched by branches and thorns. The cows parted for me.

And then I was here, trying to open the laundry door but unable to find the handle. My hand kept slipping, unable to get a purchase on anything, until the door flew away from me and I fell on the stones inside. I took the stairs on my hands and knees. The bedroom door wasn't shut properly, I think, and that's how I got in.

The scratch of a match, Miss York's face.

And now, my body still, controlled, but my brain in disarray. When the light comes, it will be different. When the light comes, I will know. I am sure of it.

The light does not help.

Marion woke me from sleep, chiding me that I would be late for duty until she looked more closely.

I dragged myself onto my elbows. Leaves and twigs clung to my dress, and my sleeves were stained with dirt.

'What has happened to you?'

I could not tell her even if I wanted to.

Marion helped me stand, leaving behind crumbs of earth on the bed, and when I turned she gasped at my back, which was much worse than my front.

I felt the twinge in my ankle and took off my shoe and

stocking. The flesh was swollen around the joint and tender to the touch.

'Let's get you out of those clothes.'

She unfastened my dress, let it fall in one big mess at my feet. She tutted as she put her fingers through my hair. It had half fallen out of its pins, one side hanging about my face, knotted and flyaway, the other side harbouring a nest of undergrowth. Her fingers trailed down my scalp, then there was a sudden sting as she reached the nape of my neck.

'What is it?' She lifted my hair up. 'Oh my goodness.'

She walked me to the small looking glass, turned me, and showed me the clump of bloodied hair. There was blood on my pillow.

'Katy, tell me what happened.'

'I cannot.'

She put her hand over her brow. 'I am sorry about how I have been with you. I should not have said what I did. But please, Katy, I am scared for you.'

'I cannot tell you because I do not know. I cannot remember.'

'You went out last night?'

I nodded, and my pulse pounded in my temples.

'Where?'

Dearest Marion, how I have missed her sweet face these last few weeks! I couldn't lose her again. 'Don't tell anybody.'

'I swear.'

'I was meeting someone... a man.'

Her eyes widened.

'It was not like that. We are engaged – we have been engaged.'

'Did he do this to you?'

'No! I... don't know. I thought he left, but...'

She made me sit on the bed once more. 'Do not worry yourself. I will tell Mrs Thorpe you have an upset stomach. Just stay here, I'll be back soon.'

I did as I was told.

Miss York came out of her section then and looked me up and down. I had forgotten she was there; she was as silent as a church mouse. She was wearing her own clothes instead of her grey uniform and looked unusually fresh in pastel pink.

'Thank you for helping me last night.'

She stood before the mirror and fixed her hat. 'So it is true, after all.'

'What?'

'What Mrs Basildon said.' She faced me. 'You can rest assured, Miss Owen, I will not help a slut again.'

She might as well have slapped me. She left me with those words ringing in my ears until Marion returned with a bowl of warm water and a cloth. She set the bowl down on the floor and began to wipe me clean, gently patting the sore at the back of my head. My hands were the worst, though, sprinkled with dried blood and crimson gashes.

'I don't like this, Katy. This is not right. What is the boy's name?'

'It's not him.'

'You said you don't know that for sure.'

'Bertie would not hurt me.'

He had told me he would never hurt me – though, of course, he had hurt me in the worst possible way. I would be pummelled and scratched and bruised all over my body, day upon day, if only Bertie would say he loved me again.

'Bertie what?'

'I won't tell you, not if you are planning on getting him into trouble.'

'Don't you think he deserves trouble after this? What kind of man leaves their fiancée in this state?'

'It was not him, Marion, I am telling you.'

'You did not do this to yourself.'

'My ankle had turned. I was bending over... Perhaps I lost my balance, hit my head?'

'Your hands?'

'I crawled out of the woods.'

She threw the cloth into the reddened water. 'I do not see how one person can get themselves into such a state. What are the scratches on your cheek from?'

I hadn't seen my face properly. I wobbled over to the looking glass again. There were four red marks on my cheek, running from the corner of my left ear down towards my mouth.

'How do you explain those?'

I had no idea.

'Tell me his name, Katy. Dr Basildon will find him.'

'It is not him!'

'Then who?'

I stared down at her, looking as much like a little grey pigeon as ever as she knelt by my bed. She was angry for me, and I was grateful for her.

'I don't know.'

Persey said very little for most of the day. We went only for a short walk, just to the mound. Indeed, it took until after midday for my head to become clearer, and still the ache in it persisted.

She read to Alice in the afternoon and insisted I have a cup of tea. She dropped two lumps of sugar into it and told me to sit in front of the fire, as if I were the patient and she were the attendant. Annie stayed by my side too, resting her head on my good foot, as if she knew the other was painful.

Mrs Thorpe let me avoid dinner, perhaps in fear that my upset stomach would return if I saw food. She noticed the scratches on my face, even though Marion had tried to hide them with powder, but she said nothing. Perhaps Miss York had been to her already. But Persey said she heard Dr Basildon ask Mrs Thorpe where I was, and Mrs Thorpe went along with the excuse of my stomach, so maybe she does not suspect anything.

It was not until we were in the privacy of Persey's room that she asked me what had happened. I did not want to lie to her; she had been honest with me – her version of honest, at least. I told her what I could, but as I put it into words, I realised how bizarre it sounded, how confused.

'I cannot remember it properly.'

'You must!' She grabbed my hands. We were sitting so close on her bed that her breath blew against my face as she whispered fiercely, 'Our memories are our most valued possessions, Katy. You must not lose them!'

I shook my head. 'I only remember bits of it, and some things I cannot be sure happened at all. I keep trying to think. It is as if there is a wall. I keep scrambling up it, and I am just about to see over the top when I fall and have to start all over again.'

'Keep trying.'

'I must have tripped. There are so many stumps there, perhaps I hit my head on one.'

She tilted her head to the side and smiled. 'You do not really believe that, do you?'

I was suddenly desperate for the privy when I had finished with Persey. I had not been all day, and I ran for it, reaching it just in time, but when the piss started, it was as if fire was pouring out of me. I gasped and tried to stop it, but it had to come. It gushed out of me, and by the time I had finished, I was panting.

I pressed two strips of paper to me, tenderly drying myself. I put my fingers there, testing how much pressure I could take. Not much. When I pulled my fingers out into the light, they were pink with diluted blood.

I lifted my skirts and let down my drawers. It was awkward in my corset – I had to raise one foot onto the seat – but then I saw them: bruises forming at the tops of my thighs.

Marion was waiting for me when I came into the room. She helped me undress, but I put my nightgown on over my drawers so she wouldn't see anything.

'How are you feeling?'

'Better.'

I flinched when she placed her cool hand on my forehead. 'Sorry, I just want to check you don't have a temperature.'

'I am fine.' We both knew it was a lie. 'I am tired, though.'

She put me into bed and patted the sheets in close. 'If you need anything, wake me.'

I smiled at her before she blew out her candle.

Then I lay there, thinking of the bruises, the stinging, the wounds. Hands had been on me, I knew it. Someone had made those bruises. Someone had caused that dreadful sting.

24

1956

The walk home was a blur. The only thing Iris saw was Kath, staring up at the ceiling, sighing as if the whole thing had happened to somebody else.

Iris had shut the diary and whispered an apology.

'It was a long time ago,' Kath had said. Her chin had trembled for the briefest of moments. 'I think I'd like to sleep now.'

Iris had tucked her up. She had wanted to say how angry she was for Kath, how she would put things right if she could, but she could not put anything right now. She was too late, so she had closed her lips and had left Kath alone, as she wanted.

Iris's footsteps echoed as she walked into the alley at the back of her house. Fred the cat jumped in front of her and meowed, demanding attention. She stroked him and let her head hang down, let her vision cloud with nothing but Fred's ginger face, his long white whiskers, his glittering green eyes, his little pink tongue.

Blood throbbed against her skull. Tears prowled behind her eyes. Pressure built, her brain threatening to explode.

Fred dashed away. She felt the cool, soft tip of his tail slip out of her hand, then a blow to the side of her body.

She was jerked upright. The blood that had pooled in her head rushed downwards and she was blinded for a few seconds as the ground swirled. A hand came about her throat and held her against the wall, not tight enough to stop the air but firm enough to keep her still. She blinked the dots out of her eyes and saw John's puce face inches away from her own.

'Shirley doesn't want to see you anymore.' A bit of his spit landed on her cheek.

'You think I believe that?' Sweat prickled down her back. Bricks scratched against her bare arms.

He spoke through gritted teeth. 'I'm telling you to stay away from her.'

'You don't scare me.'

He squeezed. The pressure in her head built as his grip tightened. She felt the pulse in her neck and opened her mouth to suck in a bit of air. Her tongue pushed against her tonsils, nauseating her.

'I could have you sacked.' John laughed, and the stench of stale cigarettes blew into her nostrils.

It was getting harder to breathe. Her eyes were stinging and watering. Her gaze slipped sideways, and she saw Fred perched on the yard door, watching them both.

'I'll tell you one more time. Stay away from me. Stay away from Simon. And stay away from Shirley.'

He shoved hard against her throat, then dropped her. Iris's knees buckled, and she crashed into the floor. Her hands flew to her neck, gently prodding it, reassuring herself with her own touch. As oxygen returned to her brain, it made the world clearer and brighter once more.

She lifted her gaze. John was gone.

Rolling onto her backside, she hugged her legs to her chest. Her knees were grazed where she had fallen on them, her stockings split, blood seeping between the fine ridges of her skin. She tried to pick a grey piece of grit out of the wound, but her fingers were shaking too much. She clutched her hands together, dropped her head into her chest, and sobbed as Fred came purring up to her, nudging his soft head against her arm.

She didn't wait for Shirley to hang up her bag. She grabbed her arm and pulled her into the corner. Shirley struggled a little, but Nurse Carmichael was too busy talking to the night nurses to take any notice of them.

'What is wrong with you?' Shirley snatched her arm away.

'Don't go back to him, please. Please!' She held Shirley's hand tight. 'He's bad, Shirley.'

'He's not. He got me this.' She beamed as she reached for the chain around her throat and pulled out a ruby necklace. 'He's sorry for what he did. He just gets a bit of a temper sometimes.'

'He came to see me last night.'

Shirley clamped her lips together.

'Did you know?'

She shook her head, but Iris's stomach dropped. Had Shirley known what John was planning to do?

'He put his hand around my neck. I couldn't breathe.'

'John wouldn't do that.'

Iris pulled down her collar to show the bruises.

'Why, though?' Shirley said. 'It doesn't make sense.'

'To scare me. He doesn't want me to speak to you anymore.'

'He thinks you're a bad influence.'

'Me?' Iris barked. 'Shirley, he is trying to control you. He doesn't want you seeing me because he knows I care for you.'

'Iris.' Shirley patted her hand. 'I know you think you're helping me, but you're not. I love John. Why can't you be happy for me?'

'Because he's beating you black and blue! For God's sake, Shirley, wake up, will you? You might love him, but he doesn't love you.'

'That's enough.' Shirley prised her hand out of Iris's grip. 'I won't have you speaking to me like that. I think John is right, and it would be best if we kept our distance from now on.'

Iris gaped at the girl she had once considered to be her best friend.

'Miss Temperton, is everything all right over there?'

Shirley turned. 'Yes, everything is fine. Miss Lowe was just filling me in on what I missed when I was ill.'

'Iris!'

Heavy feet sounded behind her. Someone tugged the sleeve of her uniform. She screamed, crouched down, and hid her face with her hands.

'Woah!' Simon backed away. 'It's only me.'

Iris's breath caught in her throat. She smoothed her hair with the flat of her palm, straightened.

'What's wrong?'

'You shouldn't sneak up on people in alleyways.' She checked to see if anyone else was in the alley with them, but found they were all alone. Though she hated herself for it, fear knotted her stomach, and she crept closer to her back gate so she could make a run for it if needed. 'What do you want?'

'I didn't have a clue about John. I need you to believe me, Iris.' He stepped towards her, and instinctively, she edged backward, her fingers straining for the latch on the back gate.

'How could you not know what he was like? You've been friends nearly all your life.'

'I know he has a temper at times.'

Iris looked to the heavens. Calling it a *temper* was a massive understatement.

'I'm not excusing him; I just can't understand why he would do what you say he's done. He has no need to.' He cleared his throat. 'I don't mean to sound crude, but John could have any woman he wanted falling around after him. Why would he need to beat them into it?'

'I don't pretend I understand a mind like his. I am only a nurse, after all.' Bitterness sizzled from her.

'You can understand where I'm coming from, though, can't you?'

'So, you don't believe what I said about Shirley?'

'It's not that…'

She unfastened her collar. She'd checked her neck in the toilet mirror at lunchtime. Her bruises were only faint – she hated to think how hard he must have punched Shirley to leave such deep ones – but they were visible nonetheless; four fat marks under her left ear where his fingertips had dug into her skin.

'He did that to me last night, right here.'

Simon tried to touch her, but she pulled away. 'Iris...' He rubbed his wandering hand over the stubble on his jaw. His skin had paled.

'Believe me now?'

'Of course I do.' His eyes were glassy. His voice had softened.

'He warned me to stay away from you all.' Her voice broke. She bit on her tongue and stared hard at the bricks, concentrating on the crinkles in the cement. She would not be frightened of a bully like John. She would not cower and check over her shoulder each time she walked home. She would not let him do that to her.

Out of the corner of her eye, she saw Simon wipe his cheek and get something out of his jacket pocket. 'I came to give you these.' He handed her a thin stack of photographs. The first one was of her and Shirley at the picnic. 'John's not in there. I... ripped that one up.'

'Don't you want to keep them?'

'I've got the one I want.' He stepped closer, and this time she did not back away. 'I miss you, Iris.' His gaze slipped to her neck and hardened. 'I'll sort this.'

25

1901

Friday, 18th January

There is something inside me. I feel it when my mind is distracted – it brings me crashing back to Friday night.

I cannot sleep. I lie there, and I can feel it wriggle, as if it is a fat slug stuck up inside me. I can feel its skin as it slides in further, and I grab at myself, trying to pick out its tail and rip it from me, but I scratch myself instead and add fresh wounds to older ones.

In the morning, I sneak to the bathing rooms before the others wake. I run the bath, hotter than allowed for patients, so that the steam rises and leaves the room in a fog. I sit in the water, watching my flesh turn pink then red, as if I could burn it out of myself.

I cut chunks off the carbolic soap and rub it down there. My God, how it smarts! But I keep rubbing until the chunk is worn down, and I am raw.

I do it again at night, when the patients are in their

beds. Miss York knows I am in there, but she says nothing as I pass her in the corridor, walking like there is a fire under my skirts.

And still, the slug survives.

Friday, 25th January

Two weeks since it happened, yet it seems like a year.

Persey keeps prodding my memory. She tells Alice to get Miss Wade to read to her in the afternoons, so that we may take our seats by the fire alone, and there, she makes me repeat the ordeal over and over again.

'Something will come to you,' she says. 'It is there; it just must be found.'

I feel like a storyteller now, spewing the words but taking no notice of them. It is like a tale from a book, not my own life at all.

Nothing new comes. I think Persey is more frustrated than me. I would forget it all if I could. I would forget the demonic figure of Bertie, for that is not my sweetheart. I would forget how the trees came alive, how the world moved around me. It is something from a nightmare, though it plagues me every minute of the day.

'The marks on your face must mean something,' Persey said.

I have not told her about the bruises on my legs, the wound inside of me. She does not need to know everything, and I must remember that her mind is more easily disturbed than most.

We talk of it until it is time to change for dinner, and then we go to the dining room as if nothing at all is wrong. I sit in the same seat, a foot away from Daniel, but I keep my eyes rooted on Persey's back until everything but her is one big, unfathomable blur. I think of "Persephone's Melody" and let the tune play in my head, so that I do not hear the voices around me.

'Hey.'

There was a tap on my elbow. The room came back into focus. The tune fell silent.

'Katy?' Daniel whispered.

I would not look at him; I tried to set my gaze on Persey, but it kept sliding off, finding different faces around the table.

'Katy, will you not talk to me?' He coiled his fingers around my forearm.

It was like a snake had bitten me. I yanked my arm free, then found him staring at me, his dark eyebrows stitched together.

'Sorry.' He rested his hand on his leg. I couldn't stop staring at it.

He had such great big hands, the same width as his thigh. His skin was darker than mine, but his hairs caught in the candlelight and gleamed golden. His fingers bulged at the knuckles, the tips of them rounded and stumped.

Slug.

'Is something wrong? You have not been yourself lately.'

'You do not know me.'

'I do.'

I looked at his face. The frown had gone, the smirk had returned. He knew me.

He knew me.

I could not run, though my legs were ready for it. I

had to stay for Persey. She was conversing with Mr Merryton, laughing at his words. His face in profile was suddenly horrifying – the cragginess of his loose neck, the giant crop of his nose. His lips parted into a smile, showing yellowed teeth. He was leaning in too close to her. I thought how his breath would stink of rancid meat and imagined the slime of his tongue pushing into my mouth.

I swallowed and tried to listen to the sound of my breath, but it was coming too quickly and still not loud enough to drown out the laughter.

The other men around the table. Bald heads glimmering with sweat. Fat cheeks wobbling. Skin clinging to bones, as if death was hanging onto them. All of them laughing, all of their teeth showing, like the trees.

And Dr Basildon at the head of the table, reaching for his wine, his long fingers gripping the glass, bringing it to his thin lips. The flash of a pink tongue as his mouth opened, his Adam's apple moving up and down in his throat as if there were something inside of him clawing to get out.

I was going to be sick.

I sprinted out of the room, raced through the house and out into the night, down the stone steps, and emptied my guts on the gravel. Doubled over, I heaved until all that came out of me was clear gloop, but still I could not stop retching. My stomach ached, my mouth was sour and too wet, my eyes stung. Everywhere hurt as I knelt beside my own vomit in the stabbing January breeze.

I squinted at the moonlit view. With the leaves fallen, I could see how the stream had swollen with the winter rains like a giant silver snake slipping through the dark fields. I followed its path but could not see the little wood that now haunted my dreams.

I slumped onto my backside and let my breathing even out. A barn owl flew overhead, screeching. Bad luck.

'Miss Owen?' Mrs Thorpe jogged down the steps to me. 'Whatever is the matter?' She saw the vomit just in time before she stepped in it. 'You look awful, go to bed at once.'

'Mrs Leverton?'

'I shall see to Mrs Leverton. We do not want to pass your illness to the patients. Go on to bed.' She helped me to my feet and up the steps but dumped me when we reached the door. 'Go around the back way.'

I lay in bed for a few hours, staring at the ceiling, until Marion came in. She didn't say anything; what was the point in asking if I was well when it was clear I was not?

After reading her handbook, she asked if she might blow out the candles, but I would not let her blow out mine. I like it bright now.

She turned her face towards the darkness. Seconds later, she was falling down imaginary rabbit holes.

The room creaks at night. I have grown accustomed to its noises. A gentle tap of the wooden boards as they cool, the hum of the wind through the cracks in the window, the occasional drip of wet clothes on the stone floor below. There are owls in the woods who hoot, and foxes who scream and bark. Sometimes there is a scuffle outside, one of the farm cats catching a rat. I can hear the rain run down the roof tiles when it is wet or patter against the windowpane when the wind is coming from the east.

Tonight, I heard nothing, for the air was still and dry, the laundry all done and ironed, and the animals apparently sleeping.

I was the only one awake in the world.

Two weeks ago, I had been there, in the woods. If I had not written that letter...

I was rushed. I was running down the hill, scared of toppling over. I stopped to catch my breath.

I heard something. I knew I had heard something. I thought nothing of it, but what did I hear?

If I had waited a moment, if I had not been so keen to see Bertie, might I have noticed a face somewhere? Had someone been following me?

I tried and tried to replay that noise, to understand exactly what it was. Surely, it had only been an animal, a weasel, perhaps, even a rat? But it was more than just a rustling. It was a clink, like glass.

And when I tried to conjure it in my mind, a new noise came. Footsteps.

The footsteps were outside my room.

I had heard them before and thought nothing of them, but now they made me shiver. I was stuck to the bed for a moment, rigid with the fear that those footsteps might come inside and repeat what had happened two weeks ago, but they continued to stalk outside.

I would not wait this time.

I crept to the window and saw Daniel in the courtyard, the glow from his cigarette highlighting his face, the moonlight glinting off his hair. He stopped, then turned to look straight at me.

I jumped away from the glass. I should have been afraid of him. But in that instant, I knew what he had done, and rage consumed me. I grabbed my cloak, stuffed on my boots, and went to find him.

He dropped his cigarette when I appeared, stamped out its orange tip, and seemed a little cowed by me. 'Just wanted to see how you were feeling.'

'Why would you care?' I spat the words at him.

'Because... I do.' He shrugged and bit his lower lip.

I took a step closer. He tensed, as if he might hedge away from me, but he stayed where he was.

'Did you enjoy it?' I whispered.

'What?'

'Did it make you feel like a man?'

He stepped back; I went in again. 'You followed me, didn't you? It was you in the bushes.'

'I have no idea what you are talking about.'

'You said you know me!'

I couldn't bear to look at him. Sickness was rising once again as I imagined him on top of me, hitching up my skirts, sliding down my drawers, opening my legs. They must have been heavy, a dead weight, and my face as blank as a corpse.

'What did you do?' I cried. 'Why? Because I wouldn't see the stars with you? Because I don't like your stupid face?'

'Katy, I don't understand.' He grabbed for me.

I screamed as I dodged him – not a scared scream, but a scream of fury.

Then I lunged.

I clawed at him and felt his skin clog under my nails. I ripped out his hair. I battered him with my fists until he was on the floor, cowering at my feet, his arms up, trying to protect his precious face. I swung my leg back and brought it down against his ribs, kicking the breath out of his lungs. He wheezed as he clutched his stomach. He was on his side, curled into himself, and I brought my foot back again and swung, my boot wedging into the softness in his groin.

He wailed, and I thought of how he had robbed me of my voice that night. I was just about to kick his head when Marion sidled into me, tackling me to the ground.

'Stop!'

She was in her nightgown, shoeless and missing her glasses.

'It is him, Marion!' I pointed at Daniel, who was just beginning to roll onto his knees, groaning as he did so. 'He did it, Marion. I know it was him.'

She crouched beside me and took my head into her arms. The fight had suddenly evaporated from me, leaving me limp. She shushed me as I sobbed, and swept my hair from my wet cheeks.

Daniel was on his hands and knees, coughing. He managed to stand, although he was wobbling. I thought he might fall over, but his body just leant into the air. 'You're a crazy fucking bitch.' He spat on the floor. Blood glistened on his lips.

'Daniel,' Marion said. 'Please don't say anything.'

'It was him,' I repeated, though I wasn't sure she heard me through my tears.

'What is she on about?'

'Something happened. Where were you this time two weeks ago?'

'What?'

'Where were you?'

He plucked a cigarette from the packet in his pocket. His hands shook as he struck the match. 'I don't need to answer any of your questions.'

He turned his back on us and staggered away as smoke silvered the air around him.

26

1956

Clouds swelled overhead. The morning was murky and cool. Iris pulled her cardigan close, thinking how distant those heady, heatwave days seemed.

She was feeling the cold because of her tiredness. It had been difficult to sleep after reading Kath's diary. Kath had seemed so detached from it, the horror in the words not at all reflected in her face.

'It wasn't the worst thing that happened to me,' Kath had said when Iris had asked how she could be so calm about it. Iris had shuddered, wondering how things could possibly get worse.

And she was also tired because of Shirley. She'd been absent from work for the last couple of days. Simon's promise kept ringing in Iris's ears. He would sort it, but how?

Iris had considered going to the police with her small bruises but realised she would be laughed out of the station. No one would believe her word over John's. There were no witnesses. The marks could have been made by anything and anyone.

It would be the same for Shirley. Both of them young working-class girls; no one would take them seriously. Iris was the only person Shirley could turn to, but there seemed no chance of that happening any time soon.

'Hey!'

Iris turned. Shirley was marching towards her. She was not wearing her uniform but a pair of pale pink trousers, a white shirt, and a buttoned-up cardigan. Coiffed out of her face, her hair was as pristine as ever, but her makeup was not thick enough to conceal the dark circles under her eyes.

'Who the hell do you think you are?'

Iris's smile dropped.

'Getting Simon involved. That really is a low trick.'

'He saw what John did to me.'

'You're lying.'

'Why on earth do you think I'm lying? John does it to you, why would it shock you if he did to someone else?'

'Because he doesn't do that to me anymore.'

'It's been one week.'

Shirley's lip curled back as she glared at Iris. 'You don't even like Simon. You're stringing him along, aren't you?' She laughed. 'Poor little Iris, I thought, she'll be a virgin forever. You're not as innocent as you make out.'

Iris swallowed. This was not Shirley; it was John.

'What has Simon done?'

'I don't know, but John's been in a godawful mood ever since he saw him. He wouldn't tell me.'

'He didn't hit him?'

'Simon?' Shirley scoffed. 'Jesus, he might look thick, but he knows who to pick his battles with.'

'And so does John.' John was a bully and a coward; he wouldn't stand a chance against Simon if Simon lowered himself to John's standards. 'Shirley, please, think about this. I know you're trying to get away from your dad, but—'

'You don't know anything.'

'John won't make you happy.'

A terrible smirk drained Shirley's features. 'He makes me happy enough.' She crossed her arms in front of her chest defiantly. Iris wondered what the bruises underneath her shirt looked like now.

'You're my best friend, Shirley.'

'I never want to see you again.' The iciness of her voice made Iris gasp.

'We have to see each other. We work together.'

'You can clean up shit and wipe snotty noses for the rest of your life.' She thrust out her left hand, jabbing the diamond ring into Iris's face. 'But I'll have a husband coming home to me.'

Nurse Okeke caught Iris's arm before she entered the ward and brought her to one side.

'What is it? She's not...'

'Not yet.' Okeke picked the cuff of her uniform. 'She's worse, though. A few days, a week at most, we think.'

Iris sagged against the wall and let her hot forehead meet the cool paintwork. She took some deep breaths.

'Would you like a cup of tea?'

Iris tried to smile, but she wasn't sure if she had

managed it. She pushed herself upright and sniffed back the tears; it would do no one any good to get upset. Bracing for the worst, she crept to Kath's bed.

The curtain had been partially drawn. Propped up against the pillows, Kath looked greyer than ever, her lips white. A deathly complexion. Her breath rasped in and out of clotted lungs. Her eyes had shrunk deeper into their sockets; only a hint of sky-blue was visible underneath papery lids.

Nurse Okeke brought in the cup of tea and placed it on the table. She gently pressed Kath's hand and leaned close to her ear. 'Iris is here to see you.'

Kath's lips tapered into a smile.

'Would you like me to read to you, Kath, or do you want to rest?'

'Read,' Kath breathed, her voice now nothing but a whisper. 'Get to the end.'

27
1901

Friday 1st February

I was sure Daniel would tell on me and I'd be dismissed, but he's kept quiet. Marion found out he was saying he'd tripped in the dark when he was having a smoke. I don't know why he hasn't reported my attack, but I assume it is a guilty conscience.

He avoids me at dinner, seating himself on the other side of the room, and I am grateful for it, though he still watches me. One time, I held his gaze. His grin had vanished, and the candlelight created deep shadows of his eyes. Was he thinking about what he had done to me? Was he sorry? I don't think a boy like Daniel can feel sorry for anything; he walks the ground as if he owns the earth and everybody on it. Perhaps he was planning how he would do it again?

I try to never be alone now. I stick to Persey's side, or else I am Marion's shadow. The sound of my own footsteps makes me hold my breath, and I strain to hear if someone is creeping up behind me. The flashing silhouette of birds as they fly beyond the window makes me shrink away from the panes. I can no longer administer medicine without shaking, for the glass bottle taps against the syringe and I am sure the sound is what I heard that night, behind me in the bushes.

I lie in the bath each morning and night, the steam veiling me, and I think I see a figure in the corner of the room, waiting beside the door.

I remember that time I woke and it had been snowing. The footsteps that morning had been fresh, had pointed towards the main house away from our room. They could not have been the footsteps of Miss York; she had left for her duties before it had snowed. Marion had not gone out either. I had felt a presence in the room that night. I put it down to waking from a torrid dream in the depths of a winter's night – who would not feel the hairs on their arms stand up? But now, as I recall how I pulled the coverlet over my head and squeezed my eyes shut, I imagine how that presence might have crept into a beam of moonlight, loomed over my sleeping body, and run its cold fingers under the covers to feel my warmth.

Marion wakes me most nights. My eyes burst open to find her face close to mine, her eyes watery and red as she grips my shoulders.

'You are all right, Katy,' she whispers. 'Hush now, hush. I am here.'

I blink the dreams away and find my candle burning low, about to extinguish. 'What…?'

'A nightmare again.' Marion rubs the permanent dimples on the sides of her nose from where her glasses usually sit. She is as tired as me. I wish, for her sake, that these dreams would end, but they are getting worse.

I am running, pounding down a steep slope, the grit on the ground tumbling beside me. My chest burns, but I cannot stop. There is someone behind me, someone coming for me.

I race over the fields, tripping on holes, my face slamming into the frosted grass, but I get up just as a hand clutches for me. I stumble on beside the stream, consider jumping into it and swimming out to sea where Edward waits for me on his boat, but I cannot find a way down from the field. So I continue forward until I see trees, and there is always the ecstasy of hope; Bertie will be there. I will crash into his arms and he will save me.

I clatter over twigs and brambles. I slip on the sludge of old leaves. I cannot find our stump. I go around and around searching for our spot, where I know I shall find Bertie, but the woods grow thicker. The branches of the trees link overhead and block out the sunlight. I cannot see anything as I fumble in the undergrowth, calling out to Bertie, and then I hear him say my name. I try to follow his voice, but he gets quieter and quieter, and the trees come closer until I face a wall of bark. And as I stare at the bark, I know someone is behind me.

The stranger grapples me to the floor and I kick out my legs, meeting only air. I am face-down and he is on me, digging into my shoulder blades, bashing my thighs apart. I am screaming into the earth for it to stop...

That is when Marion breaks through.

'Something must be done,' Marion said yesterday morning as she brushed the tangles out of my hair. 'You cannot go on like this.'

I tell Persey I am losing my mind. She still makes me repeat it all, every afternoon, and she sits there frowning in concentration. She is hunting for the slightest change in my story, as if my subconscious will give us a clue.

'Surely you must remember something new by now?'

She says she forgot exactly what she did to Edward for a few days afterwards. She says those days gave Henry time to create the lies. She was bedbound, reeling in her own nightmare, able to see only the labyrinth of white bone and red brain and black hair and bloodied hammer. She shook and shrieked for five days straight, the image burned on the back of her eyelids, and that is when the doctors visited.

When her senses returned, she pieced it all together, but Edward and his boat were gone. The doctors told her there had never been an Edward Blake as Henry stood inside the frame of the door, unable to meet her gaze.

'The first thing they question is your memory. You must hold on to it, at any cost,' she said, and pulled out her tin whistle. 'And then you must find proof.'

I watched her play and thought how little good memory and proof had been to her.

Friday, 8th February

Four weeks tonight since it happened.

It is like I have a new timeline; before and after. The *before* is tainted; the *after* is one long blur of fear and pain.

I am raw between my legs. The water each morning and night scalds my thin skin, but I like the feeling. Fire is cleansing, that is why they burned witches years ago.

In our village, there is a little hill, and Grandma used

to tell me stories of how old women were dragged on top of it in nothing but their nightdresses, their grey hair like rats' tails around their shoulders, and strapped to an old wooden post. A pyre was built around their feet, then set alight. I used to have nightmares about it – imagining my grandmother doomed to such a fate. But then she died in her own bed when I was nine, and I could rest easy, knowing she'd had a peaceful end.

I wonder, when I lie in the bath, how it would feel to burn. I close my eyes and imagine the splinters against my back, the cool breeze against my bare shins before the flames begin. I hear it – the crackle of hot wood. Heat licks the soles of my feet, pleasant at first, before it starts to prickle. My armpits sweat. It comes from below – a slow parade of agony, searing the flesh so I can smell my own skin as it cooks. My legs warp as my kneecaps burn. My nightdress is as dry as tinder; it shrouds me in orange. My hair alights, so that I have a crown of fire...

I must get such images out of my mind.

Saturday, 9th February

I went to the privy after my bath this evening. The piss stung as it seeped over my grated skin. I pressed paper to myself, then put the paper to the light. But it was clear. I thought my flesh might have been bleeding, for this afternoon, it felt like it ripped as I sat down too quickly, but it appeared to be intact.

And then it struck me.

I would have been grateful to have found blood on the paper.

Thursday, 14th February

I knew there was something inside me. The slug. It is growing.

I hit myself in the stomach, sure that I will be able to knock it out. I keep feeling a rush inside of me and I run to the privy, sure that it will gush out of me in a bloody downpour, but I find I only need to piss.

I should throw myself down the stairs. I would prefer to drink a whole bottle of gin, but I cannot do that here. And if not the stairs, then I shall have to find a woman who knows plants; rumour has it that there is such a creature a mile outside our village, her home a circle of odd-shaped stones at the edge of the forest. I have heard that girls have gone there and traded with her; ten years of life for a safe miscarriage.

Ten years less of life sounds no hardship if I can be rid of whatever it is that forms inside of me. A seed of evil. I will have the devil for a son.

Perhaps it really was the devil that night who found me. If God could do it to Mary, surely the devil could do it to me? That is why I cannot remember; he will have made it so that my memory is lost. Perhaps that is why the child will not be loosened out of me; he makes it stick.

Saturday, 16th February

We sat before the fire today, as it was raining outside. Great big drops of water made a grey curtain which blocked the view. Even Annie did not want to step into it, so we stayed inside.

I repeated the story to Persey, but even she grows tired

of it now, her eyes drooping as if I am telling her a fairy tale.

My speech ended as it always does: 'Then Miss York put me to bed.'

The wind rumbled down the chimney and made the fire splutter. Behind us, other patients played cards or read, all of us weighed down by the greyness, wishing for spring to arrive.

'I am pregnant.'

My words came out as if someone else had said them. Persey flinched, pushed herself upright in the armchair.

'You're sure?'

'I am eight weeks late.'

Persey reached for Annie and lifted her onto her lap.

'What should I do?' I was tired of trying to make decisions. I wished for someone to give me a straight road to follow.

'Get rid of it.'

Her words made me shiver. 'I have been trying.'

She stared at the ceiling. 'He is a funny man.'

'Who?'

'God. I had four miscarriages before James, all gone in the first two months. I did nothing at all when I knew I was carrying, too scared to even walk outside in fear of jolting it loose. I lay in bed every day. I remember putting my hand to myself as if I would plug the hole. And still, the morning would come when I woke to blood on the sheets, to the sense of emptiness.'

'But with James it was different?'

'I could feel his strength from the start.' She rolled her head towards me. 'This one wants to live.'

My hands drifted to my stomach. It was still flat, my

corset pulled as tight as it always has been, but everything was different.

'I cannot keep a child who has no father.'

'Tell Bertie it is his.'

Had I heard her correctly? 'But it cannot be Bertie's.'

'You do not know whose it is. Better to be Bertie's than someone else's.'

'But we didn't…'

'But you have. That is all that matters.'

'He is engaged.'

'He is a coward for what he did to you. He loved you.'

'I thought he did.'

'Then he must do this for you. Make him do it. Make him marry you.' Her eyes were black and fierce. I could not look at them.

'And hate each other for all our lives?'

'You have no choice, Katy.'

It would be a perfect solution, I supposed. Bertie would stand by me if I told him the child was his, I knew he would; even he could not abandon me if I were pregnant. And then we would be married as I have always dreamed.

But there would be the child between us, and I would know it was not his because it wouldn't have his dark hair and it would grow taller than him and, one day, he would realise I had tricked him.

But we would be married.

'I would have to leave here,' I said. 'Leave you and care for the child.'

Persey nodded. 'But you would visit?'

'Every week.' I took her hand. 'I would find Edward for you.'

'What?'

'If I am not working here, I can look for him. I will go to your house.'

'I searched everywhere for him.'

'But you said you were not... thinking straight. Perhaps you missed something?'

'Impossible.'

'A man's body cannot vanish without a trace. How was it that the servants never saw him?'

'Of course they saw him.'

'But they said they hadn't.'

'Katy, they were Welsh. My husband was Welsh and a good master and a generous landlord.'

'So, perhaps one of them knows something? After all these years, they might be willing to speak for you.'

'That is dangerous talk, Katy.' She slipped her hand free of mine and back to Annie. She was sucking in her lower lip, stroking Annie faster and faster.

'You don't want to leave, do you?'

I saw her swallow, and for an instant, she was old Mrs Leverton again, a frail woman, a stranger.

'If I walked out of those gates, I would only be going to the scaffold.'

'You would know the truth.'

'I know the only thing that matters. I killed the man I loved.' Her eyes had been shimmering. A single tear slipped down her cheek.

I had been a fool. She was right, there was no way out for her.

A great gust slapped the windows and sprayed rain down the chimney. The fire ebbed, the heat diminishing. With a dawning sensation of numbness, I left Persey in her seat and unlocked the cupboard, finding a basket of chopped wood and the fire poker. I unlatched the fire guard and piled the logs high.

I was leaning over, prodding at the amber ashes. I remembered my thoughts about burning in a pyre as the fire began to strengthen and a bright yellow gash of a flame spat at me.

The heat was growing, the wood belching out burning splinters. I held my left hand towards it, palm up, letting the flying embers stab my skin. My insides turned, the baby reminding me it would soon be ripping my skin to get out, like its father had ripped my flesh to get inside. Childbirth is the worst pain, women say. Worse than burning?

I put my hand in closer to the flames, mesmerised by the roar of yellow and orange and red, the charring of the wood, the crackling and hissing.

There was noise behind me, but I couldn't define anything.

I watched the flames, the poker in my right hand jostling the wood so that it burned harder, sparks shooting out at every angle until a sizzling piece of ash, the size of a halfpenny piece, landed on the soft flesh between my finger and thumb. I gasped and drew my hand clear of the flames. I was bending at the waist, the tip of the poker close to my right foot.

I had been the same that night – bent over, gasping with the sharp sting of pain, looking at my feet.

Someone was coming up behind me, I heard the footsteps. They had been dull that night, the hard earth muffling the sound, but now they were sharp and clear.

Someone was saying my name, though there had been silence that night.

Bent over, finding the world upside down behind my skirts, I could see a darkness approaching. And I remembered, I had seen the same thing that night. The movement of black in the greyness, coming closer, too fast for me to comprehend it.

Then an arm reaching over my back, pulling at my shoulder, knocking into my face.

Whiteness.

Something pressing into my mouth. My tongue tasting bitterness on the material. My hands reaching up to grab the arm that pinned me to his chest, his nails scraping across my cheek as I shook my head, something hard coming between my teeth. I bit down. A cry of pain. The whiteness disappeared; the arm released me.

I was free.

Then a whoosh, a crack, blackness.

There was a hand on my shoulder now, dragging me upright.

I sprang around. The hot poker whirled through the air and smacked into bone.

A cry. Gasps. I looked up to find everyone staring at me, attendants holding onto their patients like they were dogs readying for a hunt. Persey remained seated, her face white, her black eyes wide, perching on the edge of the chair as though she might leap up and wrestle me to the floor any minute. At her feet, a crumpled body, his hand cradling his face as he rolled onto his knees, his back to me.

It took some moments for him to stand. Everybody held their breath.

Then he turned towards me.

I had split the skin on his cheekbone. A deep gash oozed blood which slid down his cheek and dripped onto his stiff white collar. The red made his blue eyes shine.

'Put the poker down, Miss Owen.'

Dr Basildon took a step closer.

'Stay away!' I held the poker out before me, swooshing it from side to side to keep him at a distance, backing myself into the corner of the room.

'Take the patients upstairs,' he said over his shoulder.

There was a shuffling of feet, some moans of disappointment, Wini's stern voice as she forced them to keep moving.

Persey remained in her seat, forgotten by everyone but me.

Dr Basildon lowered his arm. He opened his mouth, moved his jaw from side to side, and winced.

'I'm sorry, I...' The blood stains were growing, seeping onto the breast of his shirt. 'I didn't mean to hit you.'

'It is all right, Miss Owen. Put the poker down.'

He was beginning to blur. It was hard to breathe. 'What is happening to me?' I said to Persey, who now made her way to Dr Basildon's side.

'Go to your room, Mrs Leverton.'

She did not listen to him.

'I can't live like this,' I said. 'Everything... everyone... I remembered something.'

'What?' Persey said, inching closer, but Dr Basildon grabbed her arm.

'A white handkerchief...' I tried to recapture the image, but it was fading.

'Go to bed, Mrs Leverton, I will not tell you again.'

'A white handkerchief. What next, Katy? What happened next?'

It was leaving me. I slapped my head; I would make the memory stay. 'I bit something... I think. And then, pain at the back of my head.'

'Put the poker down, Miss Owen!'

There was a thunder of footsteps coming my way. Mrs Thorpe shot into the day room. She pointed at me as she leant against the wall, closing her eyes, her skin mottled pink rather than its usual grey as she gasped for air. Three men ran past her, charging for me. Daniel was at the front.

I lifted my poker. 'Get away from me!' I swung it at him, making him jump back. 'What did you do?' My own voice was unrecognisable.

Daniel was perfect again, the one bruise I had given him long healed.

'What did you do to me?'

His peers glanced sideways at him. Daniel stared at Dr Basildon, scared for the first time.

'I haven't done anything, sir, I swear.'

'Liar!'

'Katy, hush.' Persey tiptoed towards me. The men started and tried to grab her, but she shook them off. 'You must calm yourself, Katy. This is dangerous.'

Her face told me all. We were lost.

The men had cornered us. They waited, ready to swoop on me. Dr Basildon's right cheek was scarlet. Behind him, under her mistress's chair, Annie cowered, her big black eyes gazing at me as if I were a stranger.

Persey touched the poker. I let her take the weight of it before she dropped it on the floor. She held me in her arms and hugged me tight as I sobbed.

Then they were pinching my skin, tearing us apart. We reached for each other, both of us crying. Annie barked as her mistress was carted away by a rough male attendant. More hands smothered me, on my arms, my legs, pushing and pulling at me as I writhed to get away.

Then the clink of a syringe. The floor on my back. A damp palm crushing my forehead. The crescent of Daniel's face upside down as he towered over me. The pierce of metal into my skin as Mrs Thorpe jabbed a needle into my neck.

Then darkness.

I write by moonlight. The candle is gone, the matches taken. Miss York and Marion are not allowed in.

My neck feels swollen where they stuck in the needle. I cannot see if I am bruised, for they have taken the looking glass too, but I run my fingers over the lump of tender skin and wince, so I imagine that I am.

I found my diary and ink pot safe under the bed when I woke. Marion must not have told about it. I will thank her next time I see her.

Mrs Thorpe saw me when I had woken. The dusk was fading, and I found her face in the glow of her candlelight.

'How do you explain yourself?' She would not sit; she stood at the foot of my bed. 'What do you think Daniel has done?'

I thought that I must tell her to save myself, so I did.

'What were you doing out at that time of night?'

I hadn't included Bertie in the story. I had no intention of doing so. 'I was going to visit my da.'

'At ten o'clock?' The candle flame made her nose shine, her eyes thin. 'Do not lie, Miss Owen.'

'I am not lying about what happened to me.'

'Who are you engaged to?'

A chill swamped my body. 'I am not engaged.'

'Miss York tells me you are.'

'We are not engaged. Not anymore.'

'Did you meet that man, Miss Owen?'

I could not lie. 'Yes. But it was not him who attacked me.' She was making her way to the door. 'Please, Mrs Thorpe, this has nothing to do with him. It was Daniel, he has been following me, he has been watching me, I am sure!'

'I have already asked Daniel where he was that night. He was playing poker before he joined the search party. Your search party.' She twisted the doorknob. 'Mr Thorpe confirms this.'

'They are lying!'

The door shut with a click. She paced two feet towards me. 'Are you calling my husband a liar?' Her voice was harder than the frost outside.

'No, ma'am, but... perhaps he is confused.'

'Get some sleep, Miss Owen, and hope you have found your senses by the morning.'

28
1901

Sunday 17th February

My strength returned this morning. I sat up in bed, let my head catch up with the movement, then dangled my feet out. My skin prickled with gooseflesh against the cold. I put my feet into my shoes, not wanting to feel the bitterness of the floor, and found my dress hanging in the wardrobe. I put it on as best I could, though when I tried to fasten the back, my arms ached from where the men had twisted them. I ran a comb through my hair, cringing as it caught in the knots.

Without the mirror, I could not judge my appearance, but it would have to do. I would go to Dr Basildon, apologise to him, beg for forgiveness, and tell him the truth.

I pulled on the door handle. It would not give. I shook it until it rattled and got to my knees to peer at the keyhole. The lock was turned.

Panic made me run to the window. Outside, the sky

above was a blanket white, the cobbles were slick with yesterday's rain. The space was empty.

I yelled for someone to let me out, but no one came.

The pane of glass is only thin; I could have broken it and jumped down, but my nerves were shattered, yesterday's bravery had vanished. I kicked off my shoes and returned to bed. My mouth had dried, and I sipped from a glass of water on the table beside me, careful not to drink all of it in case no one came back.

But they did – Marion visited me in the afternoon, scurrying inside and checking over her shoulder.

'How are you?' she whispered as she sat beside me. She pulled my hair away from my neck and frowned at what she saw.

'What is happening? What are they saying?'

'They know about Bertie. I heard Miss York whispering to Wini about it, saying how Mrs Thorpe will have you out.'

'What of Persey?'

Marion hesitated. 'She is in her rooms.'

'Is she well?'

'They have given her a sedative. She was too excited; it is not good for her.'

'Oh, God!'

'Mrs Leverton will be fine, it is not her you should be worrying about.' Marion removed her glasses and polished them against her skirt. She lifted her eyes to me, pity writ across her face.

'I must speak to Dr Basildon,' I said desperately. 'I must explain everything. He is a reasonable man.'

'He is resting. It is a nasty wound, Katy.'

'I didn't mean to hit him! I thought he was someone else.'

'Hush, now.' She stroked my head, and I lay back on the pillow.

'You must make Daniel confess. It is the only way for this all to be put right.'

She nodded but said nothing.

She did not believe me.

I have written a letter for Bertie. He must know what has happened and what is coming for him. I have the letter beside me, and I shall make a copy of it here so that I know exactly what I said. I will ask Marion to put it in the mail bag for me when she visits later.

Dear Bertie,

I do not know how to put this into words. There is no good way to begin such a letter.

The last time we met, something happened to me. I woke the next day with my memory lost and bruises and wounds upon my body, in the most intimate of places.

I know it was not you who did that to me, Bertie. In my heart I know it, but the problem lies in my memory. I cannot remember how we left it. I was sure you had gone, please tell me that you had!

My own precious Bertie, you could not have hurt me like that, could you? I know I frustrate you, and I know you are to marry another, but you would not be so harsh to me, your real sweetheart, would you?

I had to tell Marion about you. I had no choice. But I was overheard by one of the other attendants. She hates me. They do not know you by name, only that I met my fiancé in the woods.

I think I know who attacked me. His name is Daniel Cartwright. He is a male attendant here. I have heard him outside my room at night. He waits for me in the shadows and scares me. It must be him; I can see the guilt in his eyes, but they do not believe me.

I am worried for you, Bertie. Tell me you were home by midnight, that your da can vouch for you. You must come and see Dr Basildon and tell him what you know. It is the only way to save yourself and me.

They have locked me in my room. They think I have lost my wits, but I have not, Bertie. I have proof. A terrible proof, but proof, nonetheless.

Bertie, I am with child.

Please come. If you think anything of me at all, you will come.

Dr Basildon is a reasonable man; I am sure he will be discreet. If he knows the truth, he will put all this right, and Daniel will be gone, and I can be safe again, and you can marry Mabel, and no one need ever know.

I beg you, Bertie. I cannot go on like this.

I wish you would come and take me away. I wish you would hold me and kiss my bruises. I miss you with all my heart, Bertie, my little Bertie Blackbird.

Yours forever,
Katy

29

1956

Iris pressed a tissue to her eyes. It came away wet. She stuffed it between her knees.

She flicked through the last remaining pages of the diary – all blank.

Kath's eyes had closed. The tears that had fallen as Iris had been reading were now dry. Her breath was shallow and weak as she slept.

'I got the letter.' Albert clutched the foot of Kath's bed and stared down at his old fiancée.

Iris stood, an involuntary action from the shock of seeing him. She had believed he had given up on Kath again.

She offered him her chair, but he pulled over a spare one from the patient next door. He stroked Kath's foot through the blanket once he was seated.

'I went to see him – Dr Basildon. He wasn't shocked, you know, when I turned up. It was like he had been expecting me.'

'What did you say?' Iris's voice was husky with emotion. She cleared her throat.

'Not much. He did most of the talking. He told me to say it was mine.'

'The baby? How did he know about the baby?'

Albert shrugged. 'Marion probably told him, or Mrs Leverton. He said it would be the best for everyone if I said I was the father. He said he would keep it a secret for me, that Mabel and Da need never know.'

'How could he? Surely you'd have to marry Katy?'

Albert nodded. She could only see a little of his face for the crookedness of his spine.

'Not if she were in an asylum.'

Iris's breath left her. She stared at his profile in horror. A tear dripped off the end of his nose.

'He said she was showing signs of mania. She was having hallucinations and delusions which were making her violent. She needed help.' He met Iris's gaze. 'He was a doctor, Iris. He knew best.'

'So, you lied. You said the baby was yours.'

'I didn't lie. I didn't know.'

'What?'

'That night, the night she said she was attacked. We did...' He pulled an old handkerchief out of his pocket and rubbed it over his face. 'She couldn't remember it all, but we did... So, you see, the child could have been mine.'

Iris grabbed her cold tea and drank, hoping the tannin would alleviate her nausea. 'You didn't believe her.'

'I thought she could have fallen and hit her head. I hadn't read her diary then, remember. Or I thought she might be saying things to bring me back to her or to get revenge somehow. I was only going off what the doctor said.'

'What happened after?'

'I agreed to what Basildon suggested. I would tell the doctors who came to assess her the truth of what had gone on between us: I had not seen or heard anybody else that night, nor had I heard Katy scream. I assume they compiled a case to have her sectioned.'

'Didn't her family try to stop it?'

'She was pregnant out of wedlock. Rumour had been rife before that anyway. Talk of her pushing herself onto Reverend Cotton, and him being married and a man of the Church, that was why she'd been dismissed.'

'If that were the case, why did Dr Basildon employ her? He was adamant about a girl who could set an example.'

Albert sniffed. 'About ten years later, Cotton got caught with his trousers round his ankles, bending the kitchen maid over the table. She was thirteen. Another girl told the police he used to watch her through the cracks in the bedroom door, before she was sacked.'

'Do you think…?'

He shook his head. 'Katy would have told me if she'd suspected anything, but she was naive.' He patted the blanket and smiled. 'It didn't take Basildon long to get her into Smedley. That was when I received the bundle of her things, including the diary. I couldn't bring myself to look at it for years.

'Smedley was called a lunatic asylum back then. They locked all the doors. I visited her not long after she'd been brought in – secretly, of course. The screams…' He shuddered. 'All these women in these massive wards, crying and shaking.' He pressed his fingers into his eyes as if he would rip out the memory. 'She sat in her bed, quiet, looking about herself. Terrified.'

He dragged the handkerchief up to his face again. Iris didn't say anything as he cried.

'I never thought she'd be in here long. I really did think she was ill and that she'd get better and she'd come out. A few months, that's all. She grabbed me when I came to see her. She thought I was saving her.

'She didn't mention the attack again. After everything they put her through when she came here, questioning her about everything, filling her with medicines, I think she thought it really might have all been in her head. She told me she was glad I was the father because she'd be able to see her baby when she got out. I just nodded and agreed.'

'To what?'

'To keep the baby.' He dropped the sopping handkerchief in his lap. 'But, how could I? No one knew. Mabel and I were getting married that August.'

Iris didn't want to ask; she didn't want to hear the answer. 'What did you do?'

'There was a family a few miles out of the village. We did their meat and dairy. They were nice.' He stared at Iris, his eyes pleading for her to understand. 'They'd been trying for years. All the lady wanted was a child of her own.'

Iris swallowed. 'You abandoned your child to strangers?'

'They weren't strangers! And I never abandoned him. I took him the very day Katy gave birth. I asked how she was, but no one would tell me. I just wanted to know she was all right.'

Iris tore her eyes away from Albert to look at Kath. She was not sleeping, though her eyes were closed; flowing tears betrayed her.

'She wasn't all right, Albert. They took her baby away.'

'Where is he?' Kath whispered, as fiercely as she could.

Albert gripped her hand. 'I kept an eye on him. I've watched him all his life.'

'Where is he?'

'In town. That's why I moved here, so I could be closer to him, and to you. I kept my promise as best I could.' He rested his head on the bed beside her as they both wept. 'I'm sorry, Katy. I'm so sorry.'

30

1956

On the first day of her annual leave, Iris ventured to the high street. The smart black dress was a little too tight, and her black heels were too high. Dressed like this, she felt the unusual sensation of strangers looking her up and down, judging her – for better or worse, she did not know. She twisted the plain gold band around her fourth finger and searched for Benson's Estate Agents.

She found the blue sign on the corner of a small side street. It was not a large office, and she could see the dark figures of men in suits through the glass. She pushed open the door, and the bell rang.

A young man in his mid-twenties pounced on her. 'Hello, miss. Are you lost?'

'I'd like to buy a house,' she said, her dry tongue sticking to the roof of her mouth. The young man gawped. 'I mean, my husband and I would like to buy our first house. He's at work this morning and said I should come and give you our details.' She lifted her left hand to push away a strand of hair. The salesman saw the ring.

'Right, yes, lovely. Come this way.' He led her to his desk and pulled out a chair for her. She was facing the wall and had to keep glancing over her shoulder to see the other men in the back room.

'What kind of property are you and your husband looking to buy?'

She scratched her neck. 'A small one.'

The salesman steepled his fingers. 'Do you have a price in mind?'

Her gaze roamed the walls searching for inspiration. 'One thousand?'

'Right.' The salesman made a note of this figure on his pad. 'Can I take some of your details? Your name?'

'Mrs Raybould.'

A door in the back opened. Male voices grew louder and more distinct for a moment, before the door shut. Shoes padded along the carpeted floor behind her.

'Mr Benson,' the young salesman said, grinning over Iris's shoulder. 'Mrs Raybould here and her husband are looking for their first home together.'

'Congratulations.' Mr Benson came to her side. She held her breath as she lifted her eyes. 'When did you tie the knot?'

She couldn't speak. Her mouth dropped as she stared into striking blue eyes. His cold smile faltered.

'In March,' she stuttered, eventually.

'Best for taxes,' the salesman said. Mr Benson glared at him.

'Where are you living now?' Mr Benson asked, his voice slow and smooth.

'Renting, over by that new estate.' Nothing else came

to her mind. The mention of the council estate made Mr Benson's lips turn down.

'I see why you would want to get away from there. We have some quaint houses on the better side of town for a very good price. There are a couple for only fifteen hundred pounds.'

'Mrs Raybould was looking for something for a little less than that—' The salesman stopped speaking after another warning look from his boss.

Iris pushed out her chair and stood; she could not bear being under Mr Benson's penetrating glare any longer. 'Thank you very much for your help. I think, perhaps, it would be best if I returned with my husband. My head cannot understand all these figures.'

'Of course.' Mr Benson smirked and walked her to the door. He shook her hand. His palm was dry and cold, his grip limp. She smiled tightly and plucked her hand away. 'A pleasure to meet you, Mrs Raybould.'

She took the bus to Sandhills. Albert opened the door as if he had been expecting her. She asked to use his bathroom; upstairs, she scrubbed her hands with soap, splashed water on her face, and finally calmed down.

In the living room, Albert had prepared a pot of tea.

'Sugar?'

'Please.' Iris sat as Albert stirred her drink. They listened to the steady tick of the clock on the mantelpiece before either of them could find the right words.

'When did you realise?' she said.

Albert sipped from his cup. 'When he was a teenager. I

delivered the meat to the Bensons one day, and he was out practising on his horse. The resemblance was astonishing.'

'That's why Kath never got out, isn't it? Basildon couldn't let her see him.'

Carefully, Albert set his cup on the table. 'I think so. Basildon died in 1920. She could have come out then, I suppose, but everyone had forgotten about her. The shame in those days of having a relative who'd been in somewhere like Smedley... It was easier to leave her where she was.'

'You hadn't forgotten about her, though.'

He shook his head, his cowardice writ deep in the lines of his face.

'I should have known sooner that I wasn't the father. Mabel and I tried for years to have a baby.' He glanced at his wedding photograph on the wall. 'I failed her too.'

Iris finished the dregs of her tea, crunched the granules of sugar that had not dissolved.

'Will you tell Katy?' he said.

She took one last look around Albert's living room. The place was steeped in sadness, in two lives denied true happiness.

The whole thing was just so sad.

She heard the back door open as she lay curled in a ball on her bed. Mum banged around in the kitchen downstairs and set the kettle on to boil.

'Iris? You up there?'

Iris tried to swallow the lump in her throat. 'Yes,' she shouted, but her voice sounded strangled.

Her mum climbed the stairs, tapped gently on Iris's door, and peeped inside. 'Oh, love.' She strode over to Iris, arms wide, and bundled her into a hug. 'What's up? You can tell me.'

'Everything's just going wrong, Mum.' Iris's tears fell thickly.

'What is? I don't understand, Iris. You never tell me anything.'

Iris clutched her mother's cardigan and felt the familiar softness of her mum's body underneath. How could she put everything into words? The whole thing was too long and complicated.

'Is it work? Are you unhappy there?'

'No.'

'What is it then?'

'There are so many lies, Mum. Everybody just lies, all the time, even the people you think you can trust.'

'Who's lied to you?'

She shook her head. She didn't – couldn't – say it out loud, not here, in the sanctuary of her childhood bedroom.

'You know, there are different kinds of lies, love.'

Iris wiped her cheeks with the corner of the cardigan, the way she did when she was little.

'There are big lies. There are lies where people get hurt – those are the bad lies. But there can be good lies, to save someone's feelings. Your dad tells me I'm beautiful and I know that's a lie,' she said with a laugh, 'but he does it to make me feel good. Sometimes, the truth can be worse than a lie.'

She wasn't sure if her mother was right. She wasn't sure about anything anymore.

The kettle began to screech downstairs.

'Now, then.' Her mum kissed her forehead and unwrapped herself from Iris's sticky embrace. 'How about I get us a cup of tea and a fish sandwich to make you feel better?'

31
1956

'He's been here all afternoon,' Nurse Okeke said, pointing at Albert, who was sitting beside the bed. Both he and Kath were dozing. 'They were talking about their childhoods.'

'Was she all right?'

'Oh, yes. There's been a lot of laughter.'

As she neared Kath's bed, Iris saw their hands intertwined.

'Hello.' Iris gently roused the two of them.

Albert pushed himself up in his chair, suddenly self-conscious. He tried to pull his hand away from Kath's, but Kath squeezed it tight.

'Iris.' Kath reached for Iris and bound the three of them together. They stayed like that for some moments, reassured by each other's touch.

'I found him, Kath. I saw your son.'

Albert flinched; he glanced at Iris nervously. Kath stilled.

'How is he?'

'He is very well.'

'Is he kind?'

Iris recalled the cold, blue eyes, the condescending smirk. 'He is. We had tea together.'

'Is he happy?'

'Yes. He told me about his wife. He loves her very much. I have a picture of him, if you would like to see?'

Kath gasped, nodded. Albert held his breath.

Carefully, Iris peeled the photograph out of her handbag. Kath's trembling fingers covered her mouth as she began to cry.

The photograph was of Iris and Edgar. Iris had cut it down to size so that the background of The Retreat was not visible. Instead, all Kath saw were two smiling faces.

She brought the photograph to her lips and kissed it. 'My darling little boy.' Her wet eyes turned to Iris. 'Thank you.'

32

1956

'Thanks for this,' Iris said for the third time.

They'd been driving for over two hours already, the map spread out unhelpfully on her lap. She kept trying to read the place names on the signposts, but they were so long and complicated, that she didn't really know where they were.

She'd only called Simon yesterday. She'd said it was urgent, that Kath didn't have long left. Could he get a day off work? Somehow, he'd managed it, and he'd picked her up at eight-thirty this morning. She'd readied a flask of tea and brought out a slice of cold buttered toast for each of them.

They'd sat in comfortable silence for most of the journey, but the question had been niggling away at her.

'What did you do to John? Shirley said you upset him.'

'That was my intention.' Simon shifted down a gear as they rounded a tight bend. 'There are a few things John wouldn't want people knowing. I told him if he ever touched you again, I would tell his secrets to the people who mattered most.'

The mountains were growing. Waterfalls trickled down their sides and into the nearby river.

'What if he hurts Shirley?'

Simon sighed. 'Shirley has to make her own decisions. I'd step in if she wanted me to, but I don't think she does.'

She didn't press Simon to tell her John's secrets. It was enough that he had sacrificed their friendship for her. It was enough that he had forgiven her for thinking he could be as base as John.

The river was widening. If Iris's instructions were right, they should not be too far away.

They came upon a pretty village where the stone terraced houses sat on the banks of the river, their roofs lined in traditional Welsh slate. An old Norman church squatted at the head of it.

'Mallwyn,' she said, reading the sign. 'This is it; we aren't far now.'

They traced the thinning road out of the village as the river disappeared behind a mountain. The road bore a sharp left, then the river came back into view. After crossing a high-arching stone bridge, there was a tiny left-hand turn.

'Here! This is it.'

'You sure?'

'Yes!'

Simon spun onto the potholed track.

Iron gates had been pushed back and were now lost amidst the hedges. Behind the thick growth of bushes hid a small, groundkeeper's cottage.

'Keep going.'

They traced the river, driving beside lush, overgrown lawns and orchards. The road dipped lower into the heart of the valley, and then, nestled amongst the two forest-covered hillsides, Argoed finally came into view. Its red-brick facade and thick chimneys were like something out of a fairy tale. Ivy sprawled over the exterior. Trees towered beside it, their untended branches tickling the leaded windows. Weeds splintered up between the gravel on the driveway.

'What now?' Simon gazed up at the mansion before him.

Iris hopped out of the car. The oak door was as wide as it was tall, but she didn't have the nerve to knock on it. Instead, she crept to one of the ground floor windows and peered inside. The room was empty. She walked to the next window and again, found the room inside bare of furniture.

'It's deserted.' She was disappointed, although she didn't know why – she wouldn't have known what to say to the distant relatives of Persephone Leverton if they had still been living here. She couldn't exactly tell them the truth, that she was searching for a dead body.

'Let's have a look around.'

They walked the circumference of the house, taking in the sorry state of the shrivelled knot garden, peeping in through the windows to see only a few old paintings and animal heads left on the Jacobean walls.

'What are we actually looking for?' Simon said.

'I don't know.'

The view of the sun-splashed river against the dense, dark forest was dazzling. She made her way out of the once-beautiful formal gardens, over the stretch of grassland, and to the bank of the river. It had a steady, summertime flow. Skater-flies flicked on and off the surface. Beyond, a quick trill of beak against bark vibrated through the forest as a woodpecker searched for food.

She scanned the riverbank. To her left, at a fair distance away, an outcrop of land jutted into the river. The water hit into it and swirled in slow currents. She glanced back towards the house and saw the glint of a first-story windowpane in the sunlight – Persephone's window.

'I think that is where Edward might have docked his boat. Don't you?'

Simon shrugged. 'I suppose so, but it can't have been a very big boat.'

'It wasn't.'

She gazed across the river and up into the edges of the forest. 'What's that?'

Simon squinted at where she pointed: a standing, grey stone. 'It looks like…'

'A grave.'

They ran towards the arching bridge, crossed it, and scrambled down onto the other side of the river. Simon led the way, stamping on the tall grasses and trampling down nettles so that Iris would not get stung.

They were panting as they arrived beside the outcrop of land. Directly above it, on a patch of flat ground, lay the stone. It had some engraving on it, but Simon had to scratch away the moss and lichen in order for them to read it.

Annie

Beloved friend
1870

Iris gripped onto her knees to get her breath back and to stop the world from spinning. 'I thought...'

Her stomach tightened. She met Simon's eyes and knew he was thinking the same. A dog's grave would be a perfect place to bury a man who was supposed to be imaginary.

Determined to find a shovel or spade with which to exhume the grave, they raced back to the house. Surely, spare tools would be lying around somewhere in such an old estate. But before they had chance to look, they collided with a man on the track. A collie dog at his feet barked and snarled.

'What do you want here?' The man asked, with a thick Welsh accent. He must have been almost sixty, with ruddy cheeks and grubby working clothes.

Words vanished from Iris's brain.

Simon stepped forward, squaring his shoulders as if he were braver than he felt. 'We know about Persephone Leverton.'

The man dashed his hand above his dog's head. The dog cowered and fell silent. 'I don't know a Persephone Leverton.'

There was a stand-off. The dog bared its teeth at Simon.

'Roy?' A voice shouted from the nearby groundkeeper's cottage. 'What is it?'

'Nothing, Da, stay inside.'

A crunch of gravel and dirt, the squeak of un-oiled

wheels – an old man pushed himself out of the cottage in a rusted chair. 'Who are you?' The man wore a green suit similar to his son's, along with a flatcap. He peered at them through thick glasses.

'Asking about the Levertons.'

'Persephone,' Iris said, finding her voice and stepping forward.

The shadow of recognition passed over the old man's face. 'Let them in, Roy.'

'I've been waiting my whole life for you.' The old man gestured for them to take a seat on a tattered settee in front of the fire. Iris tugged at her collar, already feeling the sweat building around her neck.

'I'm Ray Brewster. You are?'

Simon and Iris introduced themselves.

'And how do you know about Persephone Leverton?'

It was hard to take her gaze away from Ray's shaking limbs.

'I care for a lady who used to look after Persephone. She wants to know what really happened to her.'

'Where was that? I never knew where she ended up.'

'The Basildon Retreat. In south Shropshire.'

He grunted. 'At least she wasn't hanged.' Ray chucked a browned apple core into the fire. 'I wondered if anybody would come. You think a secret would fade over time. It doesn't. It grows.'

His son came into the room and guarded the doorway, as unfriendly as ever.

'This is about Edward, isn't it?' Ray smiled at the shock on Iris's face.

'He was real?'

'He doesn't seem real now. It was so long ago.'

'But you saw him?'

Ray nodded. His loose, thin flesh wobbled. 'I was only a lad.'

'This isn't going to upset you, is it, Da? I won't have you upset.'

'Be quiet, Roy.'

Roy blushed and fixed his mouth into a hard line.

'It was the first time I'd ever seen blood. Human blood, I mean. So much more blood than on a skinned rabbit. She'd whacked him with a hammer. The back of his head was a mess. Da and Mr Leverton put him in my room. My blanket was ruined.' He smiled, shook his head. 'He was out cold for five days. I thought he'd died but my ma kept wetting his lips and changing his bandages.'

'He survived?' Iris breathed, as the room began to swirl.

'Only just.'

'She didn't kill him?'

Simon's little finger brushed against hers, anchoring her to the room.

'He'd lost a lot of blood. He couldn't walk for a week after he'd woken up. A headache like he'd been shot, I'd imagine.' Ray laughed. 'We weren't to tell anyone. Not a soul. We kept our word, as we always do.'

Iris tried to clear her mind. 'So, what happened to him? What did the servants say when they were questioned?'

'They lied for Mr Leverton. Said they'd never seen or heard of an Irishman called Blake. Mr Leverton had told them he'd disappeared with some silver one night, that he'd scared his wife and that was why she'd got herself all upset. An Irish thief isn't hard to believe.'

'But why did Persephone have to go to The Retreat? She hadn't killed him. She hadn't made him up.'

'She wouldn't shut up about him. Everyone knew what had been going on between them. Not right for a woman like her to be with the likes of him. My da hated her for what she did to Mr Leverton.'

'But she loved Edward.'

'That's no excuse. She was an unfit wife and an unfit mother. Sneaking around, bringing shame on the family.'

Iris bit her tongue though her insides boiled. 'What happened to her children? This place?'

'Patience married when she was eighteen, got as far away from here as she could. I never saw her again. James inherited this place after Mr Leverton passed, but he'd already gone to live in Italy by then. James died in 1940. His son died before him because of the drink, so his grandson owns this place now. Not that we ever see him. He's kept us on to keep an eye on the house. We do our best.'

'Did Mr Leverton re-marry after Persephone had gone?'

'He couldn't; he was still married to her. But he found some comfort in Clara.'

'The governess?'

Ray nodded. Iris stopped the bitter laugh before it came out. Even men could not see how their own sex deceived and lied to themselves.

'And Edward?'

'Ma nursed him back to health. He stayed here for almost two months. He used to play his little whistle at night. I liked it at first. Couldn't stand it by the time he went.'

'Wait.' Iris searched her memory for what Persephone had told Katy. 'Persephone was taken away quickly, wasn't she? Was Edward here when they took her to The Retreat?'

Ray studied the floor. 'Me and him watched her carriage go by. It was rocking, I remember that. I remember hearing her scream.'

Iris put a hand to her mouth and willed herself to stay calm. 'What did Edward do?'

'He played that bloody whistle.'

Her belly burned; anger bubbled inside her.

'Pass me that box on there,' Ray said to his son, pointing at something on the mantelpiece. 'It's cursed me my whole life.' He opened the box and pulled out a tarnished tin whistle. 'He gave it me when he left, like a thank you present. I never wanted it.' Ray handed it to Iris. 'Take it. Show your friend. Persephone was a hard-hearted bitch, but she wasn't mad.'

33

1956

They found a pub that was still serving food and ordered a plate of ham sandwiches. The rickety wooden bench outside was more welcoming than the weather-beaten locals, and so they sat there, exhausted and silent, before Simon excused himself.

The tin whistle between her hands had absorbed her warmth. Iris's fingers kept skimming over the two engraved initials, E.B.

How could you? She thought, as Edwards's ghost appeared before her.

'Get that down you,' Simon said when he returned, gesturing at the pint he'd set on the table. Edward dissolved in the air. 'I suppose it's good, in a way. She didn't kill him.'

'She died thinking she had. That's just as bad.' Iris twirled the tin whistle between her fingertips. 'If he'd never come, none of this would have happened. Persephone wouldn't have been sent away, Katy would never have got involved, Basildon might never have done what he did.'

'You can't think like that.'

She shoved the tin whistle into her bag, unable to stand the sight of it any longer. She drank her beer and absently stared at the rolling Welsh-border hills.

'I don't want to be your girlfriend, Simon.'

He laughed a bit too hard. 'Where did that come from?' He gulped his drink. 'I can't say I blame you. The last few weeks can't have filled you with confidence in the male species.'

'It's not just that.' She turned to him. It wasn't fair to keep him hanging on like this. 'You know I want to have a career. I can't be a girlfriend or a wife or anything like that. I can't stay at home and have children and cook dinners for the rest of my days. Life wouldn't be worth living.' Her cheeks started to burn. 'Even if you have grown on me these last few weeks. Rather like a fungus.'

'Thanks, I think.'

She laughed with him, relieved he seemed to be taking it well. She squeezed his arm for a second before retracting her grip.

'I'm sorry you're not enough.'

He nodded and lifted his pint for something to do. She felt like she should say more, but she'd only be spouting awkward drivel. So, the silence grew. She was just about to head to the ladies' room to get out of it, when finally, their food arrived. They descended on it gratefully.

Simon's clean red car looked awfully conspicuous on the Brookside estate.

'I'll wait here for you.'

'You don't need to, I can walk.'

He shooed her away and turned off the engine. She thought he'd best lock his doors as well, just to be on the safe side.

Next-door's children were nowhere to be seen. She knocked on number thirty-three and, like before, there was no response.

It was just like it had been: she made her way to the back room and found Mr Temperton in the same position, wearing the same clothes.

'Back again? She's not here. Hasn't been for days. Out with some boy, no doubt. Slut.'

'I'm just dropping something off. Can I go up?'

Mr Temperton grunted. She took it as a yes.

Upstairs, Shirley's room was tidier. Most of her clothes were gone, but some odd bits remained. Stockings spilled out from one of the drawers. Lipstick tubes lay scattered on the dresser. A pair of well-worn pink slippers jutted out from under the bed.

She couldn't blame Shirley for wanting to get out of this house. Iris would never understand what Shirley had been through growing up; the monster downstairs was not fit to be called a father. John offered a life of luxury, of status, of comfort, in all ways but one.

Iris wished another man had found Shirley first, a better man, but wishing didn't change anything.

She laid the photo of her and Shirley from the picnic on Shirley's pillow. She hoped the message on the back would at least be some comfort to Shirley in the dark times which lay ahead for her.

You will always be my friend.

. . .

Simon dropped her off at Smedley. She waved him goodbye before she made her way to Kath's ward. Inside, there was a hush to the place, an absence. Nurse Okeke met her at the doors, her round eyes wet. She shook her head.

Kath looked as if she were sleeping; her mouth open slightly, her eyes shut. The picture Iris had given her was face-down against her heart. Albert remained at her side, holding her hand.

'Albert?' Iris nudged his shoulder.

He tried to turn his head as much as he could. She knelt before him and saw the tears sliding down his nose.

'She's gone,' he whispered.

Iris hugged him; the act comforted them both.

'She was happy, in the end. We have you to thank for that, Iris.'

The hard ridge of the tin whistle pressed into her back. She slid it out of her bag, then dropped it in the nearest bin.

'She's at peace now.' Iris hoped Kath was in heaven with Persey and all of the Annies were running around at their feet. The thought made her smile.

EPILOGUE
1903

She is not looking. A pretty something from one of the stalls has caught her eye, like it usually does. Stupid girl.

I hitch up my skirts, ready. I start walking, slowly at first, checking no one sees me, then faster. No one will miss me, yet. No one will hear the crunch of my vanishing footsteps over the cacophony of the brass band. No one will notice the disappearance of one of the many shadows that haunt this place.

I try to run, but my legs burn, unused to the exertion. I keep going, forcing myself forward, until finally I am out of sight.

The horizon wavers. I must be quick, or else they will notice my absence.

I glide past the woods, thinking of the little graveyard between the trees where my dear Annie now rests, and over the swathes of fresh-cut grass. As I glance behind me to where the house looms, I stumble.

He is there.

His piercing blue eyes watch me from his study.

I stop. We hold each other's gaze.

I know what he has done. I knew it when Katy struck him with the poker; I saw the truth in his eyes. He knows that I know, and that is why he will not stop me now.

I turn, lift my skirts again, but there is no need to rush.

I take my time, let my breathing slow. Above, a buzzard circles, looking for meat.

The music from the fate is distant now, I block it out of my ears easily. The lake spans before me, twinkling in the sunshine like a carpet of stars. I step closer to the edge and feel the wet earth give beneath my feet.

The bite of the water takes away my breath as it creeps up my legs. My skin prickles. My hands meet the water as I step in further. Waist deep... chest deep... neck deep.

I cannot be saved. None of us can be saved. I am sorry for Katy, I am sorry for myself, but it is too late for both of us now.

The water slides over my face. My toes reach for the bottom, but it has disappeared. The world has opened beneath me.

The water will carry me to the sea, and I will be free.

AFTERWORD

Thank you for taking the time to read *Woman on Ward 13*. I hope you enjoyed it and will consider leaving a review online as it truly helps authors to get their work into the hands of those who will love it.

If you would like to hear more about my news and work and receive two **FREE** historical novellas, then please visit my website:

www.delphinewoods.com

ACKNOWLEDGMENTS

Once again, thank you for reading!

I would also like to thank my family for being so supportive and encouraging me to follow my dreams. Thank you to my mother for always being there with constructive criticism and for being the first to read my work. Thank you to my father for all his technical support. Thank you to my husband for believing in me completely.

A special thanks goes to my Aunty Jan, who helped enormously with the research of this book. It was through her that I got a real sense of what working life was like in a psychiatric hospital.

If you would like to see the inspiration for Ward 13, then find the videos on YouTube of Powick Hospital Worcestershire from the 1960s.

There are so many other sources which proved invaluable in the creation of this book. It would take too long to list them all, but if you are interested in the treatment of the mentally ill throughout history, here are a few recommendations:

- *Inconvenient People: Lunacy, Liberty and the Mad-doctors in Victorian England*, Sarah Wise.
- *The Victorian Asylum*, Sarah Rutherford.
- *Madness: A Brief History*, Roy Porter.
- The websites of the Glenside Museum and Worcester Medical Museums, both of which can be visited in person.

Finally, a big thanks to the online Indie community, who share their knowledge and expertise and continue to fill our world with wonderful new books.

ABOUT THE AUTHOR

Delphine Woods graduated with a First from The Open University in 2016, where she studied for an Open Degree, specialising in Creative Writing.

After a busy couple of years writing her collection of Victorian mystery-thrillers, she released her debut novella, *The Butcher's Wife*, in July 2019.

She lives with her husband in Shropshire where she writes in her spare room, her dog by her feet to keep her warm. You can keep up to date with her news and get in touch with her via her website, newsletter, and social media platforms.

www.delphinewoods.com

ALSO BY DELPHINE WOODS

Convenient Women Collection:

The Butcher's Wife

The Cradle Breaker

The Promise Keeper

The Button Maker

The Little Wife

Convenient Women Collection Box Set

Standalone Books:

The Last Flight of the Ladybird